AN ALEX DUI

A DEADLY PLAN

To George & Jane,
Hope you'll enjoy reading this Book

Warm wishes

Soorun Beeraje

30th December, 2022

SOORUN BEERAJE

Self- published in 2022
Copyright © Soorun Beeraje (2022)

A CIP catalogue record for this title is available from the British Library.

ISBN 978-1-913745-02-8 (eBook)
ISBN 978-1-913745-03-5 (Paperback)
ISBN 978-1-913745-04-2 (Hardback)

https://soorunbeeraje.com

AUTHOR BIOGRAPHY

Soorun Beeraje was born and grew up in Mauritius. He trained as a nurse in the UK, then progressed to becoming a lecturer in nurse education. Subsequently, he held several senior nurse education posts including that of a Vice Principal at a College of Health Studies and a Principal Lecturer in nursing studies at a University in London. He is now retired and writes crime fiction – murder mystery/thriller novels. He likes all popular sports, walking, theatre, wine and cruise travels. He lives with his wife in Surrey, UK.

BY THE SAME AUTHOR

The Fatal Tuesday

To my beloved family for their continued support and encouragement.

CHAPTER 1

Monday 10 July 2006

Gerry stepped back to the edge of the pavement, receiving a few annoyed looks from busy city people milling past her. She looked up, past the imposing corporate signage – Brown Legal – at the building in front of her. It oozes elegance and opulence, all the way up.

London was sweltering around her in the summer heat; the humidity was high, and she could hear the odd sneeze from passers-by probably suffering from hay fever. A smart suit was a hindrance in this weather; Gerry could feel the tickle of perspiration; not just the heat, she thought.

She composed herself and entered the airy atrium of the famous law firm's main building. Being a chartered accountant at Scrimshaw in the City, she had attended a few meetings at different law firms regarding their clients' transactions, but it was the first time she had been to the Brown Legal building. She was impressed with the sheer size, design and plush furnishing of the place. It was liberally dotted with exotic plants. The reception desk seemed to be miles away, tucked discreetly between a couple of palm trees with shiny foliage. *Well, here goes*, she thought, and headed for the desk. She was a few minutes early anyway.

'Good morning, my name is Gerry Hamilton. I've an appointment to see Mr Walter Coburn at ten o'clock.'

'Good morning, Ms Hamilton, how are you?'

Gerry was momentarily taken aback. 'I'm sorry, do I …?'

'I'm Jean, Ms Hamilton. I saw you at the funeral. I'm very sorry for your loss.'

Gerry's eyes flicked to the name tag on the receptionist's lapel. Apparently, Jean was who she said she was. The trace of 'Essex girl made good' in Jean's accent made her smile inwardly; an endearing flaw in the smooth corporate superstructure, she thought.

There was a brief, awkward silence, and then Jean remembered where she was. 'Mr Coburn thought it might be more comfortable if he met you in his office suite.' She handed Gerry an attractive lanyard with 'Visitor' emblazoned neatly on it. 'Just take the lift to the eighth floor and Mr Coburn's PA will look after you.'

Gerry headed for the lifts at the rear of the atrium; four of them, each spacious enough for a coach party. The ascent took milliseconds; she was glad she'd only had a light breakfast. When she stepped out, she was confronted with another Jean – this one with 'Peggy' on her lapel.

Peggy's plummy vowels were definitely not made in Essex. 'Mr Coburn won't be a moment, Ms Hamilton. Please have a seat. Can I get you anything in the meantime? Tea or coffee?'

'No thanks, I'm fine.'

She settled into a ridiculously comfortable sofa to wait. Whilst waiting, she reflected on her own desire to become a lawyer, but she ended up joining another profession. She was proud of Amanda when she announced her decision to follow a career in the legal profession. She was going to be the first lawyer in the family. She encouraged Amanda to pursue her ambition.

A few minutes passed, and she watched the office move and work around her. She was used to corporate chic, but Brown Legal was so suave, it was almost intimidating.

A door to her right opened with an imperceptible whoosh and Walter Coburn emerged, straightening his tie. Gerry had met him at the funeral, but now she saw him in his own environment, she was impressed at the air of superior gravitas he carried.

Walter Coburn was tall, a little over six foot, and his demeanour indicated that he could have been in the military. His steel-grey hair was swept back from an imposing brow; his shoulders were broad and square, and there was no hint of a paunch. His exquisitely tailored suit was charcoal grey, and he wore a blue striped shirt with a white collar and a magenta tie. He looked very smart.

Walter spotted her and, immediately, his expression changed from looking serious to appearing friendly. 'Ms Hamilton,' he said, moving towards her with his hand extended in greeting and Gerry shook it. 'It's a pleasure to see you again. Shall we?' He indicated the way to his office with an imperious sweep of a beautifully suited arm.

He ushered her into an office that stretched the entire width of the building. A perfectly designed distance from the floor-to-ceiling windows stood a desk large enough to plan a military campaign on. 'Please, take a seat. I'll ask Peggy to bring us some coffee.'

Gerry considered refusing and thought better of it. What she had to say might make the honourable Mr Coburn wish he'd ordered something stronger.

'So, how are you holding up? It must have been a terrible shock for you all, especially your parents. How are they?'

'They have taken it pretty hard, Mr Coburn.'

'Please, call me Walter.'

'Walter. And call me Gerry. We are all still in a state of shock, to be honest.'

In fact, she was understating things; her parents had aged twenty years in a month. She, herself, couldn't remember the last time she'd slept properly without the clumsy aid of medication.

'I understand. Suicide is a ghastly thing for a family to bear. I'm not sure I've got over it myself. Amanda was a…' he paused for a moment and looked into a distance, 'Amanda was a special person. She had everything to live for.'

Walter looked as if he wanted to say more, but he stopped as Peggy appeared with a tray. 'Ah, Peggy, thank you.' Gerry thought the expression that crossed his face was one of relief.

When Peggy had glided out of the office, he turned to her and smiled, back in control again. 'I'm of course glad to see you, Gerry. But I'm not entirely clear as to the purpose of our meeting. Is there something specific you wish to discuss? I assume our Human Resources department has taken care of all the mundane details.'

'Yes, they were very efficient, and very kind,' Gerry said, took a deep breath, 'I'm here on a more serious matter. I'm representing the family to express our major concern about Amanda's death. We can't accept the findings of the police report. To put it bluntly, we don't believe Amanda killed herself. Although there had been a police investigation into her death, we are not convinced that they had searched every possible avenue to establish whether she was murdered. We don't know what to do and who to turn to for help? So, we've decided to ask for your guidance on how to proceed.'

The silence that followed was profound. Walter looked aghast. 'I'm not sure I follow you correctly, Gerry. You don't think it was suicide?'

'No.'

'But if it wasn't suicide...'

'Quite. That's what I want to talk to you about. The police are very reluctant to reopen the case; they say there is not enough evidence. But frankly, they had the whole thing wrapped up and delivered in half an hour, or that's how it felt. If this was a medical tragedy, we'd be asking for a second opinion; as it is, we're at a loss what to do next, where to take our concerns. I suppose I was hoping you would have some advice for me.'

Walter took a minute to reply. He adjusted his immaculate cuffs and took a sip of coffee; his hand seemed to have developed a slight tremor. 'My first instinct is to tell you to accept the police findings, however reluctantly. But the look in your eyes tells me you are rather past that point. If you don't mind my asking, do you have any grounds for this suspicion? I don't mean to pry, but you are making a somewhat strong claim.'

Gerry took a sip of coffee before she replied, and her hand was not too steady either. She had a strong feeling that Walter was ahead of her. He hadn't told her all he knew. Either he had access to information she didn't or... could he be involved, somehow? She decided to tread carefully; the possibility, however remote, that she was in the company of a killer, or someone who knew the killer, brought a knot to her stomach.

'It's nothing definite, and I'm sure the police did what they could. But taking cyanide is a terrible way to die, and Amanda was squeamish at the best of times.

'And there was no sign that she had any problems, or that she was depressed or suicidal. She had big plans, and she was looking forward to a bright future. And where would she get hold of cyanide, for God's sake? I mean, it's not as if you can just go on the internet and order a bottle of poison.'

Walter leaned forward, steepled his fingers under his chin. 'Gerry, I have a confession to make. I was stunned when I heard it was suicide; stunned, and not a little suspicious. It so happens that I play the odd round of golf with the Chief Superintendent. I used our friendship to get a quick look at the police report two weeks ago. I felt the investigation was superficial, and I voiced my concern. Geoffrey – Chief Superintendent Macey – rather brushed me off; I think he was irritated that I had questioned his team's work ethic. But there was nothing obvious in the report; nothing they had clearly missed. I was reluctantly going to let sleeping dogs lie. But now that you have told me of your suspicions, I wonder if it's perhaps worth having another look.'

'So, you think you could persuade the police to reopen the case?' A flicker of hope danced in Gerry's heart.

'I think that's unlikely, to be honest. I rather blotted my – our – copy book with my comments to Geoffrey. But there is more than one way to approach this. Have you considered hiring the services of a private investigator?'

'Yes, I mean, I've given it some thought. But I wouldn't know where to start. I imagine a private investigator as someone snooping after husbands playing away from home, taking photos for a grubby divorce case. That's not the sort of person I'm hoping to find.'

'I agree; that's not the sort of person you need.' He straightened his spine in his seat. 'I think we can do a little better than that.'

'Do you know someone?'

'Actually, yes, I do. There is a chap, an ex-lawyer in fact, who comes highly recommended. He has a good track record, and it's not just for grubby divorces, as you so eloquently put it.'

'Do you know him?' Gerry was still suspicious and thought Walter clearly was a step ahead of her, but why?

'Not personally, but I know a couple of people who do, and they are rather impressed with him. I should also say that Mr DuPont's services don't come cheap. Have you considered the question of costs?'

'DuPont? Is he French?'

'English mother, French father, as I understand it.'

'And when you say expensive, what are we talking about?'

'I don't have the details to hand, but I can certainly find out. Do you have an idea of what you can afford?'

'Well, I have some savings, but I don't know how they would compare to a private investigator's bill. I'm sure we'll find a way, if Mr DuPont is the person we're looking for.'

Walter stood up, walked to the window and looked into the distance; the view of London was breath-taking, a panorama of wealth. He turned to her and spread his arms, a gesture she didn't quite understand. 'Look, Gerry, I have an interest in this matter; I can't say more than that, but I can offer you a proposition. I am prepared to share the costs with you; in fact, I'd be happy to take on all the costs, if it helps you – helps us – to get to the bottom of this. Would you accept my help?'

'Why would you do that?'

'Let's just say I had high hopes for Amanda, and I feel her loss rather personally.'

God, he fancied her. Gerry adopted a dispassionate expression and nodded. 'If you are happy to help, I am happy to accept,' she said, and thought: *I don't know what you're getting from this, but we can deal with that later.* At least she didn't think he was a killer now; what murderer would pay for an investigation into his own crimes?

'Good, then we are agreed. I'll contact Mr DuPont at once. I expect he will want to talk to you, and perhaps the rest of the family too.'

'I'll be the point of contact for the family; I don't think my parents are in any state to be questioned.'

Walter nodded, distracted. Since Gerry had walked in, his eyes had constantly threatened to betray him. Gerry was tall and slim, her strawberry-blonde hair tied in a loose ponytail at her nape. She wore an elegant suit with a figure-hugging skirt, over a plain white blouse. *She looks so like her; beautiful.* He inhaled sharply: *pull yourself together, man.*

'Excellent.' Walter stood and offered his hand and Gerry shook it gently. 'Leave it with me, Gerry, and let's hope we have better news when we next meet. I'll ask Peggy to see you out.'

'There's no need, I can find my way out,' Gerry said politely. She needed time and space to think.

CHAPTER 2

Walter sat for a while, musing. He picked up his coffee, took a sip and grimaced; it had gone cold and bitter. With a troubled sigh, he reached for his Blackberry and searched his contacts list; there, Alex DuPont, private investigator. There was no point in delaying it, he thought, so he thumbed the call button and settled back in his chair.

'Mayfair Investigative Agency, Jenny speaking. How may I help you?'

'Good morning. I'd like to speak to Mr Alexander DuPont.'

Jenny sensed an edge in the caller's voice. 'I'm afraid Mr DuPont is out on a case. Can I be of any help?'

'My name is Walter Coburn.' There was no sign of recognition from Jenny, so he continued. 'I am a senior partner at Brown Legal, the law firm. I am hoping that Mr DuPont will consider taking on a case for us. It's a confidential and rather urgent matter. I'd appreciate if he could come and see me, say tomorrow morning at ten?'

By the sound of his voice, Mr Coburn was clearly not used to taking no for an answer, Jenny thought, as she looked at Alex's diary. 'I can't see any appointments for that time tomorrow, but I'll need to check with Mr DuPont first. He'll be back around two this afternoon. Can I get back to you then?' She heard an impatient sigh from the other end of the line.

'I suppose that will do. Please, do get back to me promptly; as I said, this is an urgent and delicate matter. Thank you for your assistance. Good day to you.'

As soon as the call ended, Jenny did an online search for Brown Legal. She found Walter Coburn's profile on their website: a toff with links to the military and has a distinguished legal career in the City. Impressive. However, she was not sure if Alex would be able to see him tomorrow morning at ten. It could be too much of a short notice for him to attend. The first item on her list was, to let Alex know of Mr Coburn's request. She went off to make a cup of tea.

**

A little after two o'clock, Alex breezed into the office. Jenny looked up from her desk and smiled. 'So, how did it go?'

Alex shrugged. 'Well, he blustered a bit and threatened me with various forms of violence, but when I showed him the photos, he was meek as a lamb. I think he was relieved, to be honest.' He removed his jacket and launched it towards the coat rack. It fell about a foot short. He tried again and succeeded. 'Still, it would be nice to have something a little more substantial to get my teeth into. Naughty husbands pay the Agency well, but it's a tawdry way to make a living. And talking of getting my teeth into something, I'm starving.'

'Don't worry, help is at hand.' Jenny popped into the kitchen and came back carrying a sandwich: tuna, sweetcorn and mayonnaise.'

'Thanks, Jenny.'

He devoured the sandwich pretty fast. Then, he had a pink lady apple, a small pot of strawberry yoghurt and a mug of tea. After finishing his lunch, he was ready to have a chat, and went to see Jenny in her office and said, 'Now I feel much better. Where is Scott?'

Jenny buzzed Scott who confirmed he was on his way to join them.

'Did you enjoy your late lunch?' Jenny asked.

'Yes, thank you. I didn't have a lot to eat for my dinner last night and this morning I had an early breakfast, that's why I was so hungry.'

'You should have known better.'

Alex was expecting a short lecture about eating on time and as usual, he was not disappointed.

'As I have mentioned to you on several occasions, you should eat at the right time. People do not have their lunch at nearly three in the afternoon. It's almost teatime. If you carry on like this, you will end up having a stomach problem. The work can wait.'

'Don't exaggerate, Jenny. You worry too much.'

Luckily for him, Scott, his associate arrived. Jenny had to curtail her lecture.

Alex and Scott were chatting about a client. Jenny picked up her note-taking pad and was biding her time to interject and inform him of Mr Coburn's request. Alex noticed the eagerness of her face, indicating that she had a particular issue to bring up.

He looked at Jenny. 'Alright, tell us what's on your mind?'

'We received an interesting phone call in the early afternoon.'

'Really!'

'The call was from Mr Walter Coburn, a senior partner at Brown Legal, the law firm.'

'So don't keep me in suspense. What's it about?'

'He wouldn't tell me anything. But he said it was urgent. He wants you to meet him tomorrow morning at ten in his office.'

'Walter Coburn, senior partner at Brown Legal. I wonder what a corporate high-flier like Coburn wants from me.'

'He sounded desperate to talk to you. Shall I call his office and confirm that you'll be attending?'

'Yes, please; and if it turns out to be another divorce case, I'm docking your pay.'

By that time, Scott was keen to tell them about his adventures: hiding in the garden, waiting for the errant husband to appear in the window of his mistress' flat. 'And I'm sitting there with my finger on the button when this stray dog sidles up and pees on the tree I'm hiding behind. I got the shots, but the little bugger played merry hell with my shoe polish.'

'Never mind, Scott, you can afford a new pair on the fee. For a jilted wife she was very generous with her cash.' Alex rubbed his hands together, took a napkin and wiped a few crumbs off his chin.

'The meeting with Mr Coburn has been confirmed. Shall I text you his contact details?'

'No, I know where Brown Legal is. It's in Holborn. I've been there a few times in my days as a lawyer. I have a vague idea I may have met Walter Coburn at one of their wine and cheese dos.'

'How the other half lives,' sighed Jenny. Scott yawned derisively.

'I'd rather have a beer and crisps do any day,' said Alex.

'Are you calling here before you go to Holborn tomorrow?' asked Jenny.

'That's a good question.'

'Once you make up your mind, let me know.'

'If there is anything urgent for me to deal with, I'll come here first.'

'Nothing that can't wait till you come back.'

'Well, in that case, I'll go there first.'

'That's fine.'

By that time, everyone was looking tired. Recently, they had been working long hours to meet the deadlines for two clients which were achieved over the weekend. The Agency was handsomely rewarded for the services rendered.

Alex said, 'Right, I think we deserve an early finish for a well-deserved rest. I'll see you both tomorrow after my meeting with the famous Mr Coburn.'

CHAPTER 3

Alex lived in a decent size two-bedroom apartment in Mayfair; only five minutes' walk away from the Agency. It was a perfect location for him. To keep fit, he usually ran five miles on weekends in Hyde Park which was just around the corner. He occasionally thought about finding somewhere a bit bigger, but until he was ready to raise a family, he didn't really need the extra space.

The next day, he welcomed the opportunity to have a lie in. After attending to his personal needs, he went through his morning exercise routine: five minutes of sun salutation yoga, ten minutes of exercises which consisted of stretching, press-ups and half squats. Next, he had his usual breakfast: a glass of orange juice, a slice of toast and a mug of tea. After that, he dressed up in a grey suit, pale blue shirt and a pink tie. Then, he set off to Holborn.

It was only a few stops on the Tube to Holborn, so he could afford a leisurely start to his journey. The day was just beginning to warm up and the humidity was rising. He wondered if a thunderstorm was in the offing, a brief relief from the extreme heat. He sighed and headed for the Tube. By nine-thirty he was standing in front of the Brown Legal building, adjusting his cuffs and calming himself for the meeting.

He'd been out of the legal profession for a couple of years now, and his decision to change jobs had not been universally popular. His father had been particularly unimpressed. But being in the legal environment again, it evoked feelings of nostalgia that brought back pleasant memories: the good times he used to enjoy with his fellow trainees and subsequently, with fantastic colleagues. His life had moved on and he was thoroughly enjoying his new challenge.

After approaching the reception desk, he had a quick look at the name of the receptionist and said, 'Good morning, Jean. I'm Alexander DuPont, how are you today? I've an appointment to see Mr Coburn at ten. I'm a little early.' He flashed the receptionist a winning smile.

Jean blushed at the familiarity but enjoyed the momentary flirt. The man before her was handsome, and there was a distinct sparkle in his eyes. She scrolled through the diary while casting surreptitious looks at him. 'Ah yes, Mr DuPont, please take the lift to the eighth floor, sir, and Mr Coburn's PA will look after you.' She gave him a lanyard with 'Visitor' emblazoned neatly on it.

Peggy was less easy to charm. She looked at him coolly. 'Take a seat, Mr DuPont. Mr Coburn won't be a moment.'

Mr Coburn happened to be taking his time. Alex was just beginning to wonder when the lovely but haughty Peggy was going to offer him a cup of coffee when the door to Walter's office opened. *I remember you now*, Alex thought: *a man who is used to being obeyed.*

'Alex, it's good to see you again.' Walter's handshake was on the firm side, as if he was testing Alex's mettle. He squeezed back, earning a nod of approval.

Pleasantries out of the way, they settled in Walter's

opulent office and got down to business. Alex was brimming with curiosity. 'Walter, I'm intrigued; why would you need the services of a private investigator?'

'I don't, personally.' Walter looked mildly offended, as if the idea was distasteful. 'But we have something of a situation here, and it needs to be handled discreetly. With your background, I'm sure you understand.'

Cut to the chase, Walter, Alex thought, but he smiled blandly and waited for the full story.

Walter settled himself a little deeper into his chair and took a moment. 'An employee of ours...' He stopped and started again. 'I should say a former employee. We had a very promising trainee here, Amanda Hamilton. Over a month ago, she was found dead in her apartment. The police investigated and were confident she had taken her own life.'

'But you have your doubts?'

'I do and so does her sister. Between you and me, I had a chance to look at the police file on the matter. It was thin enough to slide under the door. I wasn't impressed. However, there was no obvious evidence of incompetence, so it is entirely possible that Amanda actually did kill herself. I just...'

Walter was lost in his thoughts for a moment. Alex glanced at him, wondering if the lawyer had been a little disingenuous in saying this wasn't a personal matter.

'So, who is hiring me: you or the family?' he asked.

'Well, I have offered to pay your fees. That is, the firm will pay.' Alex narrowed his eyes. Had Walter just squirmed?

'And what can you tell me about the incident? How did Amanda – allegedly – kill herself?'

'By taking potassium cyanide in a glass of Prosecco.'

'That's pretty unusual.'

'Quite.'

A brief pause followed to allow Alex some space to reflect.

'I think there might be something worth investigating here. I'll take it on. I'm not promising anything. If it turns out to be a routine suicide, I'll tell you so. As you are no doubt aware, this is not our usual line of work.'

'I know that. But a year ago, you successfully solved three criminal cases concurrently for a well-known university in London. That achievement has instantly raised the profile and status of your Agency. Currently, you are considered as one of the best private investigators to solve criminal cases. I've complete faith in your ability to tackle this complex job and solve the mystery.'

You've done your homework. 'Thank you, Walter. But as I said, if there's nothing suspicious in this, I'll tell you promptly.'

'Of course, I would expect no less. How do we proceed from here?'

'My personal assistant, Jenny, will contact your office about the fees. Meanwhile, I'd like to speak to the family and get the ball rolling.'

'About that. Amanda's sister, Gerry, has indicated you should talk to her in the first instance. She came to see me and expressed her doubts; and she intimated that the parents were pretty distraught, so one needs to tread softly.'

'I'll be discreet. Now,' Alex stood and offered his hand. Another firm squeeze by Walter. 'If there's nothing else, we need to discuss, I'll get on with the job.'

'Thank you, Alex. I'm glad you are willing to take it on. I sense I can trust you. I've made a small office available for you to conduct your interviews and so forth. I imagine you might want to talk to some of Amanda's colleagues. Please feel free to use it as you need.'

'That's very generous of you, Walter.' *Very generous; what's in this for you?*

Alex was already deep in thought as he took the lift down to reception.

On his way back to the Agency, he could not stop smiling at the turn of events. He called in a café for a cheeseburger, fries and a diet coke. The entire meeting with Walter had been friendly, informative and constructive. However, it had never crossed his mind that one day he would find himself in a position to deal with the same people he had encountered in his previous career. Then again, the job of a private investigator could take him in any direction. By working for himself, he had the choice of accepting or rejecting any case. On this occasion, he did not hesitate to accept the job. He felt the life of a young trainee solicitor had ended suddenly, and he would like to find out how she met her death.

**

He arrived at the Agency in the afternoon. Jenny was waiting patiently to find out about Alex's meeting with Walter Coburn who, on the previous day, sounded quite anxious to talk to Alex.

Both Jenny and Scott followed him to his office.

'Let me give you a feedback about my meeting with Walter Coburn,' Alex said, smiling.

'It'll be nice to know what happened?' Scott chipped in.

CHAPTER 4

The team went into the staff common room and sat in their comfortable seat to discuss Amanda Hamilton's suicide case. The addition of domestic furniture in the middle of the large office gave it the haphazard appearance of a living room hastily converted into a working space, which was not far away from the truth. In spite of this arrangement, they enjoy their private space.

After the feedback, Scott remarked, 'I'm sorry to hear about the death of the trainee solicitor. But following of what you have just said, there's not much to go on here. It's possible she did take her own life like the police report says.'

'I'm also sorry to hear of Amanda's death,' Jenny said sombrely.

'Jenny, could you give the police a ring and find out who the investigating officer was?' Alex said.

'Will do.' She went to her office.

'You may be right, Scott. There are a few things that aroused my curiosity. Cyanide is not your average method for suicide. It certainly doesn't fit with a spontaneous act. Either she was planning this for some time, or we're looking at foul play, one way or another,' Alex said, and looking pensive.

'The question to consider is why would she kill herself?'

'I guess that's the mystery for us to solve.'

Jenny arrived and she could not resist a little smirk. 'You're going to love this. The senior officer on the scene was none other than Detective Sergeant Melanie Cooper. Given your history, that ought to make things easier.'

'Or a lot harder.' Alex wasn't sure whether to be pleased or dismayed. He and Melanie had history, alright; but it wasn't all strictly professional. And the solving of the university murder had caused more than a little friction between them. Still, Melanie was a good copper, and he felt a tingle in his spine when he thought of her. *Melanie, I don't know if you're going to love this or hate it.* He was sure of one thing; he wanted to see her again.

'So, that means the pugnacious Detective Inspector Richard Jenkins is going to be involved, I suppose. I don't know how I feel about meeting him again.' Alex frowned; they had hardly begun and already the case was getting complicated. The university murder had caused quite a stir and solving it had enhanced his reputation; but the police weren't completely overjoyed to have an outsider stealing their thunder.

He straightened up and clapped his hands. 'Right, let's get started. Scott, I want you to get over to where Amanda lived. Talk to the residents and check with the neighbours if they have anything interesting to say. Jenny, can you contact the sister, Gerry Hamilton, and arrange a meeting? And ask her to bring a photo of Amanda. I think I should talk to her first. Then we'll go and take a look at Amanda's apartment. Walter told me the apartment hasn't been touched since she died; apparently the rent was paid up in advance. I think we should check it out and see if there's anything the police might have missed.'

'And who is going to get in touch with DS Cooper?' asked Jenny.

'I'll do that,' Alex replied. Jenny had that little smirk again. Needless to say, Jenny saw this as another opportunity for Alex to have a lasting relationship with Melanie. No doubt, that would make her very happy. With a bit of luck, that what Alex would like to happen as well.

CHAPTER 5

Only a year ago, Alex had his first experience of investigating a murder case with the assistance of Melanie. Although DI Jenkins did not appreciate the contribution of private investigators, he tolerated Alex only up to a point. It was widely recognised Alex did exceptionally well: he solved the case practically on his own. Melanie commended him on his superb performance. Nonetheless, he wondered how both of them would react to him as he appeared on their radar.

He was looking forward to resuming his link with Melanie, both professionally and personally. He rang her. After a few ringtones, she answered, 'Can I help you?'

'Hello Melanie, it's Alex.'

She quickly realised who it was. 'Alex, how nice to hear your voice again.' She was extremely pleased to receive a call from him. 'How are you?'

'I'm very well, thank you. I'm pleased to get you on the phone, and how are you these days?'

'Fine thanks. Always busy. I must say this is a big surprise.'

'Why?'

'I thought you would have more interesting things to

occupy yourself with than thinking of me.'

'Or course, I think about you. I suppose you're right. I always have a lot to do as regards to work and my social life. I do hope you remember my motto: work hard and play harder.'

'How can I forget anything about you, Alex?'

'Glad to hear it. Anyway, I'm afraid this isn't a social call, but more of a professional one.'

'How disappointing! What do you mean by a professional call?'

'I would like to discuss a serious issue that concerns your Department.'

'Really. Tell me you're joking.'

'No, I'm not. Honestly.'

'OK. What's it all about?'

'I understand you worked on a suicide case over a month ago about a young trainee solicitor at Brown Legal, by the name of Amanda Hamilton.'

'I remember the case very well. How are you involved in this?'

'Well, that's the thing. I got a call from a high-profile lawyer, Walter Coburn, senior partner at Brown Legal.'

'Walter Coburn. Yeah, I know of him. I heard on the grapevine he's been pumping the Chief Superintendent Christopher Macey for information about the case.'

Alex paused for a moment. He needed to tread carefully now; he didn't want to get Melanie's back up because he needed her help. 'Mr Coburn had some concerns about the case. More to the point, so does Amanda's sister. They've asked me to look into it. I'm sure you did all the right things, but something about it smells iffy to me.'

There was a brief silence. 'Look, Alex, I was under

pressure to wrap it up, and there wasn't anything obviously dodgy about it. DI Jenkins needed me elsewhere, so we didn't hang about. What makes you suspicious?'

'Nothing that I can put my finger on it yet; it's just a feeling more than anything else. Listen, I was wondering if we could get together…'

'Alex DuPont, are you propositioning me?' Melanie's laughter stirred some old memories.

'Maybe.'

'Be careful, you've already got Claire.'

'I know. I meant, could we get together and talk about the case. Also, I was wondering if I could get a look at the file.'

'I'll have to talk to Jenkins about that. You know how he feels about private investigators. I'm not sure if you're in his good books or not. On the other hand, it's a closed case, so it can't do any harm, can it?'

'I guess not. Shall we meet for lunch tomorrow and go over the details?' Alex realised he was crossing his fingers.

'I'm up for lunch, but there's no way I can get the file that quick.'

'Never mind; let's talk it through and then see where we go from there. The Excelsior at one o'clock? I'll book us a table by the window.'

'You're on. Don't expect too much, though. I think the poor girl topped herself. I've got to go; the boss is on the warpath.' She rang off.

Alex sat for a while thinking about the time he had spent with Melanie. Nothing had happened between them last time round; but he remembered their in-depth conversations about their individual relationship. They both had a partner to contend with which presented them with thoughtful complications. He sighed and moved on with his day.

**

It was nine o'clock, Gerry Hamilton arrived at Brown Legal, and she was directed to Alex's office. There was a knock on the door.

Alex opened the door. 'Pleased to meet you, Ms Hamilton.' They shook hands warmly. 'I'm Alex DuPont. And call me Alex. My deepest condolences to you. Come on in and have a seat.'

Gerry Hamilton was business-like and a little formal, but Alex could sense deep sadness and frailty beneath the composed façade. They sat in the office Walter had offered him; it wasn't as grand as the rest of Brown Legal's facilities, but it did the job. Alex wondered why she had chosen to meet him here; he supposed it was a neutral space. On the other hand, this was where her sister had worked, and that must have an emotional impact.

To start with, he felt distinctly ill at ease. He wasn't used to dealing with bereaved clients, or with victims of crime; his work was mostly corporate stuff, or high-profile divorce capers.

'I've brought the photos you asked for. This is Amanda. It was taken on our holiday in Corfu.'

Alex spent a few seconds looking at the photo: two sisters, having fun, loving their time together. They looked alike; and they were both beautiful women. 'You were close, weren't you?'

'Yes, we were. I… I miss her very badly.'

'Gerry, I have to ask; do you think your feeling of loss has influenced your thinking and hence you want the case to be re-investigated? Is it possible you are in denial about her suicide?'

'I've thought about that. I've questioned my motives, more than once. But it's more than that. It doesn't make sense for Amanda to kill herself. She was on the up; her life was going really well. She wouldn't take that away from herself, or from us.'

'Well, I can tell you I share your doubts; but I haven't had time to look into this in any depth. If it turns out she did kill herself, will you accept that?'

'If that's how it was, I'll accept it. But I don't think it was. And it sounds as if you don't either.'

'Let's just say I have a hunch, nothing more. Can you think of anyone who might have had bad intentions towards Amanda? Did she have any enemies?'

'Not that I know of. Although we were close, we didn't see that much of each other; we're both – were both – busy women. I can't say I know much about her friends, or enemies for that matter.'

'How would you describe your relationship with her?'

'We loved each other very much. Naturally, being the eldest I used to look after her.'

'Was there any competition between you two?'

'Not at all. There was no rivalry between us. We were highly proud of each other's success.'

'And can you think of any reason why she might have had access to poisons?'

'No, not at all. That was one of the things that made me suspicious in the first place. That, and…'

'And?'

'I got the feeling the police weren't too interested. After that Detective Sergeant interviewed me, I heard her on the phone. She was saying something about some gangland shooting and how her boss wanted her to get onto it. I don't think they gave themselves enough time, and they were a bit dismissive of me. I know that's not evidence, but it didn't exactly reassure me that they were doing their best.'

Alex filed that away for later. Melanie had already told him she was under pressure; he needed to know a bit more about that.

'What else struck you as suspicious?'

Gerry took a tissue from her bag, wiped her eyes. Then she was ready to answer his questions. 'There was no note; that struck me as odd. I don't believe she would have killed herself and not told us the reason why. I mean, don't people who commit suicide always leave a note?'

'Not always, no, but I take your point. To recap: you think the police might have rushed the job; the poison seems out of character; and you would have expected her to leave a note. Is that everything?'

'Yes...' There was something in Gerry's hesitation that made Alex sit up.

'Go on.'

'I know this will sound that I'm a bit paranoid, but I can't help feeling someone here might know something. I think Walter – Mr Coburn – shares that feeling. Maybe, that's why he's being so helpful.'

'Come to think of it, Walter has been extremely helpful, you're right. But I think there's perhaps more to it. I'll certainly be interviewing colleagues here; it's not unusual for office rivalries to get out of hand. Have you met any of her colleagues?'

'No, I haven't. She spoke about them as friends, though, not rivals. I think one of her old university friends works here too. Maybe, he might know something.'

'Thank you for that; I'll look into it. Gerry, I don't have any more questions for now, but once I've had a look around, I may need to come back to you. Is that OK?'

'Of course. I'm happy to help in any way I can.'

When Gerry had left, Alex made a few notes. He hadn't learned anything new, but some of the things she'd said confirmed a few of his own concerns, particularly about the police. His lunch date with Melanie was going to be a delicate affair.

CHAPTER 6

The Excelsior was buzzing. Alex waited in the foyer, casually appraising the other guests, and scanning the room to see if Melanie was already there. He was interrupted by Henri, the maître d'. 'Monsieur DuPont, *c'est un plaisir. Comment ça va?*

'*Salut, Henri, ca va tres bien, merci.*'

'Let me show you to your table, Monsieur; I see it was booked for two. A lovely lady, I hope?' Henri's eyes twinkled.

At that moment, the lovely lady in question entered the foyer. Alex felt his breath disappear in a whoosh; had he really forgotten how attractive she was? Melanie was dressed in a smart suit, tailored to accentuate her slim physique. Her shoulder-length blonde hair was held in a simple clasp and with her blue eyes, she looked ravishing. As it happened, Alex was also dressed snappily in his charcoal grey striped suit, white shirt and a purple tie with small white dots on it.

'Monsieur?'

'Oh, yes, Henri, excuse me. My guest has just arrived.'

Henri looked round and saw Melanie and said, 'Very nice to see you again, *Madame.*'

'Pleasure to see you too, Henri,' Melanie said.

A year suddenly felt like a long time, a distance of sorts.

Alex wasn't sure if he should hug her or just shake hands. Initially, he settled for a handshake and then kissed her on both cheeks. As they got closer, he felt a tingle of electricity ran through him. Probably, Melanie felt the same.

They made themselves comfortable. His eyes were focused on Melanie's face and enjoyed looking at every feature of it. It was relatively easy for them to re-connect because they had established a very good rapport at their last encounter. Very quickly, they began to enjoy each other's company.

The waiter checked with them if they were ready to order their meal. Amazingly, both ordered beer batter cod, chips and peas for their main course, strawberry cheesecake for dessert, and diet coke with ice.

'So, what have you been up to since we last met?' asked Melanie.

'I have been very busy: dealing with private clients and a few corporate cases.'

'Are you still enjoying your new career?'

'I'm indeed: it's interesting, challenging and often exciting. As the clients' turnover is quite fast, we come across a range of different cases. The volume of work keeps us on our toes. The Agency is doing very well, and our reputation is growing gradually. As a result, there's more demand for our services which is very encouraging.'

'That's nice. Do you miss being a lawyer?'

'Not really. I don't have time to think about it. Being a private investigator and running a business are my main concern at the moment.'

Their main course was served. They ordered another diet coke with ice.

'How are you, Melanie?'

'I'm good.'

'How is work?'

'Far too busy and I feel constantly knackered, but that goes with the territory.'

'Are you married yet?' He knew very well that she wasn't because he had already checked, and she did not have a wedding ring on her finger.

'What do you mean about me getting married?' she snapped.

'I thought perhaps you and Martin....'

'Don't be silly. We are still in a relationship, but marriage has never been mentioned. Anyway, are you married to Claire yet?'

'No. We've not talked about it either.'

Both were pleased to hear that the situation in their personal lives had remained the same. That meant there was still time for Alex to make a move on his favourite Sergeant.

He and Claire had been seeing each other for nearly two years, off and on, and it wasn't going anywhere. Now, sitting with Melanie, he knew why. Whilst eating their lunch, they would take a glimpse at each other and enjoy the opportunity of being together again. Both wanted to say so much about themselves and expressed their individual feelings, but these had to be left for another day. They finished their lunch.

Suddenly, he said, 'Walk me through it.'

'Excuse me?'

'The crime scene; walk me through it.'

'It wasn't a crime scene, Alex; it was a suicide.'

'Fine, walk me through the suicide scene, or whatever you call it in the trade.'

Melanie settled back in her seat and gathered her

thoughts. It was over a month ago, but a lot of things had happened since then; bad things that she had to deal with. She sighed. 'Right. Well, we got a call a few minutes after five o'clock on that Sunday afternoon from one of the first responders, the Police Inspector, about the incident. Shortly afterwards, we got there and were briefed by the Inspector. The ambulance crew and the paramedics were attending to the victim. We found a young man in real distress. He said he'd gone to visit his old friend and found her dead.'

'How did he get in?'

'He said she'd left a spare key on the lintel over the door; apparently he'd used it before.'

'And did his story hold up?'

'Yes, it did. Can I get on with it?'

'Sorry.'

'He found her lying on the floor of the living room, kind of squashed between a sofa and a coffee table. He moved the table to try and give her CPR, but when he felt for a pulse and there was none. She was cold, and he quickly realised she'd been dead for some time. He called the emergency services immediately. It turned out that they worked together and had been friends since their university days. He looked gutted, Alex. I'm not surprised; she really wasn't a pretty sight. But cyanide will do that to a person.'

'Tell me about the scene.'

'The body was where he'd described it, between the sofa and the coffee table. It was contorted, like she was trying to turn herself inside out. There was a wine glass on the coffee table. I got the SOCO people to take a residue sample from it; they found strong traces of potassium cyanide and remnants of Prosecco.

'The post-mortem report and toxicology report were

conclusive, and confirmed that she died around four in the afternoon. The pathologist said he'd examined the contents of her stomach; he found a light lunch, and about a hundred mil of Prosecco, with a liberal dash of cyanide. Very liberal, in his opinion. He reckoned there was enough to kill everyone in the building.'

'And what about the bottle?'

'The bottle?'

'The Prosecco bottle. Were there any traces of cyanide in the bottle, or only in the glass?'

'Now you mention it, I don't recall seeing the bottle. I assumed the SOCO bods had taken it for analysis; I'll need to check that in the file. We did find a small vial in the kitchen: it was obviously the container for the poison.'

'And there was only one glass out?'

'Yes, only one. We looked in the cupboards, and there were another five similar glasses, so we figured that made the set.'

'Anything else out of place?'

'Nothing. The apartment was neat and clean, not many knick-knacks around; a bit impersonal.'

'Was there a note? Usually, when people are about to commit suicide, they tend to leave a note explaining the reason for taking their life.'

'No, no note.'

'Right. I really need to see the file. Based on what I've heard so far, I don't think it quite adds up to suicide. I'm going to have a look at the place tomorrow, and it would be really useful to see the file first.'

'I'll have to talk to the boss about that. He won't be too pleased. I'll get hammered for taking my eyes off the main prize.'

'And what is the main prize?'

'There were a couple of shootings over in West Kensington; gang related. Jenkins wants it cleared up fast. What he said, minus the more colourful adjectives, was, "I want this nipped in the bud before these melts go and start a war on my turf." I'll have to watch my step.'

'You'd be doing me a real favour, Melanie.'

She liked him a lot and wanted to assist him. 'Well, don't get your hopes up. If Jenkins doesn't say yes straight off, you'll have to go through the regular channels and that could take time.'

'On that note, I hear Walter Coburn already got a look at it.'

'I don't believe this. Did he now? Then, I should just upload it onto the internet and let everyone have a good look.'

'Not a bad idea.'

'Yeah, and that's the other thing. If you find anything iffy, I'll have to go to Jenkins and ask him to reopen the case. He's not going to love me for that.'

'Hey, what could possibly go wrong? Worst comes to worst, we could end up working together again. It worked out very well for us last time.'

'I don't think Jenkins will thank me for reminding him of that. We didn't exactly cover ourselves in glory; and you came out looking like the hero who saved our bacon.'

'Wait a minute. What mattered at the time was the murder was solved and justice prevailed. I just happened to play a part in it.'

'A big part at that. I know.'

'I was only doing the best for my client.'

Melanie sighed: she could see where this was going.

'Alright, I'll go and ask him. I'll say I've heard there's some outside concerns – I won't mention you just yet – and I want to review the file which is not long anyway, so I can do it in my spare time. If he agrees, I'll let you know, and we'll work something out.'

Alex was delighted to hear it. 'Thanks, I owe you.'

'Trust me, I'll keep you to that.' Melanie winked at him.

**

Melanie headed back to the Department and went straight to see Jenkins.

'Guv, can I have a word?' Melanie saw the look on the DI's face and regretted saying anything.

'What is it, Cooper? If you want to tell me you've just arrested a melt for the gang-related shooting, I'm all ears. Otherwise, I've just seen a friend.'

She swallowed hard. 'It's not that, guv, it's the suicide case of the trainee solicitor at Brown Legal over a month ago.'

'What is it with that case? Some posh lawyer was sniffing round the Chief Super a couple of weeks ago.'

'So, I heard, guv. Thing is, I'm thinking it might be worth just reviewing the file. You know, cover our backs in case something kicks off.'

'Why should anything kick off? Is there something I should know, Cooper?'

Melanie felt under pressure and needed to come clean quickly.

'Well, I got a call from Alex DuPont…'

She saw the expression on DI Jenkins' face changed; it wasn't his happy face. *Damn, I didn't mean to do that.* She pressed on. 'He's been hired by Brown Legal and the

Hamilton family to look into it, guv. I think we'd better keep up to speed in case he finds anything. He asked if he could see the file on Amanda Hamilton.'

'So, you've already talked to him?'

'He called and asked. I said I'd see what I could do; with your permission, obviously.'

Jenkins heaved an exasperated sigh. 'Look, I'd normally say no. But since this lawyer sort has been poking his nose in, it's probably best you have another look. If DuPont wants to see the file, I suppose he can. But it stays with you; he doesn't get to take it away. Is that clear?'

'Yes, guv; very clear. I'll get on it.'

'In your own time, Cooper. I want you focused on the gang stuff first and foremost. And keep an eye on Mr DuPont; if he finds something suspicious, I want to know about it.'

Jenkins stormed off into the squad room. Melanie pitied the next person he bumped into. She went to find the file and sent a text to Alex.

CHAPTER 7

Melanie's phone buzzed: 'Hello Alex.'

'I got your text; what's the news?'

'Well, there's good news and bad news. The good news is, Richard's OK with me reviewing the file, and he's OK with you having a look at it too.'

'Right, what's the bad news?'

'It's good news really. I may have a lead on the shootings. I was planning to come over to Mayfair, but now it looks like I'll have to go to West Kensington to talk to a horribly dodgy pub landlord. Most likely, I'll be there the rest of the afternoon. Any chance you could pop over to my place early this evening? Say seven-thirty?'

Alex's heart missed a beat. 'Yes, I can do that. Will Martin be there?'

'Maybe. I haven't talked to him. Is that a problem?'

'No, it's no problem at all. I'll see you at seven-thirty.'

When Alex finished the call, he saw Jenny looking at him, that tell-tale smirk on her face. 'What?'

'It's nice to know that you are going over to Melanie's place. Sounds like a good idea.'

'Jenny, if it wasn't for the fact that you feed me, look after me and watch my back, I'd fire you on the spot.'

'Go on, you're only saying that because I'm far too good to you.'

'If your head gets any bigger, we'll have to widen the doors. Now, what have you found out about Amanda from the newspapers?'

'Not much, I'm afraid. The papers all took it at face value: Terrible tragedy, young woman cut short in the prime of her life, etc. No one seems to have raised any suspicions.'

Scott came in, like a man in a hurry. He shucked off his jacket and launched it towards the coat hooks. It landed perfectly. Alex grimaced and shook his head in amazement.

'Did you get anything from the neighbours and the residents?'

'They were all very sympathetic, but no one had any information. One thing I did find out. The owner told me the CCTV cameras weren't working on the Sunday the fourth of June, when she died; seems they were having their annual maintenance check. I called the tech company's office and talked to the two people who worked on the job. They were down in the basement all day and didn't see anything, until the ambulance turned up and then the police. I think we've drawn a blank on that one.'

'Well, you tried. We'll go over tomorrow and have a proper look at the scene. I've texted the owner and he's happy for us to have a look around. I think Walter has put in a good word for us.'

'Right. I'll put my forensics kit together this evening. You never know.'

**

The afternoon seemed to drag on forever. Alex spent the whole time in a state of nervous anticipation. He imagined

Melanie, sitting in a low-life pub in West Kensington, trying to squeeze information out of the pub landlord. He didn't like the idea of her getting mixed up in a gangland situation. But she was a big girl, and she could more than look after herself. The idea of spending an evening with her at her place filled him with excitement and dread in equal measure. Part of him hoped Martin wouldn't be there to chaperone them, and part of him hoped he would.

He made a few calls to catch up on their other ongoing cases: a finance company that seemed to be bleeding money, and a city banker who was being blackmailed. He did his best to reassure the clients that their case was being given his full attention and his team was working very hard to meet their needs.

It was six o'clock and he had to get ready to go to Westminster.

Jenny brought him a mug of tea. 'I'm off now. I've left a sandwich in the kitchen; make sure you eat it. Romance is far less fun on an empty stomach. Bye.' She was out the door before he could think of a clever reply.

He ate his sandwich and drank his tea. He then set off to see Melanie.

**

When the doorbell rang, Martin got up to answer it. Melanie felt a little surge of annoyance. 'Martin, this is my flat. I'll answer the door. Sorry. That didn't come out the way I meant it to.'

'So how was it meant to come out?'

'Um, I think I should answer the door, see who it is.' Melanie shuffled towards the door, trying to hide her embarrassment. Martin settled into the cushions of the sofa, irritated, muttering to himself. She knew who it was; that made it all the worse.

Melanie lived in a purpose-built nineteenth-century block in Westminster that had been quietly and elegantly gentrified. The Met owned several such properties in that part of London and let them out to serving officers. She felt very privileged to be able to live in such a plush location at a relatively modest rent.

The walkway had been glassed in to protect visitors from the weather. Looking through the spyhole, she could see her current visitor, looking around him at the pot plants she had arranged in the small space outside her front door.

Alex stepped in, smiling. His dark, wavy hair was tousled, as if he'd been in a hurry. 'Hello, Sergeant,' he said, grinning. 'I wonder if …' He stopped, noticed Martin. 'Oh, hello, Martin, how are you?' He made no attempt to go over and shake hands.

To his credit, Martin didn't stir from his place on the sofa and said, 'Fine, thanks.'

In fact, it was the first time they met since leaving university. They were both at Oxford together.

Melanie looked from one to the other: at Alex's lustrous dark hair (Martin's hair was flat and mousey); at Alex's brown, steely eyes (Martin's eyes were grey, and kind, but soft); at Alex's tall, athletic figure (Martin was slightly stooped from hours at his desk). She felt butterflies in the pit of her stomach.

'Well,' Alex said, apparently could sense the obvious tension in the room. 'Shall we crack on? I'm keen to see everything.'

Melanie felt as if her tongue had gone AWOL; she struggled to find an answer. Martin shifted in his seat. 'Look, if you two have something to do, I can…'

'No!' she snapped, far too quickly. 'I mean, you don't need to go, Martin, it's fine. Alex and I were just going to…' *Damn! What were we just going to do?* Answers that made her distinctly uncomfortable came spontaneously to her mind.

Alex wasn't helping. His face had settled into a submissive grin that could have meant anything. Melanie could imagine what Martin thought it meant.

She found herself imagining she was being forced to make a choice. Whose company would she rather be in? She thought about spending the evening with Alex in the comfort of her own surroundings. It was an enticing prospect.

'Alex, I think perhaps you should take the file home with you.'

'I thought your boss didn't want you to do that.'

'I know, I…' Melanie glared daggers at him; why was he making things so difficult? Why was she finding this so difficult?

Finally, realisation dawned on Alex. 'I'm sorry, I was clearly interrupting.'

'No, you weren't,' said Melanie and Martin at the same time.

'OK, I'm not interrupting. What shall we do now?'

'Umm.' Melanie felt some of her self-control returning and decided to put a lid on the situation. 'I know, Richard was pretty reluctant to let you walk off with the file, but I think he was over-reacting. I'm happy for you to take it away. Perhaps you can courier it back to me early tomorrow morning?'

'Yes, I can do that.' Alex sounded, disappointed as he realised, he was being sent home; this wasn't how he had wanted things to go. But Martin was there, and he couldn't exactly throw him out.

'Promise me, you'll get it back to me early, Alex. Otherwise, Richard will have my guts for garters if he thinks I've let you take the file away. Luckily, I got some decent intelligence out of that slimy pub landlord, otherwise I think he'd have grounded me.'

'I promise. The courier will deliver it to you early in the morning before you leave for work. I wouldn't want to get you in any trouble, you've been very helpful.'

Melanie went to the study to fetch the file. She felt ridiculously self-conscious, felt two pairs of eyes were following her; she slowed down to a casual stroll when it dawned on her that she was hurrying unnecessarily.

'Here it is. As I said, it's a bit thin.' She handed the file to Alex. Their hands touched around the manila folder. Melanie's heart leapt; invisible sparks of electricity danced around the folder in a mad corona, and she felt the buzz of them coursing through her. She pulled her hand back hurriedly.

Alex felt it too. He didn't withdraw his hand; he wanted the feeling to go on, possibly forever. 'Thanks,' he mumbled. 'I'll get it back to you first thing.'

'Well, don't stay up all night reading ten pages,' Melanie said.

'Don't worry. I won't.' Alex looked at her for a moment, smiled and left.

**

There was no need for Alex to stay up all night. He spent about an hour going through the file a few times, though there really wasn't much to read. The photos of Amanda, face an unnatural red, body contorted, left a deep impression on him. Several things bothered him; he called Scott to ask his opinion because prior to joining the Agency, he was a Detective Sergeant.

'Hi Scott, sorry to bother you.'

'No problem. What's up?'

'I've just finished reading the file on Amanda. There doesn't seem to have been much of an investigation at all,' Alex said. 'I don't understand why it was all so casual.'

'You have to see it from their point of view,' Scott said. 'Suicide is not technically a crime. The police mainly get involved as a reassurance to the families of the victims.'

'But why do they assume that it's suicide in the first place?'

'They tend to be guided by the medical responders. Ambulance crew and the paramedics are used to dealing with cases like this. They arrive on the scene and make a decision fairly quickly. If there's no sign of a break-in, a struggle, and the victim is alone, and the classic signs of suicide are there, that's what they go with.'

'But what about the lack of a note?'

'The suicide note thing is a bit of a myth. Only about forty percent of people who kill themselves leave a note; it varies a bit depending on ethnic background and class, but it's rarely more than that.'

'And poison? Doesn't that arouse suspicion?'

'Actually, it does the opposite. Poisoning is among the most common methods of suicide for women. So, for the ambulance people and the paramedics, it's a bit of a giveaway.'

'But cyanide? I mean, that's a bit extreme, isn't it?'

'You'd think so, but the stats show that cyanide is very rarely used as a murder method.'

'So why do they bother sending a detective in the first place? Seems kind of unnecessary.'

'It's belt and braces really. If a detective visits the scene, has a look around and doesn't notice anything iffy, then everybody's happy especially the family.'

'Do you think we're barking up the wrong tree here? Is it more likely suicide?'

'I couldn't say, not until I've had a good look at the scene at least.' Alex trusted Scott's opinion: he was a solid presence on the team, calm and unflappable. He didn't jump to conclusions either. 'Assumptions are like adverts,' he had told Alex one day. 'They promise a lot but you usually end up disappointed.'

'Thanks, Scott, you've really helped me out. See you in the morning.'

'Right-ho. Sleep well.'

The alarm clock was set for six-thirty. He needed to get a good night sleep. He had to get up early because the courier would be at his apartment at 7 am to pick up a large brown envelope which contained the file to be delivered to Melanie's flat in Westminster.

Alex tried but sleep wouldn't come easily. It hadn't cooled off much. The apartment was sticky and uncomfortable. In addition, every time he started to drift off, he found himself dreaming of Claire; except that she kept turning into Melanie. They drew closer; he could almost feel the moist brush of her lips on his. Then she arched away from him and continued to arch until her body was impossibly contorted. Then her face changed, and he was looking at Amanda, body twisted around the coffee table. Her eyes snapped open, angry, accusing. She didn't speak but Alex could feel the message burning in those eyes. *It's up to you now, Alex, and only you.* Eventually, he managed to get a few hours of sleep.

He woke up at the continuous beeping sound of his alarm clock. He jumped out of bed to get ready. At 7 am, the courier collected the envelope.

Then he went through his morning routine of exercises, showered and shaved, had his breakfast and got dressed in his blue striped suit, pink shirt and blue tie. He paused for a moment and thought: *let's go there with an open mind and see where the evidence leads us.*

CHAPTER 8

Before he set off for Amanda's apartment, Alex texted Melanie to make sure the file had arrived safely. Her reply was a brief yes. He sighed and pocketed the phone. It wasn't a problem, really. He had a feeling he would need to speak to her after he had examined the scene.

Scott picked him up and they drove to Chiswick which is not too far from Mayfair. The house where Amanda had lived and died was a huge Victorian pile, almost a mansion, converted in the sixties and divided into four spacious apartments. Out the back, there was a park of a garden and a view of the playing fields. The house itself was one of four equally large buildings; the rest of the street – Fairfield Crescent – was filled with more detached and semi-detached houses. It was quiet, pleasant and leafy; Alex could imagine it being a pleasant place to live.

Mr Barrington, the owner of the house was waiting for them in the gravelled driveway. He was a wiry, nervous little man with a pencil moustache and a habit of wringing his hands. He shook hands with Alex and Scott, and then his hands flew back together as if they'd missed each other.

'As you know, we're investigating Amanda's death. It's possible she was murdered,' said Alex.

Mr Barrington didn't say anything but suddenly appeared uncomfortable.

Alex looked up at the two cameras placed discreetly above the wide front door. It was a pity they hadn't been working when they were needed most. They might have had an interesting tale to tell.

Mr Barrington (a big name for a small man, Alex thought), let them in through the front door and showed them upstairs. When they arrived at the door to Amanda's apartment, he handed Alex a key. 'Right, I'll leave you to it. I don't imagine you need me looking over your shoulders.'

'Before you go, Mr Barrington,' Alex said. 'I wondered if you knew anything about Amanda's regular visitors.'

'Sorry,' he replied. 'I don't live in the house, I just rent it out. Ms Hamilton was a good tenant, and I shall miss her, but I'm afraid I know very little about her.' His hands twisted around each other again and he gave a nervous laugh; he was obviously keen to be off.

Alex slid the key into the lock, and they walked in, shutting the door behind them. 'He was a bit twitchy,' Alex said.

'Yeah, weird little bloke,' said Scott. 'Still, I don't see him as a Neuro-Surgeon, do you? Plus, I'm not sure he could keep his hands apart for long enough to do the operation.' He put his forensics kit down on the plush carpet in the entrance hall. 'Right, let's have a look at the place, see if everything lines up. Or not.'

They walked into the living room, where Amanda's body had been found.

Everything was just as the police and medics had left it: the coffee table stood at an odd angle to the sofa, indicating it had been moved. Alex could see the indents in the carpet where it normally stood.

He took a deep breath and looked around him. The room was neat and comfortable, but not especially homely. There were a few fine art posters framed on the walls; post-impressionists mostly. A tidy row of books adorned the shelf unit in the corner; best sellers, thrillers in the main, and a couple of Rough Guides to exotic locations, one to Hong Kong. Everything was covered in a thin layer of dust, giving the room a sad air, as if it had been forgotten in all the fuss.

A solitary wine glass stood on the coffee table. Scott put on a pair of latex gloves and picked it up. There was a clean ring in the dust where it had stood. 'I'll give this a check for prints. You never know.'

Alex slipped on a pair of gloves, went into the kitchen, and gently opened and closed drawers and cupboards. In the right-hand cupboard above the sink, he found four wine glasses, identical to the one on the coffee table. 'Four and one make five,' he mused. 'Interesting.' Then, he opened the left-hand cupboard; it contained china cups and everyday mugs; and a single wine glass, polished so it glinted in the sunlight from the window. *Very interesting.*

The police report had mentioned a small vial, presumably the container for the cyanide. It was on the work surface beside the fridge. 'Scott, when you're done dusting the glass, can you do this vial too?'

'Will do.'

Alex continued to look around. Something in the report was nagging at him, and he was hoping the scene would bring it to the front of his mind. The bottle! That was it, the bottle; the report hadn't included it as evidence. He looked in the fridge: no sign of the Prosecco bottle. He noticed the milk had turned into a curd; the dense aroma assaulted his nostrils as soon as he opened the door.

Next, he checked in the small waste bin under the sink. It held a couple of wrappers for posh versions of fast food from Waitrose, and a few shreds of leftover lettuce; but no bottle.

Scott came in and picked up the vial. 'It's almost cute,' he said. 'Small too; still, I don't suppose you need a pint pot to keep cyanide in.'

'No, you probably don't. But if you want to pour yourself a glass of Prosecco, even a final glass, there is one thing you would need.'

'What's that?'

'A bottle. I've had a look around, in the cupboards, the fridge and the bin, and I can't see one. It's not mentioned in the report either.'

'I suppose, if Amanda had a tidy mind – a very tidy mind, now I think about it – she could have taken it out to the recycling bin before she drank from the glass. But that doesn't fit with the idea of a woman in distress, about to take her own life, does it?'

'No, it doesn't. And it begs another question. Was the cyanide in the bottle, or only in the glass?'

'Why is that important?' Scott's forehead creased into a puzzled frown.

Alex opened the two cupboards. 'That's why,' he said, a note of triumph in his voice.

Scott looked into the cupboards: one with a row of four reasonably clean wine glasses; one with a single, highly polished glass languishing among mugs sporting jokey logos. 'Now that is interesting.'

'That's what I said.'

'This is the type of breakthrough we're looking for. I think we've got something to work on here. It's not exactly nailed-on evidence, but it's enough to put a reasonable doubt in our mind. I'm going to take a few snaps.' He left the kitchen and went to grab a digital camera from his bag.

While Scott took photos of the two cupboards, the empty fridge and the bin, Alex made notes. The combination of the missing bottle and the glass in the wrong place had set his thoughts racing. He knew it wasn't enough by itself. But it made further investigation worthwhile at least.

He went back into the living room and looked around again; nothing else seemed out of place. He tried to visualise how the incident had taken place, but he was none the wiser.

Scott had gone back to his fingerprinting. 'Any joy?' Alex asked.

'Well, I've lifted a couple of prints, all right, but that's not the whole story here.'

'What do you mean?'

'Let's start with the glass. There are some fairly clear dabs on it, and you'd assume they belong to Amanda. But they're not particularly clean. Now it might be that she was nervous, and perspiration has smudged the prints; but I get the impression that the cleaner prints are laid over others, and that's what's caused the smudging.'

'You mean more than one person handled the glass?'

'It looks that way. I can't be certain without getting it to a lab so some boffin can stick it under a microscope, but I'd put a tenner on there being someone else's prints on here. And that's not all.'

'Get on with it, man; you've got me on tenterhooks already.' Alex's voice was tinged with impatience, but Scott was enjoying himself. He wanted to keep the suspense going for a while and then disclose his finding.

'It's the vial.'

'You found prints on the vial?'

'That's the thing. I didn't find any.' Scott looked at Alex and arched an eyebrow. 'Our Amanda is beginning to look like a very strange suicide. Why would she wipe her prints off the vial?'

'Why indeed?' Alex could feel the wheels turning in his mind. The little snippets of anomalous evidence were beginning to add up into something more sinister. He jotted a bullet-point list in his notebook, scratched out a couple of items, added another couple; when he was satisfied, he looked up at Scott.

'Right; let's have a look at what we've found so far.'

'Hang on a second.' Scott rummaged in his kit bag and found a plastic carrier bag. He spread it over one of the seats on the sofa and made himself comfortable. 'OK, fire away.'

Alex couldn't help being impressed. Scott was treating the place as a proper crime scene. 'So, we have prints on the glass that Amanda apparently drank from. They are likely to be hers, but there may just be another set underneath them.

'Then we've got a vial, presumably the vial in which the poison came in, and it doesn't have any prints on it at all. The wine glasses, at least four of them, are placed together in the right-hand cupboard; but there's another glass, identical, in the left-hand cupboard, and it appears to have been very carefully cleaned and polished.

'And finally, there's the thing we haven't got: the wine bottle. So, to sum it up for this to be suicide, we have Amanda pouring herself a glass of poisoned wine. She cleans her fingerprints off the vial, the cyanide came in and disposes of the bottle, and only then does she take a drink.'

'There's the glass too.'

'Yes, yes, I was coming to that. Along with all these

glaring inconsistencies, we have the anomaly of the single wine glass, clearly in the wrong cupboard, and spotlessly clean. Like someone was cleaning up after themselves but didn't know the layout.'

Scott leaned forward, and his plastic cushion squeaked a complaint. 'I don't know about you, but I'm beginning to smell something a bit more rotten here than just sour milk and almonds.'

'Sour milk and almonds; that's good. It could be the title of a B movie. Now, where were we? I think we should go back over this place with a fine-tooth comb, see if anything else turns up. Can you have another look at the living room and the kitchen? Oh, and the police report mentioned a laptop; keep your eyes opened for it. I'll go and check the bedroom.'

Scott put on a fresh pair of latex gloves and headed for the kitchen; Alex donned some fresh gloves too and went into the bedroom. His eyes swept around the room: cosy, and bit more lived-in than the living room. And there on the bedside table was a slim, expensive laptop.

Alex lifted the laptop lid and clicked the mouse pad. Bingo. The screen came to life. The screen saver was a photograph of five young people, smiling, obviously happy in each other's company. It drew attention to Alex's memory. 'I've seen that photo before,' he said to himself. 'Now where was it?'

He clicked on a few icons at random. Amanda's inbox began to fill with new emails. Alex was tempted to trawl through them but it seemed a time-consuming thing to do just on the off chance there was a message from a killer.

He looked in the chest of drawers and the wardrobe. Amanda had exquisite taste in clothes, he thought. Everything was of high quality and obviously expensive, apart from an oversized t-shirt he assumed she'd used instead of pyjamas. He had been hoping to find a diary or an address book, but he had no luck. 'I suppose it's all on her phone,' he mused aloud. 'Now there's a thing; where's her phone?'

He went back to the living room to ask Scott if he'd seen a mobile anywhere, when something on the shelf below the books caught his eye: a photograph of five young people, smiling. 'Gotcha,' he exclaimed.

'Got what?' Scott looked up from his search under the sofa.

'That photo; she had it on her laptop as a screensaver. I guess it must have been important to her. I have a feeling about it. I wonder if we're looking at a photo of her killer. And probably one of them is the guy who found her. What's his name?' Alex checked in his notebook. 'Ashley, that's it: Ashley Bradshaw.'

'Shall we take it back to the office and let Jenny go through it? The laptop, I mean.'

'I think the police might have something to say about that,' said Alex. 'We should probably leave it for them.'

'That's not the only option.' Scott went to his bag and produced a flash drive.

'I can copy everything on it and give it to Jenny. The police need never know.'

'Scott Wallace, you are a sly and devious individual. I like it.'

'I've taken a photo of the photo too, which might come in handy.'

A couple of hours later, they were outside the house, loading a few things into the car. Alex looked over at the houses across the street. He noticed a figure in the window of the house almost directly opposite. The man looked back but didn't acknowledge Alex.

'Scott, have you noticed that bloke across the road? He seems very interested in us. I think it might be worth having a word with him at some point, if only to tell him to mind his own business. Anyway, that's for another day. Let's get back to the office, I need to make some calls, and Jenny needs to dig into Amanda's digital life.'

**

While Jenny clicked, browsed and muttered to herself, Alex took himself off to his office to make his call. He had a feeling that, with the evidence he and Scott had unearthed, the police might have to reopen the case, despite DI Jenkins' reservations.

He was about to call Melanie when he stopped and thought. He ought to give Gerry a call, for courtesy's sake and let her know how the investigation was going. But first, he decided to call Walter Coburn and update him. Walter was paying the bill, after all, and there was always the chance he could exert some influence via his friends in high places to help persuade the Met to have another look.

'Walter, good afternoon. I have some news on the Hamilton case.'

'That was remarkably prompt, Alex. Does this mean it was suicide after all?'

'On the contrary, Walter. I believe we have uncovered enough evidence to indicate foul play. It may be a little early to call it murder, but it's beginning to look that way.' He heard a sharp intake of breath on the line.

'Well, I don't quite know what to say. All in all, I'm not sure if this is good news or bad.'

Alex hadn't entirely crossed Walter off his list of potential suspects. The lawyer's attitude towards Amanda and Gerry, and his willingness to foot the bill, still didn't sit quite right with him.

'Well, I would say on the whole, it looks very promising. If it means we can bring Amanda's killer to justice, we have achieved something special. It won't bring her back, poor girl, but it may bring some closure to her family.'

'Yes, you're right. Have you spoken to Gerry yet?'

'No, not yet, but she's next on my list. I wanted to call you first because I think it's time to interview a couple of members of staff at Brown Legal.'

'Do you suspect some of my people were involved in this horrible matter, Alex?'

'Of course not. As it happens, we are a long way from the point of naming suspects. But I'd like to talk to people who knew her well, and I'd particularly like to interview Ashley Bradshaw. He was the person who found her, I understand.'

'Yes, poor Ashley; he really hasn't been the same since. Very well, Alex, I'll talk to him and contact your personal assistant, um…'

'Jenny.'

'Yes, Jenny, and arrange a suitable time for the interview. Will that be all?'

'Well, not quite. In the meantime, I was wondering if you could do me a small favour; it involves you playing a round of golf.'

**

Gerry was in her office when Alex called. She hurried to shut the door and settled into her chair, phone cradled at her shoulder. 'Mr DuPont, what can I do for you?'

'Please call me Alex. I'm phoning to update you on my investigation into the circumstances of your sister's untimely death. Is this a good time to talk?'

'As good as any, Alex. What have you found out?'

'Well, the investigation is still at a relatively early stage, and I don't want to give you false hopes, but I think I can say with some degree of confidence that there is evidence to suggest foul play may have been involved.'

Alex could hear the sharp intake of breath as Gerry digested the news. In some respects, this was the worst time for her as her suspicions had been confirmed, but no one was facing justice for the crime.

'Do you... Do you have any idea who could have done it? I'm sorry, I shouldn't be asking, I know. But it's quite a shock to hear that Amanda was – might have been – well, murdered.'

'You have every right to ask, Gerry. And no, I don't have any firm suspects at the moment. I'm at the stage where I shall be asking the police to reopen the case, though. They have greater resources than we do and it would speed up the investigation if they got involved.'

'And do you have any confidence in them, Alex?'

Alex thought of Melanie. 'Let's just say I'm quietly confident they will have more to offer than they did over a month ago.'

Gerry wasn't entirely reassured. 'I can't say I share your confidence. You seem to have got further in a few days than they did in a month.'

Alex decided to let it pass. He would like to focus on another matter. 'Gerry, there is something I wanted to ask you. In Amanda's apartment, I found a photo, of her and four other young people, probably her university friends. Do you know the other people in the photo?'

'I know the photo. She had it as a screensaver on her laptop too, I think. She did tell me their names once, but to be honest I've forgotten. I'm sorry I couldn't be of more help. Wait. Ashley, the chap she worked with, I think he was in the photo. I couldn't tell you which one is him, though.'

'That's very helpful, thank you. I'll let you get on. Please feel free to call at any time and I'll be in touch when there is something substantive to report.'

After the call, Alex pondered for a minute. He found it strange that sisters who claimed to be close should know so little about each other's lives. Gerry wasn't exactly a suspect because he couldn't see her as a cold-blooded killer. However, she played her cards close to her chest, and he had the strong feeling she was keeping something hidden from him. Whether it was relevant to the case or not was another matter. She hadn't told him anything he didn't already know; but at least she'd offered some relevant information.

CHAPTER 9

Alex was keen to contact Melanie. Hopefully, she would be able to clarify the issues he had come across whilst reading the file and visiting Amanda's apartment. He wondered whether she would be interested in doing so. In addition, how would she respond to his concerns, as this would not reflect favourably on the way their investigation was conducted. No doubt, she would have every reason to believe that their approach was being severely criticised. Alex would have to handle Melanie with care. After all, he would have to rely on her support to persuade her boss to reopen the case.

From a personal point of view, he was madly attracted to Melanie and could not wait to hear her lovely voice again. It was the second time he was hoping to work closely with her and wanted to make the most of the opportunity.

Although Melanie was relatively busy, she had been waiting for Alex to ring her. She would always find the time to speak to him. In fact, she would prefer to be in his company. But there was a problem with controlling her emotions, especially of what happened with Alex in her flat when she was giving him the file. She did not have to wait for long, Alex was on the line.

'Hello Melanie, how are you?'

'Fine thank you.' A curt reply.

'Melanie, we need to talk.' Immediately he could feel the air between them tightening, like he'd said the wrong thing.

'Alex, we can't…' She tried again. 'I think we should keep some distance, for now.' It took him a moment to figure out what she was saying: she wasn't talking about the investigation. He thought of that moment when their hands had touched. *She felt it too.* Despite the thrill he experienced every time he saw her, talked to her or simply thought of her, he needed to backtrack a bit and bring some sense to their conversation.

'Sorry, I should have made myself clear. We need to talk about the Amanda Hamilton's case.' He could practically feel her relaxing. *Whew.*

'Oh, I see. Sorry, I thought… Never mind. What have you got?'

'I've been over to her apartment for a look. I found a few things that don't quite make sense. I can't say they are evidence of murder, not for certain, but they definitely don't stack up to suicide.'

'Such as?' Melanie asked.

Alex couldn't tell if she was sceptical or just distracted.

'Mostly it's just things out of place. But there are one or two things I'm struggling to find an innocent explanation for. For instance, the vial the poison presumably came in. We need to check that. By the way – doesn't have any fingerprints on it. It's completely clean. That doesn't make any sense at all.'

'OK, I'll give you that, it's a bit odd. But it hardly adds up to murder.'

'Alright, but there's more. While Scott and I were having a look around, I thought I'd check out the Prosecco bottle. You see it smelled odd. Did she pour the cyanide into the bottle? or just poured it into the glass. The thing is, the bottle isn't there. I think that's a big miss.'

'I did say I thought the SOCO people might have it.'

Alex was ready for that. 'If they did, they forgot to mention it in the report.'

'Well, I suppose it could be that she might have taken the last glass from it and taken it out to the bin.'

'We're talking about a woman who was about to commit suicide, and in a particularly horrible way. Do you think the recycling would have been uppermost on her mind?'

'I know, it's not a strong point. I have to admit, I never thought to check on the bottle once I assumed the SOCO bods had taken care of it. Is there anything else?'

Alex had the feeling she was beginning to warm to the idea that Amanda's death might be suspicious. 'Little things. Like a glass, lovingly polished, but put in the wrong side of the cupboard on its own. Like a photo taking pride of place on her shelves and turning up again on her laptop. Like her phone going missing.'

'I must confess, it's not our finest hour, but you've got me interested. What do you think? How should we play it from here?'

This was the crucial moment. Alex had set out the bait and now, he had to reel her in. 'I think you have to reopen the case. I know you'll have to work on Richard, and that won't be easy, but I think I might have arranged a bit of help for you on that score.'

'What kind of help?'

'It's to do with the posh lawyer who squeezed

information out of your Chief Super. I've sent him off to make the right noises in Macey's ear again. I imagine it will filter down to DI level soon enough.'

'Alex, you're a crafty so and so! I'll get it in the ear from Richard for this. But you're right. If the Chief Super leans on him it will, at least, make him think about it. Alright, I'll see what I can do. I'm not making any promises, mind. If Richard thinks I should be pulling in gangsters instead of looking for poisoners, I'll have to go along with it.'

'Thanks, Melanie, I owe you one.'

'Damn right you do. I don't suppose you've got any suspects yet?'

'Not exactly. But I have a list of people whose alibis might need checking just to be on the safe side. Her laptop will need checking. And I suppose we ought to try and trace the phone too.'

'That's amazing. So, you want the Met to do the legwork for you.'

'Keep quiet about our little plan. Don't try and sell it like that to Richard either. He might think you're doing me a favour. If he does, he'll be very crossed with you from the off.'

'Alright, I know what to do. Leave it with me. I'll try and get him interested, even if it sounds a bit thin so far. You'll let me know if anything else turns up. Won't you? I need to be in the loop if I'm going to get this reopened. I'll get back to you when I've spoken to Richard.'

'Of course. I suppose this means we'll be seeing a bit more of each other.'

'I suppose it does.' Alex couldn't tell from the tone of her voice if she thought that was a good thing or not.

He was hoping for the case to be reopened soon and

worked closely with Melanie. He would be able to further develop his skills in dealing with criminal cases with her assistance. More importantly, the Amanda's case would be solved and the killer brought to justice. The Hamilton family would then feel much better.

In addition, although he would like to establish a lasting relationship with Melanie, this would have to wait. Alex was a professional, and so was Melanie. He didn't want personal issues to get in the way of an ongoing case. More than likely, Melanie felt the same.

**

Melanie wasn't looking forward to approaching DI Jenkins about reopening the Hamilton case. She walked into the squad room cautiously; she wanted to know what kind of mood the boss was in before she brought up an awkward subject with him. She breathed out a huge sigh of relief when she saw Jenkins. Apparently, he had a smile on his face.

'Cooper, just the person I wanted to see.'

'What's up, guv?'

'That pub landlord was right. That dodgy scumbag, Marku, looks like a good fit for the second shooting. I like him for it. He's in with the Vincent mob, and he's just the kind of bloke they turn to when they need some wet work doing. If he offed Murphy in retaliation for shooting Dave the Blade, then we might be able to wrap things up pretty quickly.'

'That's good news, guv. Do you need me to tail him?'

'No, that's all taken care of. We've got him under surveillance twenty-four seven now. If he makes a move, or if any of Blade's mates come looking for him, we're on it.' Jenkins sat in Melanie's chair and made himself comfortable;

she swallowed her irritation and stood in front of the desk like a visitor. Jenkins was feeling pleased with the world, and that was good for her.

'You did well, Melanie. You squeezed just enough information out of the pub landlord to get us out of a hole.'

'I'm glad it worked out, guv. I can't say I enjoyed my little chat with Doug Ramsdale, the pub landlord. He's a slimy git. I was there for nearly two hours and in all that time I don't think his eyes got as far north as my face.'

Jenkins laughed. 'Yeah, he's a piece of work all right. At least he didn't offer you a job as a barmaid.'

'I think he was leaning more towards exotic dancer, to be honest. I won't be sorry if I never see his creepy face again.' She cleared her throat: now seemed as good a time as any. *Make hay when the sun shines.* 'Guv, I need to talk to you about the Hamilton case.'

'The suicide?'

'That's right. Alex has had a meticulous look at the file and Amanda's apartment, and he thinks we might need to reopen the case.'

'Alex, eh? Are you getting on well with our Mr DuPont?' Jenkins smirked.

'Quite well. He's good at what he does, you know that. I think he might be on to something.'

'And I must say, he fancies you.' Melanie felt a deep blush starting to work its way up from her suit collar. Jenkins grinned at her discomfort and leaned his elbows on the desk. *My desk*, she thought. 'As it happens, I'm getting a few signals from upstairs about the Hamilton case. Apparently, the Chief Super thinks it would do our relationship with Brown Legal no harm if we were to take an interest. Or to put it another way, these guys might get a bit shirty if we don't.'

'So, can I take another look?'

'By all means. Any idea what we're looking at?'

'I've only had a brief chat with Alex so far, and I didn't want to get into detail before I cleared it with you. It's not so much that there's clear evidence of foul play, as I understand it; more that the suicide thing doesn't stand up to scrutiny.'

'So how do you want to play it?'

Melanie was pleasantly taken aback; it wasn't every day that DI Jenkins asked her for advice.

'I think I should meet Alex and hear what he's turned up so far. If it looks like he's on to something, I'll review the file and reopen the case. I might need to pull in a couple of uniforms to do a bit of leg work.'

'Sounds to me like you already think it's a murder investigation.'

'Let's just say I've got an itchy feeling about it. If it looks like murder, we'll need to check a few alibis: talk to her friends and work colleagues. Alex thinks her phone's missing too. I could get one of the uniforms to chase it up. But let's see what the score is first.'

'Alright, I'm happy to sign off on that. But remember, we might still need you if things kick off with Marku.' Jenkins pushed the chair back and stood up, trying in vain to straighten his rumpled suit. 'Give me a shout when you've spoken to DuPont. If we need hands, I'll collar a couple of plods for you.'

'One other thing, guv.' Melanie had inched her way round the desk and taken her seat. Now it was Jenkins who looked like the visitor. A sharp intake of breath told her she'd scored a point. 'I want to be clear about our role here. If Brown Legal sees Alex as the main player, are we supposed to be the hired help?'

'Yeah, it's a tricky one, isn't it?' Jenkins shrugged. 'The Chief Super said as far as he was concerned Alex DuPont is an independent investigator. If our paths cross, then we cooperate. So, we're kind of working in tandem. Obviously, if he finds clear evidence of foul play then we need to step in; until then, we do the basics and keep a watching brief. If you do any favours for him, keep it under the radar. I don't want every private dick in London ringing up later and asking for help. Keep me posted.' With that, he sauntered back to his office, hands in pockets, whistling tunelessly.

Melanie sat back and thought about it. Until she knew everything Alex had found, she couldn't do much. She sent him a text, and went to get the original file, and bring herself up to date.

She was halfway through a second read of the file when Alex called. 'Hi Melanie, how did it go?'

'We're on, at least provisionally. I've reopened the case, but it's a paper exercise unless clear leads turn up. You need to tell me everything you've learned and then we can have a chat about how we move forward. The DI got a pull from the Chief Super so he's on board.'

'Excellent. I'm happy to share everything. Shall we discuss it over dinner?'

'Do you ever do any work in the office?'

Alex laughed. 'There's nothing wrong with convivial surroundings for discussing a murder case. This evening around seven-thirty? Usual place?'

'Do you ever eat anywhere else? OK, I'll see you there. Bring everything you've got.'

'I will, Detective Sergeant Cooper, I will.'

**

'I see, dinner with the lovely DS Cooper,' said Jenny, a wicked smile playing across her face. 'How romantic!'

Alex blushed. 'Are you eavesdropping on my private conversations?'

'Oh, I'm sorry,' she said innocently. 'I thought it was work.'

'Talking of which, don't you have any work to do? I can find you something boring if you like.'

Jenny did not reply and made a quick exit.

'I'd best get on.' He headed for his office. As soon as he stepped into the room his phone buzzed: his father. 'Dad, what's up? You don't normally phone me during work hours. Is everything OK? How's Mum?'

'Your mother is fine, Alex. I'm just calling to see how you are. Ever since that business with the university, your mother worries about you. She thinks, and so do I, that you were safer when you were working as a lawyer. I'm not sure I like the idea of you getting involved with murders.'

Alex shifted uncomfortably in his seat. 'I'm fine, Dad. I can look after myself.'

'And what are you working on? Another corporate case?'

Alex thought about telling a white lie, but his father always knew when he wasn't telling the truth. 'Now you mention it, I'm investigating a possible murder.' He swallowed and thought: *Dad wasn't going to like that.*

'Ah, Alex.' Alex could sense the Gallic shrug of the shoulders. 'You see what I mean? You were a very successful lawyer.'

'I'm a very successful private investigator, Dad.'

'Yes, yes, but shouldn't you leave murder to the police? Can't you hand it over to that nice detective; what was her name?'

'Melanie, actually. It looks like we'll be working together on this case.'

'Ah, I see.' There was a pause just long enough for a raised eyebrow. 'She is a rather attractive lady, *n'est pas*? And how is Claire, by the way?'

'Dad, I appreciate your, um, concern, but I have enough on my plate right now without you matchmaking for me.'

'I only want what is best for you, my son. Speaking of which, I was talking to your uncle. He had a conversation with a friend of his, a letting agent. This friend told him he could make a lot of money on his Mayfair apartment, your current office; short-term lets for rich Arab clients. He is tempted, I think.'

'Dad, I know you don't mean to threaten me, but that sounds just a little like an ultimatum.'

'Not at all, not at all. It's just something to think about. If you were a lawyer, someone else would be paying the rent.'

'I'm doing just fine here. If uncle Guillaume wants to rent this place out to rich Arabs, he can tell me that himself.'

'I'm sure there is nothing in it; Guillaume just likes to – how do they say it – cover all the angles. But think about what I am saying, Alex. You would make your mother feel more at ease if she didn't think you were in danger. And I was very proud of you when you were a lawyer.'

'And you're not proud of me now?'

'Of course, I am. I didn't mean it like that.'

'That's how it sounded.' This conversation really wasn't going the way he wanted. Alex regretted what he'd said, immediately.

'Oh dear! I think perhaps I found you in a bad moment. I will speak to you soon.'

Alex stared at the phone in his hand, wishing he could rewind the whole conversation. His father could be a difficult man sometimes. *But so are you, Alex, so are you.* He would have to call back and make peace with the old man, and soon.

**

Although Alex would be having dinner with Melanie to discuss the case and share information, he was also looking forward to spending some quality time with her.

He changed into his blue striped suit, blue shirt and fuchsia tie, then walked to the Excelsior. He got there ten minutes early and decided not to order a drink but wait for Melanie. After a couple of minutes, Melanie arrived. She wore a pink dress and a pale blue cardigan. Everyone watched her with keen interest as she passed. She scanned the restaurant and saw Alex sitting at a table apart from the others. They were delighted to see each other and exchanged greetings. Alex kissed her on both cheeks.

'You look gorgeous, Melanie,' Alex said.

'And you look very dapper.'

The waiter ushered them to their table in the restaurant by the window.

'This table's a bit off the beaten track. Doesn't Henri like you anymore?'

'I asked for a table out of the way so we could talk. I don't think the other customers need to hear about cyanide whilst eating their delicious food.'

'No, especially not if they're drinking Prosecco.'

Alex laughed amiably. 'I've ordered us a bottle of Haut Medoc. It's about as different from Prosecco as you can get.'

'Wise decision.' Melanie thought she saw a hint of

worry on his face. 'Are you OK, Alex? You don't look your usual self. More importantly, I've been here over a couple of minutes or so and you haven't flirted with me yet.'

This time his laugh held a trace of bitterness. 'I'm getting a bit of pressure from my dad. He says my new life as a private investigator is worrying my mum. He'd like me to go back to work as a lawyer. He even hinted he might persuade my uncle to take back the Mayfair office.'

'Gosh! What are you going to do? Make peace with him and your uncle, or move to another site?'

'I don't really know right now. I'm hoping he will change his mind and allow me to continue with my business.'

'Do you think he will carry out his threat?'

'Difficult to say. I've not been in this situation before.'

'As I see it, you have been very successful in your new role and are increasing your revenues due to high demand for your services. You have been cautious with the type of work you undertake. Your Agency is fast gaining a good reputation in the City, and Brown Legal hiring you, could only testify to that notion.

'To be fair, you're making more money with your business than you would have earned in any law firm. You have enjoyed the freedom and independence that many of your peers craved for and rarely achieved. I think your parents should be hugely proud of you for the incredible amount of success that you have achieved in such a short period of time.'

'You are of course right. The Agency has done extremely well. But my father wants a son who is working as a lawyer and not as a private investigator.'

'I wouldn't like to be in your shoes right now.' She shook her head.

'They won't fit you anyway.'

'Alex, we are talking about your future and you're trying to be funny.'

After a good giggle, although Melanie was not amused, he said, 'You've got to laugh otherwise you would go crazy.'

Following a brief pause, Melanie said, 'How are you going to handle it then?'

'I intend to carry on operating as I have done up to now, maybe, on another site. I've got the taste of running my own business and I feel good about it. No need to give it up.'

'That's the spirit, and that's the Alex I know and admire, you'll be fine.'

'We'll cope somehow. Let's wait and see what action my dad will really take.'

'What does your mum think about all this?'

'Well, she doesn't like the idea of me being in danger. But she likes seeing my name in lights. That's something that doesn't happen to many lawyers, unless they're caught with their hands in the till.'

'Because she loves you.'

'I know she does. But I do have a plan on how to persuade my father to see things my way.'

'What is it?'

'Let's just say I have more than just a vested interest in solving this case. If I can get a good result; this will show him, I'm equally successful at my new profession, then he won't have a stick to beat me with. Also, he would not think that solving my first murder case, with your help of course, was just a flash in the pan.'

'Then let's see if I can help you out. I'm in the boss's good books right now, but a high-profile murder result wouldn't go amiss. Spill the beans, Alex, let's see if we've got a real case on our hands.'

Alex had ordered a plate of mixed starters and dips, and they picked distractedly at their food as he went through his findings. The Haut Medoc was rich and fruity, with a hint of blackberries. Melanie perked up after a couple of sips and focused on the discoveries he had made. She made notes as they talked.

Alex explained Scott's suspicions about the fingerprints on the glass Amanda had drunk her last draught from. Coupled with the complete lack of prints on the vial, it clearly didn't make sense in a suicide.

He told her about the curious arrangement of wine glasses in the kitchen cupboards. Then he went on to the items missing from the scene: the bottle, first and foremost, but also Amanda's phone.

'There's one other thing. It may be nothing, but I have a feeling about it. There is a photo on the shelves in the living room: a group of friends, five of them including Amanda. She had the same photo on her laptop as a screensaver. I think it was important to her. I'd like to know who they all are. It's possible one of them could lead us to the killer or may have something to do with her murder. At the very least, we need to eliminate them from our enquiries. I think one of them is the guy who found her, Ashley Bradshaw. I'm interviewing him tomorrow at Brown Legal, and I'm hoping he can help me locate the others.'

'OK, I think you've found enough evidence to suggest it wasn't suicide. And if it wasn't suicide…'

'It's safe to say it wasn't an unfortunate accident. It's not like someone laces her own drink with cyanide by mistake and drinks it.'

'Umm…. So, we're looking at murder by person or persons unknown.'

'Yes, but not a stranger. Poison isn't an opportunist weapon. This was intimate. She let this person into her apartment and shared a glass of wine with him/her. You don't do that kind of thing with someone just off the street.'

'Of course not.'

Alex smiled and took another sip of wine. 'What do you think? Have we got enough to get DI Jenkins interested?'

'More than enough, I think. Bless him; he needs something to take his mind off those morons with guns. Don't ask.'

'What happens now? Do I just hand it all over to you lot, or are we working together?'

'Word has come down from on high that we are to give you all the support we can, without turning into your sidekicks, obviously. I've been authorised to enlist a couple of uniforms to do the donkey work. They can start on the people from the photo, once you've got their names from Ashley, they can check who's got an alibi for that Sunday afternoon.'

'And what about you?' There was a look in Alex's eyes she couldn't quite work it out. Whatever it was, it wasn't just business.

'I'll have a look at Brown Legal, run some background checks. I'll talk to the family again too. Now that we're looking at murder, they may have some ideas.'

'Good, then I guess we're all set. I'm looking forward to working with you again, Melanie. I think we make a good team.' He smiled, and this time there was genuine warmth in it. Melanie felt the colour flooding her cheeks. *It's the wine*, she thought. *Who am I kidding?*

CHAPTER 10

Ashley Bradshaw was a tall man with long limbs and a boyish face with wavy blond hair. He gave the impression, Alex thought, of someone who had not yet fully grown into his frame. For such a large man, he had slim, sensitive hands, like a talented pianist.

They sat in the small office at Brown Legal, facing each other across a plain desk, devoid of decoration except for two mugs of tea and a slim office folder.

'Ashley, I know this is going to be difficult for you, so take your time and, at any time you need to take a break, you do so. I'm not here to interrogate you, I just want to know what happened to Amanda on that Sunday afternoon.'

Ashley nodded. The boyish enthusiasm with which he had greeted Alex had gone now, replaced by a more sombre expression. 'Of course, Mr DuPont, I'll do anything I can, to help. Amanda was one of my favourite people. Ever.'

'You were students together at university?'

'Yes, we both studied Economics at Bristol where we first met, and we've been...' Ashley took off his wire-framed spectacles and wiped at them distractedly. 'Sorry. We were friends from then until... Until she died.'

'Take your time, Ashley, I know this can't be easy for

you. So, you were close friends; was there ever anything more between you two?'

'You mean like, were we in a relationship? No. I mean, she was lovely. In fact, she was really beautiful, but that wasn't how we connected. We were just very good friends.'

'And you ended up working for the same firm.' Alex smiled encouragingly.

'Yes. Total coincidence, actually. We'd joked about keeping our applications secret from each other and then, on the day I came here for interview, there she was, dressed in her best suit and looking at me like I'd just jumped out of a cupboard and said "boo!" We had a good laugh about it afterwards. Then when we both got offered a trainee position, we were really pleased. It was like our student days would just go on forever.'

Ashley paused again, and looked into the distance, into a future that would never happen. He sighed. 'But nothing goes on forever, does it?'

Alex gave him a moment. 'So, was it just the two of you at university?'

'No, there were four of us who made friends during Freshers Week. We all hit it off really well: we called ourselves the Gang of Four. Then, we turned into the Famous Five when Charlotte came on the scene.'

'Charlotte?'

'Yes. She was my girlfriend for the best part of our time, so she tagged along with me when the gang met up. After we broke up, she still tagged along some other times, but it wasn't the same, really.' Alex noted the sudden change in Ashley's expression; he'd gone from happily nostalgic to sadly reflective in a moment.

Alex took the photo out of the folder and showed it to

Ashley. 'Is this the Famous Five, then?'

'Yes, it is. We had a laugh taking this. We used one of those digital cameras with a timer on it. We had ten seconds to get into position; we were laughing so much it took us several goes before we were all in shot. Charlotte got quite annoyed with us in the end.'

'Can you tell me the names of all the people in the picture?'

'Yes of course. You know me and Amanda. Then there's Charlotte, Charlotte Palmer, that is. The guy with the frothy curls is Timothy, Timothy Williams; he works in the City these days, as a high-flying finance analyst. The serious-looking guy is Jeremy, Jeremy Higgins. Actually, he can be a lot of fun, but he had his glum face on for the camera.'

'And do you know where Jeremy is these days?'

'He lives in Paris. Last I heard he was working in some rather chic jeweller's boutique.'

'Have you all stayed in touch?'

'Off and on. I see Tim for lunch once in a while; he only works down the road. I haven't seen Jeremy since he moved to Paris about a year ago. And Charlotte… After we broke up, things were a bit difficult for Charlotte, I think. Since university I haven't heard from her. I don't know what she's doing these days.'

'I'll need to get in touch with all of them at some point,' said Alex. 'If you have contact details for any of them, I'd be grateful.'

Ashley took out his phone. 'I've got numbers here for Tim and Jeremy. I don't know if Jeremy's number is up to date. I haven't used it in a while. I'm afraid I don't have any details for Charlotte. You don't think any of them had anything to do with Amanda's…?' Alex wrote the numbers down.

'It's just a detail, Ashley. What the police call eliminating them from our enquiries. I'm sure they are all in the clear.'

Ashley's shoulders settled in relief. 'I'd hate to think any of our little circle had bad intentions towards Amanda. She was the sweetest person.'

'And what about work? Did Amanda make friends here?'

'Well, she was very popular; she was that sort of person, easy to like. I don't think she had any other close friends here, though. Maybe Steve, in a way.'

'Steve?'

'Steve Mortimer. He's part of our trainee intake. He kind of latched onto me when we first got here. We share a passion for football – Amanda used to say it was my only defect. Steve's a Tottenham fan, of course, but I forgave him for that.'

'And you?'

'I'm a gooner, for my sins.'

Alex must have looked puzzled. 'That's to say I'm an Arsenal fan. Arsenal and Tottenham are rival north London clubs.'

'Ah, thank you. I'm a Manchester United fan myself. Were Steve and Amanda friends?'

Ashley paused and looked up, as if he was doing a sum in his head. 'I guess you could say that. To tell you the truth, I think Steve has – had – a bit of a crush on her.'

'Do you think she felt the same towards him?'

'No, I don't think she even noticed him, to be honest. When I say they were friends, I mean the three of us used to go for a drink the odd evening. Steve was always a bit tongue-tied when Amanda was around, but he often asked me to invite her.'

'Do you know if they spent any time together when you weren't around?'

'No, I... Wait. Amanda told me he invited her for a drink one evening. They only did it, once. I think she felt uncomfortable around him. He was a bit over-attentive, if you know what I mean.'

'Did she have any other work friends that you're aware of?'

'No, I don't think so. She had a few admirers, that's for sure. I think the old man was a bit soft on her.'

Alex looked puzzled again, but this time it was an act. He had a feeling he knew who Ashley meant.

'The old man is what we call Walter, because he kind of looks after our cohort. God, don't tell him I said that or what I said about him and Amanda. I don't think my life would be worth living.'

'Don't worry, your secret's safe with me.'

'Thanks, Alex, you're a decent sort, even if you are a United fan.' They shared a quiet laugh. After a few moments, he moved the conversation on to more serious matters.

'Ashley, this next bit will be tough for you. I need you to tell me about the day you went to visit Amanda and found her body. If you need to take a break first, feel free.'

Ashley's face fell. He'd been expecting this, thought Alex, but now it came to the crunch he wasn't feeling good about it.

'No, it's OK – I guess I knew it was coming, might as well get it over with.'

Ashley stretched his arms out, fingers interlinked, palms outwards. He squared his shoulders, took a deep breath and steadied himself. 'Amanda texted me on the Saturday and asked me to come over on the Sunday at 5 pm. She said there was something she wanted to talk to me about, something confidential. I thought it was probably about Hong Kong.'

'Hong Kong?'

'Yes, the firm has a branch in Hong Kong. It deals with international commerce mainly, shipping and so on. Every year, a couple of trainees get to go there for work experience. Not the most interesting work, but it's great to spend a year in such an exotic place. Well, as you can imagine, the competition is fierce.

'Amanda and I both applied and we got lucky. She was really looking forward to it. I thought she wanted to talk about it. There's a lot of practical stuff to do in preparation. Now I think on it, though, I'm not so sure. She wouldn't have said it was confidential if it was about HK, everyone knew we were going.'

'Did Steve apply for the Hong Kong seat?' Alex asked.

'You know your legal jargon, Mr DuPont. Yes, Steve applied but he didn't make the cut.'

'I was a lawyer myself, in an earlier life. How did he feel about that?'

'He was disappointed, naturally. But he's a resilient character, and I think he got over it quite quickly.'

Ashley had lost his thread. 'Where was I? Oh, yes. Anyway, at first, I said I'd pop over in the evening. It's not far from where I live in Barnes. But Amanda asked me to come a bit earlier. Apparently, she was expecting someone else in the evening. I remember I teased her about there being a new man in her life. Now I think about it, her reply was a bit off, like she was annoyed with me. I got there just before five o'clock and rang the bell but got no answer. As luck would have it, one of the other tenants was coming home and let me in. I knew Amanda kept a key on the lintel over the door. I thought I'd let myself in and surprise her.'

'How did you know about the key?'

'Oh, it's funny really. A couple of months ago, she borrowed a rather expensive textbook from me. It was something we needed to cover for the HK seat. Then she went away unexpectedly for a few days. I think her mum was unwell. Anyway, when I texted her to ask for the book, she told me that her neighbour, Imelda, would let me in if I rang her doorbell and then she told me where the key was, so I could let myself in and pick up the book.

'She told me afterwards that she'd hoped I'd hit it off with Imelda. She thought it would do me good after Charlotte. Imelda's quite something, very Latin, very beautiful. To tell you the truth, I found her a bit intimidating.

'Anyway, that Sunday, it was Imelda who let me in. We had a chat for a few minutes. I still couldn't pluck up the courage to ask her out. Then, I grabbed the key off the lintel and let myself in.'

Ashley faltered. The colour slowly drained from his face as he relived the next few moments in his mind. 'I opened the door and called out her name, in case she was asleep or something. No reply. I stepped into the living room and that's when... that's when I saw her.'

He stopped and wiped his spectacles again, taking a bit more time than was necessary. 'She was lying on the floor, kind of trapped between the sofa and the coffee table. I rushed over to see if she was OK. She wasn't, she really wasn't. I moved the coffee table so I could get to her. I felt really weird about touching her shoulder. Her face was a deep red, and there was an expression on it, like a horrible smile, an angry smile.'

A rictus, thought Alex; a tell-tale sign of cyanide poisoning.

'She was sort of pressed into a strange shape. I thought she'd fallen and got tangled around the leg of the table. But when I moved it, she stayed in the same position. Anyway, I gathered my courage, and knelt beside her...' A choked sob escaped his lips. 'I... I felt for a pulse in her neck; I think I must have seen that on TV somewhere, one of those crime series. No pulse, her skin was really cold, and it had a stiff, waxy feel to it.

'I stood up and called 999. I wasn't sure who to ask for, so I said ambulance. The ambulance operator asked if I'd tried CPR or anything to revive her. I said I hadn't and told him she was so cold, and she looked so... horrible. I thought she must have been dead for ages.'

Ashley stopped and searched his pockets, confused. Alex produced a couple of tissues and handed them to him. 'Thanks, I thought I had some with me. So, I waited for the ambulance crew and let them in. They took one look and seemed to know what had happened. They said I should wait there and one of them called the police.'

'What did you think at the time? Were you surprised they called the police?'

'To tell you the truth, I was way past worrying about stuff like that. I was numb. My best friend was dead, and it looked like she'd died in some awful way. I stood in the corner like the school dunce and sort of watched the ambulance people doing their jobs. Shortly afterwards, the local police arrived. The Inspector got in touch with the detectives. They got there quickly. A female detective led me out of the house and asked me a few questions. I don't think I was very coherent, and now I can hardly remember what she asked me.'

'Did you feel like you were under suspicion at all?'

'Do you know, now you ask me, I should have, probably. But I was so upset I didn't care what anyone thought. I haven't heard much from the police since, so I haven't given it any thought. It's different now, I guess. Do you think they'll see me as a suspect?'

Alex tried to reassure him. 'I think that's unlikely, Ashley. Amanda died around four o'clock, an hour before you arrived. I assume you can account for your movements before that.'

'Yes. Ah, I remember now; that's pretty much what the detective asked me. I was on a Skype call with a Chinese friend who lives in Hong Kong. I was asking her about the place: what I should see, where I should go and eat, that sort of thing. Ling Mai gave me the whole Rough Guide spiel: the sights, the best tours, the restaurants, street food. When she gets into her stride she can go on a bit.'

Alex looked down at the notes he'd made. He wanted to make sure he hadn't missed anything. He also wanted to check for any inconsistencies in Ashley's account. 'I just want to go back a bit. Amanda really didn't give you any idea what she wanted to talk about?'

'No, not a clue. Now you say it, it's a bit weird, isn't it? I mean, what could be so important she couldn't text me? But considering what happened... Oh. That's terrible. Maybe, she knew something bad was happening. Maybe, if she'd texted me, I'd have known who it was: the killer, I mean.'

'Do you think it was murder?'

'Well, I don't see why I'd be talking to a private investigator if it was suicide. I mean, isn't that why you're here?'

'Yes, you're right. There is some evidence to suggest it

wasn't suicide. I'd prefer if you kept that to yourself for now, Ashley. I'm sure it will all come out eventually, but for now consider it *sub rosa*. I've only got one more question, and then I'll let you get on with your day. Do you have any idea who might have had enough ill-feeling towards Amanda to kill her? You knew her pretty well, after all.'

'Yes, I knew her as well as anyone did, I suppose. And no, I honestly can't think of anyone who hated her...' Ashley's eyes dropped to the desk for a moment. Alex felt a subtle frisson of suspicion. *He knows something*, he thought. *Something or someone; but he's not going to tell me, at least not yet.*

Alex stood up. 'Ashley, thank you. I know how difficult this must have been for you. You've been very helpful. I'm a lot clearer about the circumstances. And now I know what a gooner is.'

Ashley's laugh was a pale, dutiful thing. They shook hands and, without another word, Ashley left the room. Alex watched him go, and turned back to his notes, deep in thought. He didn't suspect the distraught young man for a moment. But he was holding something back, Alex was sure of it, something significant. At some point, they would need to have another conversation: a serious one.

Alex phoned Walter and asked him if he could see Steve Mortimer at one that afternoon. Walter got back to him quickly and confirmed his meeting with Steve at Brown Legal had been arranged.

CHAPTER 11

Gerry was having a busy, irritating morning. The Paris conference was only a few days away, and she needed to clear up the Trevellyan account before she went. She could manage that, but she wasn't sure how she was going to fit her awkward conversation with Hugo Zelov into her Paris schedule.

Hugo, a businessman from Marseilles, had made some irregular requests lately. These had been passed on to her. Gerry knew he was a valued client, but she was beginning to have suspicions about him. It was just possible he was using the firm to launder money. And bona fide clients did not launder money.

She booted the PC into life and was sorting her Paris schedule when the phone rang. 'Gerry, I have a Detective Sergeant Cooper on the line. Can you take the call? I can put her off if you like. I know you're snowed under.'

Angela, her pint-sized, super-efficient PA, often acted as her minder, fielding difficult calls or pushy clients for her.

'No, it's OK, Angela; I'll take the call.' Since her conversation with Alex she'd been half expecting the police to get back in touch, if only to apologise. 'Detective Sergeant Cooper, what can I do for you?'

'Ms Hamilton, I was wondering if you had time for a chat.'

'Not much, I'm afraid. I'm up to my neck at the moment. I have a conference to attend in Paris early next week and I have to clear up a few things before then. Is it urgent?'

'Not urgent, exactly, but it would be good to meet. I understand Alex DuPont got in touch with you.'

Great, she thought, *the police are going to get in Alex's way; typical.* 'Yes, he did. We had a most enlightening chat.'

There was a pause. Gerry waited, tapping her fingers on the desk. 'Look, Miss Hamilton. I think we all got off on the wrong foot after the unfortunate events. I'm calling to tell you that we are reopening the case.'

'Has Alex found the evidence you missed?' Gerry couldn't keep the note of triumph from her voice.

'So to speak, yes. I think we need to talk. Could I meet you for coffee later today?'

Why not, she thought. At the very least, she would get to watch a police officer grovelling and get an apology from her. 'Very well. I could clear a space around three if that works for you. I won't have much time, though. As I said, I'm pretty busy.'

Another pause, and the rustle of paper. 'Yes, I can make it for three.'

'There's a café in Covent Garden called Café Bella. I'll meet you there.'

'Fine. See you later.' She rang off.

**

Alex strode into the atrium of Brown Legal building. Needless to say, he was becoming quite familiar with the place. And Jean was becoming quite friendly with him.

'Hi Alex.' She winked at him; a slow, sly wink, full of promise.

'Hello, Jean. Do you wink at all the boys?'

'Leave off; it's more than my job's worth. You seem all right, though.'

'Thank you; I'll put that on my CV. You're all right too, Jean, and a bit of all right.'

Jean blushed and waved a hand in front of her face. 'Blimey, is it me or is it getting a bit warm in here?' She cleared her throat and put her office voice back on. 'What can I do for you, Mr DuPont?'

'Call me Alex; I felt like we're good friends already. I'm here to see Steve Mortimer. I might be a bit early.' Now it was Alex's turn to wink. 'I suppose we could just flirt for a bit.'

A statuesque woman in a rather tightly tailored suit came into the atrium from the lifts. Her hair was expensively dyed and she wore enough make-up for two.

'Look out,' whispered Jean. 'It's the dragon.'

'Mr DuPont,' said the dragon. 'I was hoping to catch you before your meeting with Mr Mortimer. I'm Sally Prentice, Head of Human Resources.'

'Mrs Prentice, what can I do for you?'

'*Ms* Prentice. I thought it might be useful to have a little chat. I'm pretty plugged in to everything here and I can fill you in on any issue you need to know.'

'And what is it you think I need to know, *Ms* Prentice?'

Sally Prentice was taken aback but managed a smile. 'Well, I imagine you would like to know about poor Amanda's colleagues. I can tell you a little about each of them, so you can cross them off your list of suspects.'

Sally was here to put out a few fires before Alex had actually lit any. He glanced over at Jean, she had her head down but he could see the laughter lines clearly.

'That's very kind of you, Sally. May I call you Sally?' Alex gave her his best winning smile.

Now it was Sally's turn to blush. 'As you wish, um…'

'Alex.'

'That's right, Alex. Shall we sit for a minute?' She indicated a plush sofa under a tropical vine.

'Amanda was very well liked here. It was a terrible shock to us all when we heard the dreadful news. And now that you're investigating a murder, well, I can tell you, that's set the cat among the pigeons.'

'It's really nothing to worry about, Sally. And this matter is no reflection on Brown Legal; it's just an unfortunate tragedy. I would, of course, be interested to hear what you have to say, and I'll make some space in my diary for you just as soon as I can. In the meantime, I have an interview to attend to.'

Sally could tell she was getting the brush-off, but there was little she could do about it. And the investigator chap was really quite a dish. She swallowed her irritation and stood up. 'Well, I'll get my PA to call your office and arrange something, perhaps next week?' She looked hopeful.

'I'll get my PA to call yours, don't worry. I'm away next week but I'm sure we can arrange something convenient to both of us. Now, if you'll excuse me.'

'Yes, of course. It was a pleasure to meet you, Alex. Call me anytime.'

'Likewise.'

'Oh, and one more thing. If the finger of suspicion should fall on a member of staff, I'd be grateful if you could give me a heads up. That would create something of a situation, and I might find myself needing to put out a few fires.'

Alex smiled inwardly.

Sally stormed off in the direction of the lifts. Alex gave her a minute as he didn't fancy sharing a lift with her. He sauntered over to the reception desk. Jean was giggling behind her hand. 'Well, I never! You're not just a private investigator, but a dragon killer too. I'm impressed.'

'Thank you, Jean; that's high praise coming from you. I might put that one on my CV too.'

'Go on with you. Steve will be arriving in the interview room – we all call it that now – in about ninety seconds, so you'd better get your skates on, dragon boy.'

**

Steve Mortimer cut an odd figure for a lawyer in a City firm. He was a little under average height, and his jet-black hair was buzz cut, a striking contrast to his pale face. He was standing in the middle of the office when Alex arrived.

'So, you're a private investigator. I don't really understand why you wanted to see me.'

Alex couldn't decide if the man was just cocky, or nervous and hiding it: a mix of both, probably. 'It's just routine, Steve. I have to talk to everyone who knew Amanda, and I gather you knew her quite well.'

Steve sat down, lounging in his chair with a manspread that belied his size. 'I suppose Ashley put you onto me?'

'Yes, he did. He said the three of you went for a drink together fairly regularly.'

'Yeah, we did. Amanda was a nice girl; I mean really nice. I enjoyed her company.'

The smirk that followed the words put Alex's back up. *I bet you did*, he thought.

'And was it always the three of you or did you and Amanda go out without Ashley?'

'As it happens, we did, the odd time.' Steve's accent was in danger of slipping into Cockney: fake, but strangely appropriate.

Alex fixed him with a steely look. 'Define "the odd time", Steve.'

The cockney wide-boy façade began to evaporate before Alex's eyes. Steve drew his knees together and leaned forward in his chair, the look in his eyes somewhere between earnest and pleading. Beads of sweat suddenly appeared under his hairline.

'Maybe, I was laying it on a bit thick. I liked Amanda; I really liked her a lot. We only went out the once, to be honest. I think I may have come on a little bit too strong, and she obviously wasn't interested. I can't blame her; she was out of my class, to be honest. I didn't push it after that.'

Alex changed the subject abruptly. 'Tell me about Hong Kong.'

'I wish I could. I won't be going to Hong Kong anytime soon.'

'Were you disappointed?'

'I won't lie; I was gutted. It was the opportunity of a lifetime, and I blew it. I didn't prepare myself enough on the boring commercial stuff. Ashley and Amanda breezed through it. I was pleased for them, really.'

'So, no grudges, then?'

'Grudges, no, of course…' Steve stopped in mid-sentence and his face became even paler. 'I didn't kill her, Mr DuPont, I couldn't do that to her. In fact, I couldn't do that to anyone, I don't have the guts for it.'

Maybe not, Alex thought, but you're hiding something, and you're desperate to keep it hidden.

'I'm not suggesting you killed her, Steve. That would be jumping to conclusions. And I'm sure you can tell me what you were doing that Sunday afternoon.'

'Oh, you mean an alibi. Yes, I have an alibi. I was at a football match: Tottenham v Burnley. I was in north London the whole time.'

'Was anyone with you?'

'No, I went on my own. I think, I've still got the ticket somewhere.' Steve started rummaging in his suit pockets. 'There, look. I knew I had it somewhere.'

Alex thought it was curiously convenient that Steve had the ticket on him. Did he really go to watch football in his work suit? He decided not to say anything for now.

'Isn't it out of season?'

'Yes, it's out of the regular season. It was an under-twenty match, a friendly.'

Steve gave him one of those superior 'you don't know anything about football' looks and relaxed.

'There's something else. I'd like to show you a photo.'

Alex produced the photo of Amanda and her friends; it was getting a bit crumpled now. He made a mental note to have a fresh copy made. 'Do you recognise anyone here?'

'Well, I know Amanda – knew Amanda – and I know Ashley, obviously. I'm afraid I don't know any of the others.'

That's curious. Alex was sure Steve's eyes had flicked to someone else in the picture, but he couldn't tell if it was because he knew them or he was just scanning them to make sure.

'You're certain; you don't know any of the others?'

A DEADLY PLAN

'Certain. I don't know any of the others.' Steve's voice was confident but he refused to meet Alex's eyes, and his repetition of Alex's question was unsettling, like he was reading from a script. The beads of sweat on his hairline had been joined by a few friends.

'Thank you, Steve. You've been very helpful. If I think of anything else, I'll be in touch.'

'Is that it? Can I go now?' The look of relief on his face was close to comical.

'Yes, that's it, you can go now.' Alex threw the repetition trick back at him.

Steve didn't seem to notice. He was too busy hustling out of the room.

Alex jotted down a few notes. Quite a few of them ended with question marks.

90

CHAPTER 12

C afé Bella was a chic and medium size coffee shop. Melanie arrived punctually, to find Gerry waiting for her. She squeezed into a seat at the window table and then realised she'd have to stand up to take off her jacket. Gerry looked on, more than a hint of sardonic amusement on her face. Melanie thought: *Great, I've only just arrived and already I've messed it up.*

Gerry had a Latte glass on the table in front of her. She didn't look as if she was going to offer. So, Melanie ordered an Americano.

'Gerry.' Gerry raised an eyebrow at the familiarity, but Melanie ploughed on.

'I owe you an apology. We all do.'

'I appreciate that, but I hope you haven't dragged me away from a busy desk just to say sorry.'

'No, I wanted to explain a few things about the original investigation and what we plan to do now.'

'Go on.' The frosty glare from Gerry was a real contrast to the Americano; the first sip burned her tongue.

'You probably feel we sold you short first-time round. In a way we did, but there are some protocols around apparent suicides. The ambulance crew were satisfied that's what they'd found. In those circumstances, the police have only a minor role to play. We weren't shirking our responsibilities; we were going through the normal procedure.'

'You had bigger fish to fry; gangland shootings. So much more exciting than a dead woman in Chiswick.' Melanie got the distinct impression Gerry was fighting back tears, despite the sarcasm.

'I'm sorry you overheard that. Yes, I was under pressure, but as I said, in the circumstances as we understood them, there was no reason for a full investigation. Obviously, now Alex has turned up some anomalies in the case...'

'Alex? You know him, then.'

'We've worked together in the past. I trust him, and I trust his instincts. He has found some very suggestive evidence. Nothing concrete, but enough for us to reopen the case. I just want to reassure you that this time round, we'll be doing everything we can to get to the bottom of it.'

'How does Alex fit into all this? I hope you'll let him do his job. He seems to be rather good at it.'

Ouch; she really doesn't like me. 'We'll be working in tandem. If we can help him, we will and vice versa.'

'What are you actually going to do? It's been over a month now, and we're no nearer to finding out who killed my sister.'

'We'll talk to Amanda's friends, see if anyone held a grudge against her. And we'll talk to people at Brown Legal, her former colleagues. Most murders are carried out by people well-known to the victim.'

'You should have a chat with Walter.' An odd expression flickered across Gerry's features.

'Walter Coburn? You think he might be involved?'

'I do have a funny feeling about him. I think he fancied

92

Amanda. He gave me the once-over when I went to see him. We look – looked – alike, and I think he was a bit shocked by that. Another thing: I really don't understand why he insisted on paying Alex's fees.'

'I see.' Melanie made a note of that. She hadn't thought about Walter being a suspect. 'I'll talk to him. In the meantime, I'd like to show you something.' She reached down for her bag, knocking the table. The coffee cups shifted, and a dollop of Latte landed on Gerry's purse. She wiped it off hurriedly. Mumbling an apology, Melanie produced the photo. 'I'd like you to have a look at this. Do you recognise any of these people?'

'I've seen this before. Alex showed it to me, and I remembered it from Amanda's apartment. I can only repeat what I told Alex; I don't know any of them.'

'Ah well, it was worth a try. I won't take up any more of your time, Gerry, as you said you've got a lot to do.'

'Yes, I am very busy. Look Sergeant, I can see you're serious about resolving the case, and I'm grateful. I'm sorry if I sounded cynical earlier. It's just I was sure Amanda didn't kill herself. It had been years since she had depression, and…'

'Depression?' Melanie was taken aback. This was news to her.

'When Amanda was on her gap year prior to starting at university, she met a man who treated her rather badly. It took her a while to get over it, and our family doctor diagnosed depression. He was confident she would pull through it, and she did.'

'Well, that's useful information. Why didn't you tell us before?'

'I didn't think it was relevant, it was a long time ago.'

93

Gerry got up to go, and they shook hands awkwardly. On the drive back to the station, Melanie went over what she'd learned. Two things stood out: Gerry's suspicions about Walter, and the episode of depression. Talking to Walter would be difficult. She decided to let one of the uniforms check his alibi. But Gerry's revelation about Amanda being depressed was another thing entirely: was there a reason to suspect suicide after all?

**

'Melanie, what's up? Is this a work call or were you missing me?' Alex sounded cheerful, too cheerful for Melanie's mood.

'Just checking in with you, Alex; we're working together, remember?'

'In tandem, you mean. Isn't that what DI Jenkins called it?'

'Whatever. Thanks for the contact details from the photo. I'll get the plods on it first thing tomorrow. Listen, I just had an interesting chat with Gerry Hamilton.'

'I bet she was pleased to see you.' Alex was enjoying himself.

'Yeah, really. She made me feel as welcome as a fly in a salad. Thing is, she told me, in passing that Amanda suffered from depression a few years ago.'

'That's very interesting.' Alex sounded as if someone had popped his balloon. 'So does this mean you're leaning back towards suicide?'

'Not necessarily, but it means we can't completely rule it out. The evidence is suggestive. But if she did kill herself, it could all be explained clearly. I'm not saying I doubt you, Alex, but we need to keep it in mind.'

'And where does that leave us?'

'It doesn't change anything. We still need to check the alibis and talk to the people she knew, friends and colleagues. I'll see if I can talk to the GP, clear up the depression angle.'

'Good plan. By the way, I interviewed two of her colleagues today. Ashley Bradshaw and Steve Mortimer. Ashley gave me the idea Steve might be worth talking to. So Walter organised for me to see him in the early afternoon.'

'Love interest?'

'In a one-sided sort of way. It seems our Steve was sweet on Amanda, and he'd lost out on a work trip to Hong Kong, a trip Amanda and Ashley were going on. Quite a prestigious one. Obviously, he was gutted.'

'Right, how did the interview go with him?'

'It was very interesting, actually.'

'You think we've got a suspect?'

'Not sure about that, but Steve has got a secret he really doesn't want to share with us. He has an alibi which we need to check.'

'Do we need to bring him in and put the pressure on?'

'Not yet, but we may have to at some point.'

'Anything else for me?'

'Maybe one other thing. Ashley also told me he thought Walter Coburn was a bit taken with Amanda. I think you ought to check his whereabouts on the day in question.'

'Amazing. You're the second person to tell me that today.'

'Really, who?'

'Gerry said the same thing. In addition, she was a bit suspicious that he'd offered to pay your fees.'

'What are you saying, Melanie? You think I've got in some dodgy relationship with our Walter?'

'It's not all about you, Alex; reel in your ego. She wondered why he felt strongly enough to pay the fees, and I think it's a valid question.'

'Yes, it is. All the more reason to check his alibi.'

'Are we done now?'

'By the way, did the SOCO people picked up the Prosecco bottle?'

'I was going to tell you. No, they did not come across any bottle.'

'OK. One other thing, I'm thinking I might pop over to Paris on Monday.'

'Good on you. Is this a romantic city break with Claire?'

'Nothing like that. One of the people in the photo lives in Paris. I thought I'd go over and have a word with him.'

'Paris will be pretty crowded next week, then.'

'Why, is there some sort of event on that I haven't got wind of?'

'No, but Gerry Hamilton is going there to attend a conference. Perhaps you'll bump into each other on the Avenue des Champs-Elysees.'

'Is she now? Maybe, I should arrange to meet her somewhere close where her conference is being held.' Melanie heard a shuffling sound, like Alex was shifting in his seat. 'I don't suppose you're free next week. You could tell Jenkins it's a work thing.'

'I don't think so, Alex. Jenkins won't let me swan off to Paris just like that, we are very busy at the moment.'

'In case you're worried about us staying at the hotel, I can book two rooms if that will help.'

'Say something sensible, if you don't mind.'

'You tend to spoil the fun, don't you? We could have a wonderful time together in Paris: seeing the iconic sights, eating the gourmet food, drinking the delicious wine, attending a show at the Moulin Rouge or the Lido and strolling down the Avenue des Champs-Elysees or the bank of the river Seine.'

'Honestly, I don't wish to be a spoilsport, but I can't go to Paris with you, alright.'

'If that's the way you want it, fine.'

CHAPTER 13

Melanie was sitting at her desk in her office, going over her notes. Gerry's revelation about Amanda's encounter with depression bothered her, and she was trying to fit it into the bigger picture that was starting to emerge.

The two uniformed officers who had been assigned to the case were working the phones, establishing alibis and taking notes: they had been at it for a couple of hours now, checking the alibis against timelines and gradually building a framework that she – and Alex – could use to move forward.

DI Jenkins came in and headed straight for her desk. The smile was gone, replaced by a face that, if it was a weather forecast, would say there was a storm coming. 'What's up, guv?'

Jenkins parked himself in front of her desk, and leaned his hands on it, fingers spread across the surface. He had big hands and they seemed to cover most of the available space.

'I've just had a phone call from the Chief Super. He's just had a phone call from Walter Coburn. They weren't talking about their golf handicaps, whatever that means.'

Melanie plumped for playing the innocent. 'So, what was it about, guv?'

'Walter Coburn wants to know why he's being treated as a potential suspect. He's not the only one. Macey wants to know, and so do I.'

'The fact of the matter is that he is a potential suspect. There's no getting round it. We had to establish an alibi for him, same for all the others. He's involved, so he gets treated the same. We wouldn't be doing our jobs properly otherwise.'

Jenkins sighed. 'I know and you're right. But we have to tread carefully with the toffs.'

'Wait, let me get it clear. He did have an alibi, right?'

'Cast iron. He was playing golf with one Chief Superintendent Macey. All afternoon, followed by drinks in the clubhouse.'

'In that case, he's in the clear. What's the problem?'

'The problem is he's a toff, and he expected special treatment. I know it's normally the plods that do this stuff, but he felt he should have got a call from one of us, suitably respectful, asking him very gently if he could tell us where he was on the day in question. He was cheesed off at having a lowly plod questioning his whereabouts.'

'Funny, isn't it? Most people would feel better if they got a call from a uniform. If a detective called, they'd think there was a problem.'

'Dare I say it, we still need to placate him.'

'Why don't we just tell him – or Macey – that the plods made a mistake and took his name from a list reserved for us to handle?'

'Great minds …, Melanie. That's exactly what I said. Hopefully the Chief Super is telling him that now. But I think one of us needs to give him a call to apologise for the mistake and tell him we'll be much nicer to him in future.'

'When you say one of us…'

'Exactly, I mean you. Butter him up a bit and then we won't spend the rest of the week going around with something smelly sticking to the soles of our shoes.'

'I expect he'll still find something to make his nose wrinkle.' Melanie wasn't looking forward to a grovelling phone call to Walter Coburn but it could have been worse.

'How is it going otherwise? Are we getting anywhere?'

'I think so, guv. I'm going to call the Hamilton family's GP later.'

'Something come up?'

'Might be something, might be nothing. Gerry Hamilton let slip that Amanda had suffered from a bout of depression a few years ago. She said it was all over and done with, but I want to talk to the doctor and get his opinion.'

'She might have topped herself after all?'

'I'm not saying that, not for definite. But it might put a spanner in the works at some point so I thought it was best to put it to bed if I can.'

'Keep me posted. And don't forget Coburn. I don't want him leaning on Macey so Macey feels he has to lean on me. Apart from anything else, that means I'll feel I have to lean on you.'

Jenkins heaved himself upright and headed for his office. Melanie exhaled, resigned to the task at hand and might as well get it over and done with.

She reached for the phone on her desk just as her mobile buzzed: Alex.

'What's up?'

'Just to let you know, I'm going to run what we've got past the team now, and if anything comes up, I'll give you a call. What are you up to?'

'I'm planning to call the GP in a bit. But first I've got to placate one very miffed senior partner at Brown Legal.'

'How about this! Walter didn't like being asked for an alibi.'

'He shouted at the Chief Super, and the Chief Super shouted at the DI, and, well you know how it goes. So, I've been instructed to make nice with the lawyer and then everyone feels better, apparently.'

'Sorry, Melanie. I've kind of dropped you in it.'

'Not your fault. But try and bring me some good news soon, eh?'

'I'll do my best.'

**

Before he could get to the team meeting, Alex got a call from his mother.

'Alex, how are you? I hear Robert was browbeating you again about not being a lawyer anymore. Ignore him, son, he'll get over it. We're proud of you, whatever you do.'

'Does that mean my next gig as a male stripper is OK with you?'

'So long as I don't have to watch, I know where you've been.'

They bantered for a few minutes until she got to the point. 'How is this latest case going? Robert said it was another murder.'

'It is. And would you believe it, it's about a lawyer no less.'

'Be careful, won't you? I worry about you, especially after what happened last time.'

'You mean what nearly happened, Mum. I can look after myself. Oh, by the way, it looks like I'll be in Paris next week, something to do with the case.'

'Have you booked in with your aunt Sophie Bouchard? She'll be offended if you don't stay at her hotel. She'll probably drop me off her Christmas card list.'

He was ready for that. 'I've already done it. She's a fusspot, but I'm very fond of her.'

'You'd better be careful in Paris. You never know these days.'

'Don't worry about me. I'm not exactly infiltrating the Parisian underworld. The person, I need to see, works in a posh jeweller's shop.'

'Well, I could do with a new pair of earrings if you see anything nice.' Alex's mother wasn't bothered about fancy clothes and furniture, but she had a soft spot for jewellery.

'I think this place might be above my pay grade. There's a flea market nearby, though.'

'Huh! I expect your dad has a suitable French expression for what I think of that.'

Alex got to the point. 'Mum, listen, I won't be able to make it this weekend. I need to do a few things to prepare for the Paris trip.'

'Or to put it another way, you don't fancy facing your dad because you think he's going to give you a hard time about not being a lawyer. I'm disappointed, Alex, but I understand. He can be a bit difficult at times, but he loves you and he's very proud of you.'

'It doesn't always feel like that.'

'I think you two are very similar. That's why you set each other off so easily. OK, take care now. Bye Alex.'

'Bye, Mum.'

When she rang off, Alex felt calmer. She hadn't said anything about Guillaume taking the Mayfair's office back, so he figured he was in the clear for a while.

**

Jenny and Scott were already sitting comfortably.

'Let's have a look at what we've got so far. Jenny?'

'It seems Amanda didn't have much of an online life, probably too busy. Her emails were mostly work and family; a few friends, but nothing suggestive. She had a Facebook account but hardly ever used it. One thing, I did notice a few snide comments from one poster, Amanda had unfriended them. They were mostly innuendoes about her and Ashley. I don't know if that means anything.'

'Scott?'

'My boffin friend agrees with my assessment of the glass, but unfortunately, he says the prints underneath are probably too smudged to get even a partial from. He's going to have another go over the weekend, but he says not to hold my breath. I've called the security people at Tottenham stadium, and I'll go and see them on Monday. Apparently, there's a lot of footage so it might be a long day.'

'Is your boffin mate any good with photographic stuff?'

'If he isn't, I'm sure he knows someone who is. Why, what do you need?'

'I think it would be useful if we had individual pictures of the people in the group photo. You can use them when you scout the neighbourhood again, see if they jog any memories.'

'I'll ask him.'

'Excellent. Jenny, while I'm in Paris can you set up interviews with Timothy Williams and Charlotte Palmer? You'll have to get Charlotte's contact details from the police. If you can arrange it for Wednesday, and make them later in the day if possible, so I can confer with Melanie first and find out what the plods have discovered. I don't think they're involved but I may as well get them out of the way.'

'Alex, are you sure you don't want me to come to Paris with you?' Scott said.

'I can rearrange the Tottenham thing easily enough. Only, I've got a ticklish feeling in the back of my head about this trip. You might need a minder.'

'Scott, I know Paris like the back of my hand. I've got family there. I'll be safe as houses. Don't worry and that goes for you as well, Jenny.'

**

The GP wouldn't give any information over the phone, so Melanie had to make the trip to Twickenham. The surgery was in a leafy, well-to-do neighbourhood and the sort of place that looked like no one ever got sick. Doctor Mayhew was hale, hearty and pushing on a bit in years. He ushered her into his office and offered her tea.

'Detective Sergeant Cooper, isn't it? You wanted to know about Amanda Hamilton. You understand, I have a duty of confidentiality to my patients. But in the circumstances, I'll tell you what I can.'

'Thank you, Doctor Mayhew. Amanda's sister told me that Amanda had suffered from a bout of depression in her late teens.'

'Yes, she was quite ill for a while. I treated her with anti-depressants and found her a therapist. She recovered pretty well; all things considered.'

'All things considered?'

'Depression isn't like a broken arm. You don't just fix it and forget about it. There is always the possibility of a recurrence.'

'And in Amanda's case, how likely would you say that was?'

'Hard to say. I haven't seen her since she went to university and then moved to London to take up a job with that law firm. She seemed a resilient young woman, though. Still, who knows, eh?'

'Do you know what triggered the depression?'

'I suppose the therapist would know better, but I gathered there was a young man involved. Amanda wasn't very forthcoming with me. I got the impression she was rather ashamed. In fact, now I come to think about it, I believe it was Gerry who told me about that.'

Interesting. Melanie made another note, scratched it out, wrote it in again.

'You've been very helpful, Doctor. I won't waste any more of your time.'

Doctor Mayhew chuckled: a fragile, throaty sound. 'You are very kind, Sergeant Cooper. I rather suspect I've been of no help at all.' He chuckled again.

Melanie drove back to London thinking she was no clearer than when she'd set out. She trusted Alex – more than trusted him – but the nagging doubt wouldn't go away. If Amanda had become depressed again, then all their investigations were just a wild goose chase. And that didn't feel good.

**

The garden in Victoria Embankment was practically empty. Pigeons foraged on the path around him for the remains of a million lunches. Parakeets, a livid green against the grey London sky, screeched and chattered. Steve made his way to the bench under a spreading Canadian maple and sat down; same place as always, like Charlotte had said.

The voice from behind him startled him.

'What did the private investigator have to say?' asked Charlotte.

He looked up. She was behind and slightly to his left, partly hidden in the shadow of the tree. 'He asked me all the stuff I expected. I don't think he learned anything new,' said Steve.

'Did he ask about me?'

'Why should he?'

'No reason. Just checking.'

She leaned over and looked down at him. 'He'll question you again; you need to keep your wits about you. Don't try to be clever with him; you're a terrible actor – I should know. And our Mr DuPont is no fool, so keep to the story. If he finds out about us, he'll be on you like a shot.'

'Why should he find out? And anyway, you didn't kill Amanda: did you?'

The question was genuine. Steve wasn't sure what she was capable of, but he wouldn't put it past her.

'No, I didn't kill the evil bitch. I'm glad she's dead, though. At least it saves you from constantly looking nice and being pleasant to her.'

'I didn't mind. She was very beautiful to look at and I felt good when she gave me her sweet smile. I fully enjoyed the experience. So, no harm was done.'

'I don't need to hear that.'

'No, sorry. Can I … Can I ask you something?'

'What?'

'Now she's dead, our little arrangement; I mean, there's no point to it now, is there?'

'Our little arrangement stays in place until I say otherwise, Steve. Do you understand?'

'I suppose so.' Steve leaned forward and rested his head

in his hands. 'It's just... I've done everything you asked me to do. I've done my best, and now I've got this investigator breathing down my neck. I think you could cut me some slack, after all this time. What do you say?'

He looked up and around. He was alone in the garden. She had disappeared.

CHAPTER 14

On Saturday morning, Alex did a five-mile run in Hyde Park. Afterwards, he did his routine exercises. He showered and shaved; had his usual breakfast and read the newspapers. Following that, he decided to catch up on domestic chores, not his favourite hobby. He filled the washing machine and the dishwasher, got the hoover - Mr Dyson's new toy out and hoovered the whole apartment.

He was still tidying around, and about exactly halfway round the living room when the phone rang. 'Saved by the bell,' he laughed and reached for the phone. He sat on the sofa in the tidy half and looked over at the rest of the mess.

'DuPont cleaning services; how can I help?'

'I've got a police station looking like a pigsty if you're looking for work.' Melanie laughed briefly. 'On the other hand, knowing you, you'd probably spend your working time nosing around in all our secret little places.'

'Melanie, you should learn to trust me. I'm one of the good guys.'

'The bad guys must be worse than I thought then.'

'Tell me, have you turned up anything new or are you just looking for a place to stay for the weekend? I've got a very clean apartment you could use; well, precisely fifty percent clean, but I'm working on it. And you get me into the bargain.'

'I just had a mental image of you in a pinafore waving a feather duster. Not a pretty sight, I would say.'

'You are a very strange woman, DS Cooper. I didn't realise you were into cosplay and incidentally, I do love a girl in uniform.'

'I'll treat that comment with the respect it deserves.' Melanie's tone changed, all business now. 'I've had a chat with the doctor.'

'And? Did he have anything useful to say?'

Melanie paused. Alex thought he could hear her thinking. 'Yes and no. Amanda did have an episode of depression. Doctor Mayhew said she had recovered fully, but he couldn't rule out a recurrence.'

'Nothing definite, then.'

'No. But he did say one interesting thing.'

'Go on.'

'He told me Gerry was aware of the whole thing. I don't know if that just means sisterly concern or something else, but it made me think.'

Alex filed that away for later. 'So now you've spoken to him, what do you think?'

'I think we need something concrete before I'm convinced it's murder.'

'Melanie, don't jump ship on me now. I know we'll get the evidence, I can feel it in my bones.'

'Until we do, I'm on the fence about this one. I'm not saying you're wrong, Alex. But without a stronger lead, or a viable suspect, it's all still up in the air. Sorry to sound like the devil's advocate, but I have my doubts.'

'The evidence we've got so far is suggestive, you said so yourself.'

'Suggestive isn't good enough for the CPS, though, is it?'

'Let's see where we are after my trip to Paris. If you still think it's iffy, we'll worry about it then. The thing is, I don't want to feel we're on different sides.'

'We're not, not really. It's just…'

Alex let out a breath he hadn't realised he'd been holding. 'Come on, Melanie, this is murder and you know it is. You can feel it just like I can.'

'Let's leave it until you get back from Paris, like you said. I need… I need some time to think.'

Alex started, drew back and looked at the phone in his hand. Had something just shifted?

'Are we still talking about the case?'

It took a few moments for Melanie to answer.

'Alex, I think, I mean I feel… God, what am I saying? Ever since you came back into my life, I've felt at sixes and sevens. Having you around is a big distraction in my life, a disruption more like. I really don't know if that's good or bad.'

'I could take a step back, if it helps. I mean, we're both spoken for, so to speak. God, now I'm doing it too.'

'But you can't, can you? First of all, we have to work together until this case is resolved. We can't do that without seeing each other. And I get the feeling you don't want to step back. If only I knew where I stood with you. You don't treat Claire all that well. And even if we were both free, it's not as simple as that, is it? I'm not sure if I want to commit myself to a long-term relationship.'

'Your doubts, are they're really about the case, or what?

You're confusing your feelings with your work. And you can't tell me how to act with Claire. You've got form there too: look how you treat Martin.'

'Alex DuPont, are you accusing me of being un-professional? And my relationship with Martin is none of your business.' She was practically hissing at him now.

'Oh, right; you can tell me how to act with Claire, but I can't say anything about you and Martin. That's rich.'

'I didn't mean… Oh, you're impossible!'

The line went dead. Alex fumed at the phone for a few moments, then he put it down and fumed at himself. *You idiot.* Now he did not know what to do. He thought he should have stuck to talking only about work instead getting involved in a personal and sensitive conversation. He found himself in a conundrum. He wondered if he should give Melanie a ring and sort out their disagreement. After careful consideration, he decided it would be better to let things evolved instead of initiating a move, professional or personal. It could upset her more. He still had the whole weekend to consider it.

CHAPTER 15

S t Pancras station was never empty, but it was, mercifully, less crowded than he'd expected. Alex steered his wheeled suitcase between small group of tourists, past the food court and headed towards the trains. Jenny had booked him a first-class seat and he was looking forward to a comfortable journey.

After the row with Melanie, the weekend had turned out better than he expected, in more ways than one. His laundry was up to date, at least, and the apartment looked better for his furious spring clean. He just wished he'd been able to spring clean his head as well. In any case, on Saturday afternoon he played football with friends and had a few pints of beer with them. On Sunday, he did his five-mile run in Hyde Park, spent his time with some friends in Leicester Square. In the evening, he went out to dinner with Claire.

He settled into his plush seat. The carriage was empty, which was a relief, he would be able to do some thinking and reading about the case. The last thing he needed was a chatty stranger interrupting his concentration. At ten o'clock, the station robot announced their departure, and he watched the last few passengers rushing to get on before they were left behind.

As the train was pulling out, he had a cup of coffee and a croissant in the buffet car. After a few minutes he took his files out of his case and spread them on the table. He was looking forward to being in Paris again. He'd always loved the city, and he'd have some spare time to wander around and enjoy the atmosphere, so very different from London.

Before he left home, he'd texted Gerry to let her know he would be in Paris too, and to ask if they could meet. After Melanie's revelations from her visit to the doctor, he wanted to talk to her: she wasn't a suspect – not exactly – but there was something she was holding back and he wanted to know what it was. Perhaps she'd be less guarded on neutral ground and reveal more.

Jeremy had agreed to meet him the following day at lunchtime in the shop: *Boutique Bijou,* an ostentatiously classy jeweller's shop, just a ten-minute walk from Hotel Bouchard, run by the lovely, but bossy, Sophie Bouchard, a maternal cousin of his father's.

'Well, Jeremy Higgins, let's have a good look at you,' he said, taking the freshly copied photo out of the file. He didn't think Jeremy was the most likely suspect, but he didn't like loose ends.

The young man in the photo would have been vaguely handsome except for the acne scars that marred his face. He looked to be about normal height, shorter than Ashley and Timothy, but probably a bit taller than Steve. He wasn't smiling in the photo. Alex remembered Ashley saying he'd had his grumpy face on for the camera. Now he looked more closely, he wondered if grumpy was Jeremy's default setting.

Jenny had looked into Jeremy's background. Alex took out her notes and read them. Jeremy Higgins had studied Philosophy at Bristol, gained a first-class honours degree and played scrum half for the university first team. He'd left for Paris immediately after graduation and found a job in *Boutique Bijou* within a month of arriving. Now, he was the under-manager. Alex assumed he spoke fluent French, although there was no note of him, having French family connections or having taken a course in French while he was a student. A quick study, then.

With the file notes spread out in front of him, Alex tried to form a picture in his mind of the web of relationships around Amanda. It felt frustratingly incomplete. He was about to shuffle them around, to see if anything came to mind, when his phone pinged with a text message. It was from Melanie. She had written a single word, all in lower case as if she was whispering, *sorry.*

**

Alex enjoyed both the Kent and the French countryside all the way to Paris.

The train stopped at Gare du Nord. It was a welcome sight. The station was a monument to grand, nineteenth-century design: an ocean of glass above and in front, a utilitarian grid of platforms beneath. He went through the security checks then, caught the Metro to Charles de Gaulle-Etoile. It took around forty minutes to get to his destination. Upon arrival, he left the station, walked up the steps and came out onto the pavement of the Avenue des Champs-Elysees. The place was buzzing with people, mostly tourists, walking, talking and laughing. It was a real pleasure for Alex to be there. The monument of the Arc de Triomphe was quite close. He went to have a look at this iconic landmark and stood on the edge of the grassed area to admire its splendour.

After walking crisply across a couple of Avenues, he

arrived at the Hotel Bouchard in one of the side roads. Hotel Bouchard was an eccentric stack of architectural leftovers squeezed between a bank and a bookshop. Sophie Bouchard was on the front step, waiting to welcome him. 'Alex, *Mon Cheri*, you are late,' with the customary *Hugs and Kisses on both cheeks* in typical French style.

'Hello, Aunt Sophie. Delighted to see you.'

'Come on in, let the porter takes your suitcase to your room. I've given you your favourite room on the second floor, as always.'

'*Merci, merci.*'

A few minutes later, his luggage safely stowed away, Alex sat in the ground floor parlour: a crowded, chintzy arrangement of wing-back chairs and rickety tables, while Sophie regaled him with family gossip. He had some pastries, a slice of strawberry cake and two cups of tea that helped to settle his rumbling stomach. She finally took a breath and appraised her English nephew. 'So, you are being the great detective, eh? And are you chasing criminals in Paris?'

'No, I'm here to interview a witness in a murder enquiry.'

'Ah, you sound like a TV detective! Dangerous job, isn't it?'

'I'm doing someone a favour. Usually, I deal with wealthy clients' personal problems and large corporations' issues.'

'Do you know where this witness is?'

'I believe he works at *Boutique Bijou*, the luxury jeweller's shop on the Avenue des Champs-Elysees.'

'Do you know where it is?'

'I've a good idea.'

'Are you on your own?'

'Yes, I am.'

'It's not safe for you to conduct your investigation in this large city without any assistance. I know a *gendarme* very well and I'll ask him to keep an eye on you. What am I talking about? It's your second cousin, Gerard. He is a senior police officer in Paris. For the sake of the family, he should help you out. In any case, Gerard would do anything for me. I'll contact him.' She winked as if she'd revealed a dark family secret.

'That's very nice to know but I'm fine and can manage on my own.'

'Alex, this can be a dangerous place, you understand. I'll make sure that Gerard provides you with the necessary help. Also, if you come across any problems, ring the hotel immediately.'

Alex was not expecting all this fuss from Sophie. He had no choice but to go along with her suggestion. C'*est la famile, n'est pas?*

'OK, that's settled.' Sophie was delighted. 'Go and have a shower and change. You look like a man who just got off a train. I've booked us a table at that posh French restaurant you like.'

The rest of the evening was taken up with food and family. By the time they got back to the hotel, Alex was tired, full and a little drunk. He said goodnight and headed to his room. Seconds after his head hit the pillow, he was fast asleep.

**

Hugo Zelov was not having a good day. One of his night clubs had been raided by the Marseille drug squad. They hadn't found the drugs, which was good. But his nephew,

André, who managed the club for him – and sold the drugs to the punters – was under the care of a struck-off doctor now on Hugo's payroll, having his stomach pumped out, which was definitely bad.

And now this call from the English woman, warning him that some English private investigator was snooping around his business interests in Paris. He had vaguely recognised her voice but couldn't place her. And she'd called from a burner phone, so his tame techie couldn't trace the call.

He didn't understand why she was protecting his interests. In Hugo's world, everyone looked after their own interests, which meant everyone had their own agenda, was busy screwing everyone else. He couldn't see what this woman's agenda was. And who was this guy she was setting up? She said he would be the fall guy if he didn't take care of the investigator. Which, in Hugo's opinion, meant she wanted Hugo to drop some very special crap on him. And that begged the question: was she also planning to drop some crap on Hugo?

Whatever she meant, Hugo had to look after himself first. If this weird English woman had other things going on, so be it. If there was a threat to his Paris operation, he had to push it away or if it came to it, snuff it out.

Hugo had a diverse portfolio of business interests; some of them were even legal. But his line in recycled gems was particularly lucrative, and the last thing he needed was some inquisitive Englishman sticking his nose in. He picked up the phone.

'Herman, I need a favour.'

'Sure, Hugo, I owe you one.' Damn right, thought Hugo. He had taken a big risk in bumping off Herman's main rival. The police had put real heat on him for that, but he was a survivor, and he wriggled out of it. Meanwhile Herman was home and dry.

'Are any of your boys in Paris right now?'

'Yes, David and Antoine are picking up a shipment for me.'

'Ah, that's good to hear. Listen, this is what I need them to do…'

**

It was the bright sunlight shining through the curtains that woke Alex up. He jumped out of bed; had a wash, shave and shower. Then, he dressed up in his navy chino trousers and pink polo shirt. He had no choice but to plan his day over a sumptuous breakfast. Sophie had pulled out all the stops. 'A good breakfast is the best cure for a hangover, Alex, and it will set you up for the day,' she said as she plonked a heaving plate in front of him.

But he wasn't aware that he had a hangover, he felt fine. He was used to eating a light breakfast. So, coping with the massive breakfast would be a real challenge. To please her, he did his best and left the rest. All the same, he had to complement her. 'Ah, Aunt Sophie, what would we do without you?'

'Perhaps I should move to London and be your housekeeper, eh?'

Alex did not reply to that tempting offer. He just smiled.

He had arranged to visit Jeremy at the shop at lunchtime. He could spend an hour talking to him and clear him from the list. In the meantime, he would stroll over to the conference centre and see if there was a suitable café nearby to meet Gerry in.

'Right, I'm off; I'll see you later, Aunt Sophie. Be good while I'm gone.'

'Ah, you rascal, I am always good, I am an angel.' They were standing in the small reception hall of the hotel. Sophie glanced out the window and noticed a man in a wine-coloured windcheater loitering outside a lingerie shop across the road. Hmm; he didn't look the sort to be browsing at women's underwear, at least not in public. She kissed Alex on both cheeks and watched as he walked off towards the Avenue des Champ-Elysees. The man in the windcheater waited a couple of beats and followed. Hmm.

Sophie picked up the phone and called Gerard. 'Gerard, my sweet, I need you to do your aunt Sophie a little favour…'

**

Boutique Bijou looked ridiculously expensive. There were only a few pieces in the shop window, but each of them was worth almost as much as Alex's apartment. He checked himself in the window's reflection to make sure he didn't look too down at heel and walked in.

'Bonjour, I'm here to see Jeremy Higgins.'

The sales assistant was an over-dressed waif, a super model on her day off.

'Ah, I'm afraid Mr Higgins isn't here. He left about half an hour ago.'

'Oh, that's strange. I arranged to meet him here at one o'clock. My name is Alex DuPont.'

Alex took out a business card and handed it over. The supermodel perused the card and looked up. 'A moment, please. I will fetch the manager.'

The elegant lines of the manager's suit were slightly

spoiled by a supersize rectangular wristwatch, 'Monsieur DuPont, I am so sorry. Jeremy had to rush away. He had a bit of a shock this morning and he looked quite unwell.'

'I'm sorry to hear that. A shock? Not bad news, I hope.'

'Who can say? We had a customer earlier, an English lady. When she came in, Jeremy looked as if he had seen a ghost. They spoke for a few moments, and after she left, he excused himself and said he wanted to take some time to recover.'

'That's inconvenient. I was hoping to talk to Jeremy.'

'Actually, he left you a note. At least, he told me to tell you this and I made a note of it.'

He produced a piece of paper covered in an elegant scrawl and passed it to Alex.

'I'm sorry; could you read this out for me? The handwriting is rather, um, unusual.'

The manager sniffed haughtily and cleared his throat. 'I am unable to meet you at the appointed time. I can see you this evening, say about six-thirty, at the entrance of Carré Marigny garden.'

Now it was Alex's turn to sniff. 'I suppose that will have to do. Thank you for your help, Monsieur. I hope I haven't inconvenienced you.' He turned to go, and then turned back. 'Oh, there is one more thing. I wonder if I might have a look at your security camera feed. I am curious about this English lady.'

'This is a little irregular, Monsieur, but I suppose, if it helps...' He shrugged and held out his hands, palms up.

They went to the office at the rear of the shop. The manager booted up a laptop and clicked a few times. 'Ah! There you are, Monsieur, your English lady.'

Alex watched as the shop door opened and a tall, blonde woman walked in: Gerry Hamilton.

**

As Alex walked out of *Boutique Bijou*, he noticed a man in a wine-coloured windcheater standing in front of an upmarket travel agency. He didn't look particularly upmarket. When he caught Alex's eye, the man bent down as if he needed to tie his shoelaces: odd, for a man wearing loafers.

Alex walked on, not entirely sure where he was heading. He stopped at a shop selling ornate mirrors and looked at his reflection over his shoulder, the man in the windcheater turned away and became very interested in a display of antiquarian books.

Alex had never been trained to lose a tail, but he'd seen enough movies to know the general drill. He slowed down and sped up at irregular intervals. He took the Metro for one stop, got off and doubled back. After a while, he felt sure he had lost Windcheater Man.

He came to a small patch of greenery and flowers with a cast-iron bench and sat down. Within a few seconds he had company. Two men sat, one either side of him. He wasn't particularly worried about them. They looked like common thugs, and he was confident he could handle them. But they sat so close that they had trapped his arms between them. It would be a struggle to free himself and get on equal terms.

'So, Mr English, you are enjoying your sightseeing of Paris?' Windcheater Man was the boss. Apparently, he spoke English with a heavy, guttural accent.

Alex spoke native-level French, but he decided to play the innocent abroad. 'I was, until two goons came along and spoiled my day. Do you normally sit this close to people, or are you just very pleased to see me?'

'No, we are not pleased to see you. And we are not the only people who are not pleased.' Windcheater Man reached into his pocket. He didn't pull anything out. A couple of large shadows had fallen across the ill-matched trio on the bench.

'So, Antoine, you are a long way from home? Oh, don't look so surprised; your accent is a dead giveaway. Marseille. Did you have *peng* for breakfast, huh?' Alex got the joke. So did Antoine and David, but they didn't appreciate it. When people from Marseille said the French word for bread – *pain* – for them, it came out as *peng*. At least, it did when Parisians imitated it.

Alex looked up. Two men stood in front of them, obviously police officers; the man who had spoken looked oddly familiar. His partner opened his jacket, revealing a shoulder holster. 'Let's stay friendly, Antoine, or things could get a little noisy around here.'

Antoine looked over his shoulder, gauging the chances of escape. Behind them stood two burly *gendarmes* in uniform. One of them tapped a wicked nightstick across the palm of his hand, a grim smile on his face.

Alex spoke to the men in front of him, in perfect Parisian French. David looked at him in mild surprise. 'Officers, this is a pleasant surprise. I have a feeling it has something to do with Aunt Sophie. Am I right?'

'Indeed. Sophie noticed this individual,' he pointed at Antoine, 'loitering outside the hotel. When you left, he followed you. She gave me a call and told me my English second cousin might be in a little spot of trouble. Naturally, I came to see what the fuss was about. Blood is thicker than water, *n'est pas?*'

'You must be Gerard. I thought I could see the family resemblance.'

'Yes, I am Gerard.' He signalled to the two uniformed

gendarmes with a nod. They produced handcuffs and took hold of Antoine and David. 'My colleagues here will take your new friends to the station. I'm sure we can find something interesting to talk about.'

'Thank you, Gerard, I owe you one.'

'Not at all.' He took out a business card. 'Here is my number, Alex. After what has just happened, I think it would be a good idea if we stayed in touch.'

**

Alex was now at a loose end, at least until six-thirty. He looked at his watch, it was coming up to three o'clock, just the time for a conference tea break. He walked briskly to the conference centre and stood outside on the broad steps. He was right: people were coming out of the main hall, looking at phones and chatting.

He was in luck. Gerry appeared on the steps, looking at a company Blackberry. When she noticed Alex, she stopped in surprise. She didn't look totally pleased to see him.

'Alex, what brings you here? I got your text and I was just going to reply.'

'I was hoping you might have a few minutes to talk now. It looks like you're on a tea break.'

She looked at her watch. 'Yes, I have fifteen minutes before the next session, let's find a place to sit and we can talk.'

There was a raised flowerbed in the drive sweeping away from the centre to the gate. It had a marble ledge wide enough to perch on, so they perched.

'What's the conference about?'

'Digital currencies and problems with blockchain development. Sorry, I can't explain that in simple English.'

123

Gerry's smile was disarming, but it didn't reach as far as her eyes.

'And what else have you been doing in Paris?'

'Oh, you know: sightseeing, a little shopping.'

'Shopping for jewellery, for instance?'

The look that crossed her face was difficult to read, but it wasn't friendly.

'Have you been following me, Alex?'

'No, it's just a peculiar coincidence. I went to see Jeremy Higgins earlier today. The manager of the shop said he'd seen a ghost.'

'He wasn't the only one. I went there to see the manager, and then I saw Jeremy and recognised his face from Amanda's photo. I was taken aback, but he looked completely shocked.'

'Why did you want to see the manager?'

'One of our clients at Scrimshaw is a... businessman from Marseille called Hugo Zelov. Not your typical businessman. I met him once, a couple of years ago when he was in London. He had a prison haircut, a nose that looked like it had been broken more than once and had super-size hands.

'Anyway, Mr Zelov appears to be laundering money, and he's using our firm to do it, not a comfortable situation for a reputable City firm. We also heard he was using a couple of Parisian jewellers to fence stolen gems. I was hoping to call him and find a subtle way to get him off our books.'

'And did you?'

'Did I what?'

'Call him.'

'Not yet. Why do you ask?'

'I had a brief encounter with a couple of guys from Marseille earlier today. I don't think they had my best interests at heart.'

Gerry looked genuinely upset at that. 'I'm sorry about that, Alex, but I don't see how it could have had anything to do with me or the dubious Mr Zelov.

Are you alright?'

'I'm fine. A cousin of mine turned up with a couple of friends and we sorted things out.'

'You never cease to surprise me, Alex.'

'I might say the same about you, Gerry. While we're on the subject of surprises, I heard some surprising news about Amanda: it's to do with a bout of depression. Can you tell me anything about that?'

'I mentioned it in passing to DS Cooper. It was a long time ago. I didn't think it was relevant.'

'Your sister may just have killed herself, Gerry. And her bout of depression was only a few years ago, and you didn't think it was relevant?'

She looked sheepish at that: sheepish and guilty. 'I don't think it changes things. Someone murdered Amanda, you know that.'

'Something else… You told me that you and Amanda were close, but you hardly ever saw each other. Do you want to tell me anything about that?'

'I told you; we were both busy…' Gerry stopped and looked deflated. 'Look, I haven't been entirely honest with you, Alex. Amanda and I were close, very close. But five years ago, things took a strange turn. Amanda got involved with a man and so did I.'

'You mean the same man?'

She looked at the pavement under her feet. 'Yes, the

same man. It didn't end well, for any of us. Amanda got depressed, and we drifted apart. For a while, to tell you the truth, I hated her.'

Gerry stopped and looked into Alex's eyes. 'But I got over it, we both did. I had nothing to do with her death. Nothing.' She stood up and straightened her suit jacket. 'I have to go now. The next session is about to begin.' Gerry turned abruptly on her heel and walked away. Alex watched her go. She looked a little unsteady on her feet. He sighed and headed back into the streets of Paris.

**

Alex had a very late lunch in a little café. He made some fresh notes, and then he remembered the text from Melanie. He replied, keeping it simple: *It's OK, I'm sorry too.*

Afterwards he hurried back to the hotel. Sophie was waiting for him in the hallway, a broad smile on her face. 'So, you met Gerard, and in strange circumstances, I hear.'

'Yes, I did. Thank you, Aunt Sophie. You got me out of a spot of bother. I'm afraid I can't stay for dinner, something has come up. And my train back to London is at nine o'clock. I'll just get my bag and be off.'

'Alright, it was wonderful to see you again. Give my best regards to everyone and have a pleasant journey back to London. Take good care of yourself, Alex.'

They said their goodbyes with the customary hugs and kisses. Alex picked his suitcase and left.

**

The Carre Marigny garden was quiet; few green benches were occupied by people sitting and chatting. Alex chose a bench in the shadows; he wanted to watch Jeremy's approach unnoticed.

It was a little after six-fifteen. He had a few minutes to relax and think over the day's events. He decided to give Gerard a call.

'Ah, Alex, I was expecting a call from you. You want to know about our friends from Marseille, eh?'

'There is something in particular I want to know, Gerard. Did either of them mention the name Hugo Zelov?'

'It's funny you should ask that. They don't work for Hugo Zelov directly. But they seemed to think they were doing him a favour by acting heavy with you. Does that make sense?'

'Yes, it does. In more ways than one.'

'You are an enigmatic Englishman. You want to tell me more?'

'I need to sort it out in my head first, Gerard. But when I have, you will be the first to know. I have to go now. *A bientôt.*'

Jeremy had just turned the corner into the garden. He walked slowly, his footsteps heavy, his head down, a picture of misery, or worry, or both.

Alex raised a hand in greeting. Jeremy came over to the bench and sat down heavily, staring into the distance. There was a brief, awkward silence.

'We meet at last, Jeremy. I was a bit surprised to find you'd run out on me.'

'It was nothing to do with you, Mr DuPont. I'd had a shock and I needed some time to process it.'

'So I understand. They look very alike, don't they?'

Jeremy finally turned and met Alex's gaze. His expression was unreadable, blank except for the constant movement of his eyes.

'When she walked in, just for a moment, I thought I

was looking at a dead woman. I felt like I was going to faint.'

'I didn't realise you felt so strongly about Amanda. I know you were friends at university. Was there something more between you two?'

The question startled him, the mask slipped for a moment, and Alex could see a well of troubled thoughts. 'No, we were just friends. But for those three years, the four of us, we were very close.'

'As I understand it, there were five of you.'

'Ah, Charlotte, yes. She was part of the group, but not really part of us, if you know what I mean.'

'I can't say that I do.'

'Charlotte came with Ashley. She was part of the package, you might say. In many respects, she didn't really fit in.'

'Why not?'

'She was insanely jealous of Amanda. She thought Ashley was sweet on her and she didn't like that one bit.'

'But she and Ashley broke up.'

'They did. But Charlotte always held a candle for Ashley. And seeing him so close to Amanda... I think she found it very difficult to cope.'

'Did it ever come to a head?'

Jeremy shifted like his clothes had stopped fitting him. 'I couldn't say.'

Alex made a note in his head and changed the subject abruptly. 'Does the name Hugo Zelov mean anything to you?'

That brought a reaction. Jeremy seemed to break into little pieces for a second, like an anthill kicked by a dog. He regained his composure quickly, but with difficulty. 'I can't say I have. Is he – was he – something to Amanda?'

'No, I don't believe so. I was just curious.'

The look he gave Alex was narrow and hostile.

Alex changed the subject again. 'The day Amanda died - Sunday the fourth of June. Where were you, Jeremy? Can you account for your movements?'

'I was sightseeing. I went to a few famous places and sat in cafés, people watching. I do that a lot.'

'Was anyone with you?'

'No, I was on my own the whole day. I don't have many friends here, Mr DuPont. To tell the truth, I've become a bit of a loner since my student days.'

Alex stood up and offered his hand. 'Jeremy, you have been most helpful.'

Jeremy shook his hand. 'I don't see how. I had nothing to do with Amanda's death. I heard she'd committed suicide. I'm surprised to see a private investigator snooping around a suicide.'

'So, Gerry didn't say anything about Amanda's death?'

That slight shift again. Jeremy was hiding something. He seemed to lie with his whole body, not just his voice. 'No.' he glanced at his watch on his right wrist, an expensive model. Alex noticed his hands: they were slender and tapered and looked strangely feminine.

'I may well need to talk to you again, Jeremy. If you feel the need to run off again, don't run too far.'

Alex left him there in the garden, elbows resting on his knees, head down, entirely alone.

**

He just made the train back to London. He didn't get his notes out on the return journey as he had too much to think about. Also, he needed to get it all sorted out in his mind before he wrote it down.

He was in London before he knew it. It was amazing how quickly one could get to London from Paris, he thought, as he stepped down onto the platform. You could be there and back in a day. Now, that was something else to think about.

CHAPTER 16

The following morning Alex arrived at the Agency. Jenny and Scott had been waiting patiently to hear of his visit. Whilst they were having their morning tea, he gave them the feedback. Both were stunned when they heard about the fracas he encountered.

'I told you I should have gone with you.' Scott was practically bristling with agitation. 'I don't know, Alex. You were in Paris only for a short time and you ended up facing the Parisian low lifes. What were they like?'

'They weren't Parisian, they were from Marseille.'

'Same difference. Or do thugs from Marseille punch with a different accent?'

'Funny you should say that.' Alex remembered Gerard's Parisian joke.

'Still, it's all the same when you're on the wrong end of it.'

'Maybe.' Alex stopped abruptly. 'Hmm. Jenny, can you dig up what you can about a criminal entrepreneur in Marseille called Hugo Zelov? I'm curious what kind of business activities he has in Paris; drugs, perhaps.'

'Do you want to hear what we were doing while you were getting yourself in trouble in Paris?'

'In a minute, Scott. Jenny, I think it's worth having another look at Jeremy. While you're at it, can you check something for me? I want to know if it's possible to get from Paris to London and back on a Sunday, within the time frame of Amanda's death.'

'Is our Jeremy a suspect?' Jenny asked astutely.

'Not yet, but there was something off about him. And he doesn't really have an alibi for the day Amanda was killed. He says he was sightseeing, but he's been in Paris for almost a year. You'd think he'd have seen the sights by now.'

'OK, leave it with me.'

'And one more thing, can you have a look at the shop he works in – *Boutique Bijou*? I'm curious why Gerry chose that particular jeweller to visit when she was checking up on Hugo. It could be a coincidence, of course. But it stinks.'

'Now you're back, I suppose you'll just be swanning off to meet the lovely Melanie.'

Instantly, Alex looked a bit worried.

'Ooh, I think I've touched a sore spot. Are things alright with Melanie?'

Alex scratched his chin, looking distracted. 'Of course. I need to call her after we've finished here,' he said, composed again. 'Tell me what you've found, Scott?'

'My boffin guy got back to me with some news. He had another look at the prints on the wine glass. He used a new piece of kit they've just got in and he says there's definitely another set of prints under Amanda's. Funny thing is, he says he can't tell straight off if they come from a man or a woman. Usually it's easy, apparently, but these are a bit of a mystery.'

'Can he ID them?'

'Well, that's the tricky part. He says he's managed to isolate a couple of partials, but it may not be enough for a proper ID. However, there's enough there to match with a full set of prints from another source if we need corroborating evidence.'

'Excellent. It doesn't get us anywhere right now, but if we narrow the field down a bit and it may come in very useful indeed. What about Steve's alibi?'

'I spent a couple of hours with the security guys at Tottenham Stadium. We were able to narrow the search down a bit from the ticket, luckily. And I think we might have got a result. Unless he likes taking the scenic route, Steve would have to use one of two entrances on the north side of the ground.'

'And what did you see?'

'Nothing. In particular, no Steve. It seems he's not just a toe rag, he's a lying toe rag to boot.'

Alex thought on that for a second. 'Well, that's suggestive, but it's not definitive. If we have any further reason to put Steve in the frame, you'll have to go back to the stadium security people and check all the entrances, just to make sure.'

'Thanks, Alex, I'm really looking forward to that.'

'Perks of the job, Scott.' Alex said. 'I think I'd better go back and talk to him again. In any case, Jenny, any luck with your search on Timothy and Charlotte?'

'I did some background checks on them. Timothy is from Nottingham originally. He went to Bristol to study Applied Maths and Economics. After university he moved to London and started working for a firm called...' Jenny clicked a couple of times. 'Delacroix. An American outfit apparently. He's a derivatives analyst, whatever that means. I couldn't see anything suspicious in his background. He has a girlfriend, who works at the same firm, and he seems to be clean.'

'I'll go and talk to him anyway, just to eliminate him from our list, if nothing else. Also, he might be able to shed some light on the relationships between the other friends in the group. I have a gut feeling that by understanding the dynamics of the Famous Five, might give us an insight into motives. What about Charlotte?'

'Yeah, that was interesting.' Jenny drew her hands together under her chin and looked at the file. 'Quite interesting.'

'Come on, Jenny, cough it up.'

'You've got no patience, Alex. OK, where was I? Charlotte Palmer. I don't know if she's dodgy but she's kind of connected. Her family is loaded. I'm surprised she bothers to work, to be honest. But work she does, for an insurance firm called Angleton Insurance in Aldwych. She does something I can't even pronounce but it seems to make her a bigwig of some sort.'

'And how is she connected? Does she do something unpronounceable for Brown Legal?'

'No, the connection is her dad. Brown Legal do his legal stuff. And he's a member of the same golf club as Walter Coburn.'

'Which means he knows Macey too. Well, that might be a clue. More to the point, it might mean we get some blowback if we start investigating her. We'd better tread carefully with Charlotte Palmer.'

'Oh, and one more little thing.' Jenny consulted the file again. 'It seems Charlotte might have a taste for designer drugs. She's had brushes with the police, both here and in France: no charges were brought in either case. It sounds like the French police were keen to do so, but she had a good lawyer and they backed off in the end.'

'Very interesting.' Alex took a sip of his tea. 'So, have you got interviews set up for Timothy and Charlotte?'

'Yes. Charlotte at two this afternoon. She asked if you could come to the reception at the Angleton building, and she'll get a room for your meeting. And Timothy at five in a café next to where he works. I'll ping you the details.'

'Perfect. That should give me enough time to check in with Melanie and get my notes in order. Another thing, I'd better call mum and dad. I'm sure aunt Sophie has filled them in on my adventures in Paris by now. I'm not looking forward to that conversation.'

**

Melanie's morning had started badly and was still going downhill. Jenkins collared her the moment she walked in. 'Cooper, I've had another call from on high.'

'What is it this time, guv?'

'The Chief Super called me and asked why we were interviewing someone called Charlotte Palmer. Apparently, her dad is one of his golf mates, and he got a bit shirty when he heard his daughter was under suspicion.'

'She's not, guv, at least not yet.' That wasn't the answer Jenkins wanted to hear. He leaned his considerable bulk over her desk.

'And then I got a call direct from Walter Coburn. He was asking if Ms Palmer needed legal representation for her interview. As a matter of interest, why are we talking to her?'

'There was a photo in Amanda Hamilton's living room, and this was also on her laptop as screensaver. Ashley Bradshaw was in it and a couple of other people: university friends of Amanda's. One of them is Charlotte. Alex thinks…'

'What does Mr DuPont think? Remember we have a dog in this race too.'

'He thinks the photo might be extremely important. Tell the truth, I think he's a bit fixated on it.'

'Well, you tell him to be nice to her, and don't get heavy. I've got enough toffs breathing down my neck as it is.' Jenkins straightened up and put his hands in his pockets. He looked very worried.

'What's up, guv?'

'Yeah, well that's the other thing. That Albanian melt, Marku? He was seen visiting a lady friend in Earl's Court. Now, he disappeared from her flat. I need you to check it out. He's our best lead so far and I want him back within our sights as soon as.'

'On it, guv.' Melanie didn't have the first idea how she was going to find a lone, dodgy Albanian in a city of nearly ten million people. But she was sure of one thing, it was going to be a pain.

Her phone buzzed: Alex. 'So, you're stirring up the hornet's nest again.'

Alex sounded puzzled. 'Am I? What have I done now?'

'Charlotte Palmer. Her dad is a mate of a couple of people we know.'

'Ah!' She had an image of his face as realisation dawned. 'Yes, we saw that. Her dad is rather well connected.'

'Too right he is. Jenkins is leaning on me to lean on you. He wants you to be nice to her and make it very clear she's not a suspect.'

'I'll do my best, but I can't assume she's not a suspect until I know more. Did her alibi check out?'

'Yes, it did. She was at home with her parents for Sunday lunch and stayed around until evening. Her mother confirmed it, in between telling me off for having the temerity to ask. So how was Paris?'

'Interesting, too interesting in parts.' Alex gave her a run-down on the events of the past two days. Melanie's heart fluttered when he told her about his encounter with the two thugs.

'Are you OK?'

'I'm fine. A cousin of mine, who happens to be an Inspector in the Paris serious crime squad, turned up with a couple of his mates and took them in.'

'You do lead an exciting life, and what was Jeremy Higgins like? Was he worth the trip?'

'I think he was. His alibi wasn't up too much, and there is something about him. I can't put my finger on it, but there's something there.'

'Funny, he got a visit from Gerry.'

'There's that too. I'm beginning to think she has more to tell us or to put it another way, she may still be hiding something.'

'Well, most murders turn out to be by the nearest and dearest. But from what you found out, maybe they weren't so near and dear after all.'

'Exactly. And her connection to the gangster who set those thugs on me is food for thought. I mean, it could all be a coincidence, but it makes me feel uneasy about it all.'

'But you don't think she's a suspect?'

'No, I think it's more complicated than that. But I haven't ruled her out yet. She keeps turning up in the wrong places.'

Melanie nodded, and then she realised she was on the phone. 'You're right, Alex; there is more to Gerry than she's letting on.'

'I think so. Anyway, Scott and Jenny were busy too. I'll run through their findings.' He rattled off a bunch of bullet points from a list. 'There you have it. I think we're getting somewhere, though I'm not absolutely sure where yet.'

Melanie looked down at the notes she'd made as Alex was talking. 'I think we need to have another talk to Steve. Shall I get him to come into the station? You can sit in. You've already talked to him so, you've the background. We might be able to put a little bit of pressure on him and see what pops out.'

'That's a good idea. I've been thinking the same. Let's get on with it straightaway.'

'Ah, there's a bit of a problem there.'

'What's up?'

'You remember I mentioned the mad Albanians with guns? Well, one of them, our best lead in the gang shootings, has done a runner. The DI wants me on it. To some extent, I guess I feel responsible partly because it was me who fingered him out in the first place, via that dodgy pub landlord with the breast fetish.'

'Does that mean we need to put everything on hold?' She could hear the frustration in his voice.

'Only for a couple of days, sorry. In any case, you've got other stuff to be going on with.'

'And what about the prints?'

'Prints?' She looked back at her notes. 'Oh yes. Can you ask Scott to get his boffin mate to send them to us? I'll ping you an email address. There's a bit of a queue for IDENT1, so don't hold your breath.'

She could practically hear a sound on the line like someone tapping irritated fingers on a desk. Alex sighed audibly. 'When can we get together for a proper catch-up? Just work stuff, obviously.'

Neither of them had mentioned the argument over the weekend. Melanie thought she should leave it that way. 'Not tonight, Alex; I'm going to be scouring the streets for the phantom Albanians. Let's talk tomorrow, after you've seen Charlotte and the other guy; ah yes, Timothy. Sometimes I can't read my own handwriting.'

**

Alex made an awkward call to his parents and settled down to make some notes for his interviews with Charlotte and Timothy. He was taking the notes off the printer when Jenny bustled in. 'I've got Ashley Bradshaw on the line. He sounds very upset. Can you take the call?'

Alex looked at his watch. There was time, just. 'OK, put him on.'

'Ashley, what can I do for you?'

'Mr DuPont, I didn't know who to call: you or the police? I thought you might be more, um, sympathetic to my predicament.'

'I'm all ears, Ashley.'

'Last night, quite late, I got a worrying call. It was a woman, but I didn't recognise her voice. It sounded like she was talking through a handkerchief.'

'And what did she have to say?'

'She threatened me, Mr DuPont. Her exact words were, "I'm going to destroy you." Then she rang off. I don't mind telling you, I'm scared.'

'And you have no idea who it might have been?'

'None at all. What should I do?'

'Well, you could drop your phone off here this afternoon. I'll ask Scott to check it and see if he can trace the call. I also think you should call the police.'

'I can't do that. They'll want to talk to people at work, and I don't want word of this getting out. It might jeopardise my chances of going to Hong Kong. Can you look after it for me? I'm happy to pay your fees.'

'We'll do our best, Ashley. Pop over with your phone and leave everything to us.'

'Thanks, Mr DuPont. I feel…' he paused, and Alex could hear the uncertainty radiating down the line. 'Ever since Amanda died, it feels like everything is spiralling out of control. I don't understand why it should be coming back on me like this.'

Neither do I, Ashley. 'Don't worry; it's likely just a crank call. We'll get back to you as soon as we've got something.'

Ashley rang off and Alex called Scott into his office. 'Ashley Bradshaw got a threatening phone call. He's scared out of his wits. I've asked him to bring his phone in. It's probably a long shot, but can you see if you can trace the call?'

'No worries, I'll have a look. This case is generating a lot of loose ends all of a sudden.'

'I'm afraid so. I wonder if we've spooked those responsible for murdering Amanda and they are trying to get things under control. Probably, they are trying to cover their tracks, thus preventing us from solving the case.'

CHAPTER 17

Alex did not have time for lunch. He decided to go and see Charlotte. She worked for a high-end insurance firm with its office in Aldwych that screamed wealth and influence. Alex waited for several minutes in reception until Charlotte appeared from the lifts, a little frazzled. 'I'm sorry, Mr DuPont, a particularly needy client delayed me for a few minutes.'

'No problem. And please call me Alex.'

'Alex, then. I've booked an office where we can talk in private.'

As they stepped into the lift, Alex took Charlotte in with a sideways glance. She had red hair, dark enough to almost be auburn, around an elfin face. She was attractive, but something in her expression was sharp. What his mother would call 'difficult'. He imagined her getting angry easily and that might be an intimidating prospect. Perhaps, she was just annoyed about her needy client.

The office was about the size of Alex's apartment and beautifully furnished. Charlotte invited him to sit on a plush leather sofa and perched herself on the other end, facing him.

'You wanted to talk about poor Amanda, I presume. Such a waste of a young life.'

'Can you think of any reason why she might want to kill herself?'

'No, but I hadn't been in touch with her for quite a while. Who knows what could have happened since then?'

'And can you think of anyone who might want to kill her?'

'Kill her? I thought Amanda committed suicide.' Her expression didn't give much away. She appeared shocked at the thought of murder, but her eyes were busy, calculating.

'We are working on the theory that she was murdered. The circumstances surrounding her death suggest it was most likely to be someone who knew her pretty well.'

'Oh, I see. That's the reason you are talking to all her friends. It makes sense, I suppose.' That calculation was still going on, Alex noted.

He took out the photo and showed it to her. 'Can you tell me about this?'

'It's just a photo, Alex. I think it was taken late in our last summer term. We all used to hang out together: me, Amanda, Ashley, Jeremy and Tim. Those were happy days.'

'And were those days always happy, Charlotte? Did everyone get along with each other all the time?'

Charlotte took a few seconds before she answered. She obviously suspected that Alex knew something, but she didn't know what. Her reply was non-committal. 'There was the odd bust-up; bound to be over time.'

'And was there ever a bust-up between you and Amanda?'

'No.' She looked into Alex's eyes; his expression didn't change. She carried on. 'Amanda and I weren't that close; we were just university friends. But there was nothing to fall out over, really.'

'Tell me about Ashley.'

She frowned. *He does know something.* 'As you probably already know, Ashley and I went out together. We hooked up shortly after we started at uni and were together for just over two and a half years, then we broke up.'

'And was it amicable?'

'Yes, I'd say so. Ashley may feel differently, but there were no hard feelings on my part.'

'And there was nothing untoward afterwards happened between you and Amanda?'

'No, why should there be?' Her eyes narrowed slightly.

'Ashley and Amanda were close, weren't they?' Alex leaned forward, gauging her reaction. Something flickered across her face and then it was gone.

'Yes, they were, um, very good friends. I'm sorry, Alex, and excuse me if I'm being dim, but is there a point to these questions?' She smiled, but the smile was cold.

'I'm trying to understand a whole set of relationships, Charlotte. They may have no bearing at all on Amanda's death. But then again…' He left the words hanging.

'Well, I can't help you with that. As I said, it's been a while since I saw any of the people in this photo. I'm sorry about Amanda, sincerely sorry, and I wish the others well. But they are not part of my life anymore.' This was said with such quiet conviction that Alex almost believed it.

Charlotte allowed a few moments of silence before she spoke again. 'Is there anything else I can help you with? I hope I don't sound like I'm brushing you off, but I am particularly busy today.'

'Then I won't keep you, Charlotte. However,…' Alex stood and proffered his hand which she shook. 'I may need to contact you again, if anything comes up.'

'Of course; anything I can do to help. Poor Amanda, she had so much going for her.' That should have sounded wistful, Alex thought, but instead it sounded as if Charlotte's secret calculation had just come to a satisfactory solution.

**

Ashley walked into the coffee shop, his mind elsewhere; after last night, he needed something to wake him up. He saw Steve on a stool at the window counter, his head in his hands.

'Cheer up, Steve, it was only two-nil. And it's only a summer friendly. Still, it should have been six; they battered you.'

Steve looked up and smiled but it was a pale, vague attempt. 'Oh, hi, Ash; yeah, it wasn't our finest hour.'

Ashley grabbed his coffee and came to join him. 'I could get you a season ticket to the Emirates for your birthday, if you like.'

'It's never that bad, mate.' Steve's expression said the opposite.

'So, what else is up?'

'I guess that investigator bloke rattled me a bit. I was sure Amanda had killed herself – I still am – but when he started on about her being murdered, it put the wind up me.'

'It's not a nice thought, is it?'

'No, it isn't. And I got the feeling he thought I was involved somehow. I mean, I could be reading too much into it, but he didn't seem to believe anything I told him.'

'Well, unless you're a serial murderer in your spare time, I wouldn't worry about it.'

'That's fine for you to say. That DuPont bloke was all over me like a rash. The thing is, there are things – personal things – I'd rather keep private, and if he keeps on like this they might come out. I wouldn't like that one bit.'

'What kind of things?'

'They wouldn't be private if I told you, would they?'

'Excuse me; I was only trying to help.'

'Yeah, sorry mate, I know that. Look, I'd better be going. The old man has probably got his stopwatch out. See you.'

Steve raised himself off the stool and made his way out, shoulders hunched as if he was feeling cold. An odd pose on a hot day. Ashley watched him go, puzzled. He felt as if he'd just had a baffling conversation with Steve. What could Steve be hiding that he didn't want Alex DuPont to find out?

**

Alex spotted the offices of Delacroix easily enough. The signage was loud and brash, out of place among the sober plaques of other long established City firms. The café was just a couple of doors away, beside the entrance to a Wren church he couldn't remember the name of.

Timothy Williams was taller than he looked in the photo and as thin as a rake. His dark hair fell over brown eyes that were kind and perpetually amused. Alex liked him immediately.

'Timothy? I'm Alex DuPont. And call me Alex. Can I get you anything?'

'No, please allow me. This is my home turf and you're a guest.'

They settled at a window table with teas and chocolate brownies. Alex wolfed his in one go, he hadn't had lunch yet. Timothy nibbled at his like a mouse at a piece of cheese, enjoying every crumb.

'First of all, call me Tim. If you say Timothy, I'll look over my shoulder in case you're talking to someone else. I gather this is about poor Amanda. I can't imagine I'll be much help but, please, fire away and I'll do the best I can.'

'Tell me about Bristol, Tim. About the Famous Five.'

'Well, we were probably happier as the Gang of Four if I'm honest, but that's how things worked out.'

Alex showed him the photo. Tim laughed, nostalgic. 'Yes, I remember when we took that, one of those cheap digital things with an auto-shutter on it. The reason I'm not smiling is because I was trying not to laugh. The first time we tried to take the shot I fell over Ashley's leg and ended up on my backside.'

'You were happy back then, weren't you?'

'I was. I think we all were, or most of us, most of the time.'

'Tell me more about that.'

'Ah!' Tim gave an amused grin, enjoying himself. 'The relentless sleuth zeroes in on the hapless victim. What do you really want to know, Alex?'

'I want to know if there were any… tensions in the group.'

'Bound to have some tension with two women and three men: it's an odd number, isn't it? Yes, there were, and towards the end of our university days they kind of erupted. Charlotte and Ashley were at each other's throats, or at least she was at his. And she was jealous of Amanda: quite jealous, actually.'

'And this was about Ashley.' Alex felt he could be direct with Tim because he gave the impression that he clearly didn't have anything to hide.

'Yes, it was. Charlotte thought Ashley and Amanda

146

were secretly an item, or that Amanda was chasing him and keeping him away from her. She never got over their relationship, and the idea that someone else might have her precious Ashley made her very angry indeed.'

'Angry enough to kill?'

'I don't know about that. I mean, if looks could kill, yes, she'd have reduced poor Amanda to ashes on the spot. But she doesn't strike me as a murderer. I don't think she'd go that far.'

'Did things ever kick off?'

'Not in public. But there was an incident, a few months before we left. She had some sort of epic row with Ashley, and he ended up being kicked out of the hall of residence.'

'That seems a bit drastic for a disagreement.'

Tim looked a bit more serious. 'Well, by all accounts it wasn't just an argument. Charlotte accused Ashley of assaulting her. She insisted on getting the police involved, though it didn't come to anything. But Ashley had to move out. I think it was the hall manager's way of avoiding more trouble until we were all safely on our separate ways.'

'Can you remember the manager's name?' Alex's pen hovered over his notebook.

'Laura something. Wait, it was Laura Goldsmith.'

Alex wrote the name down and underlined it. 'And where were you on Sunday the fourth of June, Tim?'

'Ah, the alibi. I was in there,' he pointed to the frontage of Delacroix, 'Working. I know, it's sad.'

'Were you alone?'

'Goodness no, I'm not the only sad one. There were four or five of us there. We went for a drink together after we'd finished up. I can give you their names if you like.'

Alex wrote the names down, but he was sure he

wouldn't be following them up himself. He felt he could trust Tim. The plods could have a look if they needed to. 'One last thing, tell me about Jeremy.'

'Well, what I can say about him is that he's an odd fish, bless him.' Tim noticed Alex nodding. 'You've met him, then?'

'Yes, in Paris. I didn't quite know what to make of him, though.'

'Neither do I, and I spent the best part of three years in his company. He gave me the impression he wasn't used to being part of a group. He joined in with everything we did, and he was a good sport when we teased him. But I felt he was more of a loner than a team player.'

'Have you stayed in touch with him?'

'Not really. I send him the odd text and get an occasional one-word reply. I think he's forgotten about us, most of us at least.'

'Most of you?'

'Yes, didn't you know? He was quite sweet on Amanda. He never did anything about it, at least not while we were at uni, but I think he had an almighty crush on her. It's funny, really. At one point, I thought Charlotte had her eye on him, and I don't think he'd have said no. But it never came to anything.'

'You think he was holding out for Amanda?' Alex was thinking about Jeremy's reaction when Gerry walked into the shop.

'Maybe. But I used to run into Amanda every so often, and she never mentioned him, so I don't think he got in touch with her after uni.'

'Tim, you've been a real help. Thank you for taking the time to see me.'

'Not at all, I sort of enjoyed it. I've never been interrogated before, apart from by my mum, that is.'

Alex laughed. 'Well, you can relax. I don't think you're a murderer, and your secret work fetish is safe with me.'

Tim laughed too and shook his hand. 'Anyway, I think I'll knock off early and get some proper food. That brownie was great, but it was about two thousand calories short of what I need.'

Alex's stomach rumbled in sympathy.

**

He was tucking into a chickenburger when his phone buzzed.

'Alex, what are you up to?' Melanie sounded excited.

'I'm enjoying my chickenburger and fries in a café.'

'Where?'

'Why? You want to join me? It's not far from where I live. I can ping you the details.'

'Fancy a drink after? I've had a result and I want to celebrate.'

Within an hour, they met in a small pub just off the bustling area. It was practically empty, and Alex got the feeling the barman would have shut up shop if it wasn't for them. Melanie had a glass of Merlot and Alex had a pint of Beer.

'Well, have you solved the gang shootings yet?'

'Not quite, but we're well on the way. I didn't really know where to start looking for Marku, but I had an idea I should go back and talk to the dodgy pub landlord again. I took Connors along for a bit of muscle – he's not much use for anything else, bless him – and the pub landlord would have something else to look at apart from my boobs.'

Alex, instinctively, had a quick look.

Melanie noticed Alex's eyes wandering. 'Don't you start as well.'

'I'm not doing anything,' Alex said, looking like an innocent schoolboy.

Melanie smiled and continued with her feedback. 'Anyway, we stepped into the pub and there was our Marku cradling a whisky at the bar. He tried to run away but Connors got him in a bear hug until I cuffed him. He's safe and warm in the nick. Jenkins thinks we've got enough on him to get a warrant to search his flat. So, the upshot is I've got time to concentrate on the Hamilton case now.'

'Great. Let's have a think about our next steps and divvy up the jobs. Cheers.'

They both got notebooks out and Alex gave her a summary of his day and what he'd found out. Melanie looked like her doubts had evaporated, finally.

'I think Steve Mortimer is the priority. I like him for this, or at least for being involved. What do you think, Alex?'

'I think he's hiding something significant, that's for sure. I can't see him as a murderer, but that doesn't mean he's innocent. What about Charlotte?'

'Well, the last thing we need to do is drag her into the station. We'll have lawyers coming out of our ears and senior officers crapping on our heads. But you're right, we need to talk to her again. Why don't you arrange another interview and I'll tag along?'

'Alright I'll do that and let you know. And what should we do about Jeremy?'

'He's a bit of a problem child, isn't he? Do you think your French mate could bring him in?'

'Gerard? Yes, I think he'd be happy to help. And he's

my cousin or second cousin maybe. My French family's so big I'm not really sure where we all fit in.'

'Wonderful. We could set up a Skype call with the French cops and listen in or ask a few questions ourselves.' Melanie's eyes were alight with enthusiasm.

'That just leaves us to deal with the prints. if you can get them sorted, that would be perfect.'

'On that score, we may have to wait, I'm afraid. I can't hurry the techies up. They work for an outside company, and we don't get to talk to them. But we've got enough to be going on with here.' She paused. 'And I'm sorry about last weekend. You were right. I was mixing business up with my personal feelings, and that wasn't very helpful.'

'So was I, Melanie. I think we were both out of order. No hard feelings?'

They clinked glasses, finished their drinks and got up to leave. The barman hurried over to collect the glasses and clean the table, whistling happily. I was right, Alex thought: *he'll be closed in a few minutes.*

Outside, they stood for a moment on the pavement in the cool night air. They got close and looked at each other with warm eyes. He pulled her gently towards him. She did not resist. He was about to kiss her on her lips when she hastily said, 'I've got to go now.' She moved a few steps away from him and then caught a taxi. Both waved goodbyes to each other.

CHAPTER 18

Scott and Jenny were already at the Agency, drinking tea and nattering about the arrests for the gangland shootings. Then, Alex arrived.

'The papers reckon the police have averted a proper gang war,' said Scott. 'Just as well, I don't fancy having to duck for cover every time I go out for milk.'

'I know about the incident, Melanie told me all about it,' said Alex.

'I checked with Eurostar, it was possible to travel from Paris to London on Sunday fourth of June and go back on the same day,' Jenny said.

'That confirmed my suspicion. Good work, Jenny.'

He went into his office and booted up the PC. 'Jenny,' he called from behind his desk. 'Can you try and get me an appointment with Mrs Goldsmith, the manager of the university's hall of residence in Bristol. It is important that I meet with her quickly. I need to discuss some emerging issues with her.'

'Is this a campus university?' asked Scott.

'What is that?' Jenny was also curious.

'Yes, it is a campus university where students' accommodation is sited on its grounds.'

'What does a residence manager do?' asked Jenny.

As Jenny did not get the opportunity to study at university, she was always interested to know about the various functions of the institution.

'I believe she is responsible for the overall running of the hall of residence ensuring that safety, security, cleanliness and protection of the property are maintained. Also, the university residence policies are adhered to,' said Alex.

'OK. I'll go and phone Mrs Goldsmith and see if I can get you an appointment,' said Jenny, and went to her office.

Shortly afterwards, Jenny informed Alex. 'Mrs Goldsmith says she has some time free this afternoon if you can make it.'

'Excellent, tell her I'll be there around two-thirty if that suits her.'

**

He'd left Jenny and Scott a list of instructions. Jenny would get in touch with Melanie to set up the second interviews with Steve and Charlotte; he was curious how Steve would react to being in a police interview room rather than a city office. Scott would go back to Chiswick and do a bit more door-stepping.

'Seems a waste of time,' said Scott. 'The neighbours were a washout last time.'

'Someone may remember something, even if it's just a small detail. The plods don't have the time or staff to do it. See if you can get the attention of that bloke who was staring at us last time we were there. He might be just the kind of curtain twitcher we need.'

He made a few phone calls to calm the nerves of the agitated clients. At eleven o'clock, he got into his car and was on his way to his destination. He figured out it would take him at least two hours to get to Bristol.

Due to the heavy traffic, it took him thirty minutes to get onto the M4. The weather was fine: dry and sunny with a light breeze. Whenever he had the opportunity, he would go to the West Country to visit relatives, so he was familiar with the road. Although he had a fast car, Aston Martin, he habitually kept to the motorway speed limit. The music on Radio1 entertained him. As he drove, he compiled in his mind a list of questions for Mrs Goldsmith. He hoped her memory was up to the task. After an hour drive, he stopped at the motorway café where he usually took a break. He had a croissant and a cup of tea. Then, he continued with his journey. He did not have far to go.

**

Upon arrival at the hall of residence, he parked his car in the visitors' parking area and walked towards the entrance of the building.

The hall of residence was set in beautiful gardens. The building itself was an attractive modern construction. Alex thought of it being a lovely place to live for three years.

Mrs Goldsmith welcomed him. 'I trust you are Mr DuPont, pleased to meet you. I'm Laura Goldsmith, manager of the hall of residence. And please call me Laura.' They shook hands warmly.

'I'm indeed. Pleased to meet you as well. Thank you for the nice welcome. And call me Alex.'

'Well Alex, the call from your PA rather took me by surprise, how can I help?' Laura Goldsmith was younger than he had expected. She wore a smart business suit and her hair was cut in a fashionable asymmetric style. She looked a bit flustered, as if visits from private investigators were definitely not part of the normal routine.

'It's nothing to worry about, Laura. I'm just hoping you can help me with some background information for a case I'm working on. It involves one of your former residents.'

'Really? Is one of our ex-residents in trouble?'

'Can we find somewhere quiet to talk? It's a rather delicate matter.'

Laura took him to her office, down a secluded corridor on the ground floor of the hall. There were photos of current and former residents, arranged on the walls, otherwise it was free of decoration.

'You remember your residents fondly, I take it?' Alex smiled and Laura blushed.

'Yes, I suppose I think of them as my wards while they are here. Some of them keep in touch after they leave.' She focused her full attention on her visitor. 'Which one of my residents has been naughty?'

Alex thought about softening the news but in the end, he took the direct approach. 'Amanda Hamilton, who lived here until last year, I believe, was found dead a few weeks ago. We have reason to think she was murdered.'

'How… awful.' Laura was struggling to control her emotions. 'I remember Amanda very well: a lovely young woman, and always surrounded by friends. Why would anyone want to kill her?'

Alex half regretted telling Laura. He wondered if it would colour her answers to his questions. She was obviously protective of her 'wards' and would want to shield them from suspicion.

'Let me say, it's no reflection on the hall of residence, or you, Laura. I'm here merely to get some background information, so I understand Amanda's relationships a little better. I've met a few of her friends from their student days and they strike me as a solid, loyal group of people.'

'Yes, they were and I imagine they still are.' Laura seemed reassured by Alex's comments. He produced the photo and laid it on her desk.

'Ah, yes.' Laura's eye lit up with recognition. There was genuine fondness there too and a hint of something else, more troubled. 'They were a nice bunch: five of them lived here, in different flats.'

'Laura, I understand there was an incident involving Charlotte Palmer and Ashley Bradshaw here, towards the end of their third year.'

That troubled look returned. 'I thought you might want to ask about that. Yes, it was unfortunate. Poor Ashley: he didn't deserve it.'

'I gather that Ashley had to leave the hall of residence after the incident.'

'Yes, he did. The police were involved, though it didn't come to anything; it was one person's word against another. But Charlotte was very upset, and her father had an undue influence on proceedings. It turned out he had agreed to fund for the Lab extension, and the Vice Chancellor was under pressure to placate him.'

'Can you tell me what happened?'

'I'll tell you what I can. To be honest, some of it remains a mystery to this day.'

HALL OF RESIDENCE, APRIL 2005

Charlotte stared out of her bedroom window at the beautiful gardens: she was fuming. She'd had enough of student life, and she'd had more than enough of the Gang of Four. Still, after the final exam she would be free. She thought about the summer ahead and began to make plans.

'Marseille. Yes, Marseille,' she said to the window, and smiled at her reflection. Her family had a beautiful apartment in the city, at the port end of the Canebière and she'd stayed there last year on her own for the first time. That's when she had met André. He was the manager of a seedy little nightclub down by the Port de la Joliette, but that didn't stop him from selling a delicious range of designer drugs to the clientele.

André had a mane of lustrous black hair that hung down in loose curls to his shoulders. He was proud of it, kept it beautifully. His hair framed a feline Mediterranean face that was handsome despite the knife scar that disfigured his left cheek.

He had given her a cute little pink pill. 'On the house,' he said with a wolfish smile. It made her feel really good really quickly. They spent their time together and eventually, they had a fling.

André had shown her a side of the city that tourists didn't normally get to see. His uncle, who owned the nightclub, was some kind of gangster, a brute of a man who leered at her. She didn't care. She was having the time of her young life.

She would look André up and spend a week or two in a pleasant haze. She combed her hair, looking in the mirror, her tongue playing over her lips. She was feeling excited at the prospect of being in Marseille and seeing André again.

A knock at the door interrupted her, spoiling the mood. She opened the door to find Ashley standing there, looking sheepish. 'What do you want?'

She regretted snapping at him immediately. She wasn't angry at him, not really. It was that bitch Amanda who had caused all the trouble.

'Look, Charlotte, I appreciate you're upset...'

'Upset? Why should I be upset? My boyfriend has been stolen by some evil little strumpet and he doesn't have the courage or decency to resolve the situation. Everything's just fine, Ashley, really.'

'No one stole me, Charlotte. We broke up, remember?'

'Oh, yes, remind me. You dumped me because I liked you too much, wasn't that it? Perfectly logical, obviously. Stupid of me to think otherwise.'

'You know it wasn't like that.' They were both shouting now. They could probably be heard all over the hall and in the gardens. Charlotte didn't seem to care.

Ashley lowered his voice, with considerable effort. 'OK, Charlotte, I can see I came at the wrong time. I think it's best if I keep out of your way for a while and let you get it out of your system.'

'Get it out of my system? What, you think I'm addicted to you and I need to go cold turkey? Get over yourself, Ashley. And just keep her away from me or I won't be responsible for my actions.'

Ashley left, defeated. Charlotte tried to remember why she was in love with him and couldn't. In time she'd remember, of course: Ashley had captured her heart, for good or for ill. But in the meantime, the wicked André and his pretty pink pills seemed a much better idea.

**

Charlotte finished the email and sent it off to André. She spoke rusty, school French and he had learned some English from movies and music videos, but they managed to communicate well enough.

She lay back on her bed, dreaming of good times in

Marseille. The knock on the door was another interruption. 'God, what am I?' she muttered as she made her way to the door. 'Hall reception?'

It was Amanda, the last person she wanted to see. Amanda pushed her way into the room, anger etched on her beautiful face. 'Charlotte, we have to talk.'

'No, we really don't, Amanda. Not unless you want to apologise for stealing my man and pretending nothing happened.'

'I didn't steal anything or anyone from you. I'm not interested in Ashley, not that way. We're good friends, that's all.' Amanda's face was flushed, but not as flushed as Charlotte's.

'I don't have time for this rubbish, Amanda. I should be revising for the exams, ironing my socks or something. Pretty much anything that isn't talking to you. I don't like you, Amanda, and I don't believe you. I'd much rather you were somewhere else, or dead possibly. That would be just fine by me.'

'Charlotte, I came here thinking we could clear this mess up and leave university with no hard feelings. I see now I was wrong. You don't want to talk to me because you don't want anyone to puncture your fantasy balloon. I really don't understand what Ashley saw in you.'

'What you see isn't always what you get, Amanda. I've got connections: people you really don't want to meet.'

'Are you threatening me?' Amanda's voice had risen. She was on the verge of shouting now.

Charlotte's voice rose a level higher. 'Go to hell, Amanda, and stay out of my sight. If I see your smarmy, pretty face again I might not be able to stop myself from spoiling your good looks.'

Upon hearing that, Amanda's anger had turned to fear. She backed away, towards the door, felt for the handle behind her and fled, in tears.

Charlotte smiled a victorious smile and slammed the door shut. Her French daydream had dissolved, but that didn't matter now. She'd got one over that stupid bitch and she felt good about it. She went back to her laptop and started to compose an email to her father, asking for the use of the Marseille apartment for a couple of weeks in summer.

She thought about sending André another email, asking him if he fancied scaring an enemy of hers, just for the hell of it. André would love the idea, it would make him feel like a big-time international criminal.

He was bound to know some shady characters in London who could follow her around, put the frighteners on her. Her cheeks warmed at the idea. She imagined Amanda, scared out of her wits, looking over her shoulder constantly.

She decided against it, reluctantly. Her family ties had got her out of trouble a couple of times in the past, but threatening violence might be a step too far. She settled for soft-soaping her dad.

When she'd finished, she went back to the window and looked out over the gardens. Birds were singing, and spring flowers made vibrant splashes of colour against the lush green of the meadows. It was turning into a good day, she thought.

There was another knock at the door.

HALL OF RESIDENCE, THE PRESENT

'When Charlotte came to see me, she had a livid mark on her right cheek. It looked as if someone had printed three fingers on her in red. She told me Ashley had slapped her.

She insisted I call the police and I reluctantly did so.' Laura was in full story mode now, remembering it all, but Alex stopped her for a moment.

'You're sure it was on her right cheek?'

'Yes, absolutely certain.' Laura fished in one of the desk drawers and brought out a folder. 'You're not the only one with photos; look.'

The bruise was livid, just as Laura had said. Three bars of pain across her cheek, looking for all the world like a child's painting of fingers; a narrow, shorter mark just above her chin, presumably the fourth finger; and the first sign of a swelling under her eye. Alex exhaled sharply, almost a whistle.

'Whoever did this put considerable force into it. It's not just a slap on the cheek, is it?'

'Absolutely. The thing is, try as I might, I can't see Ashley doing this. Not to Charlotte, not to anyone. But if he didn't do it, who did?'

Alex was really puzzled. He knew Ashley was right-handed. How had he managed to slap her so hard on her right cheek? 'OK, tell me about the police investigation.'

'Well, it wasn't a full-blown investigation. Charlotte's father was pushing for that, but the university authorities wanted it handled low key, and I agreed with them. And anyway, Charlotte's story didn't really stand up to scrutiny.'

'What makes you say that?'

'In fact, she happily admitted that Amanda had gone to see her after Ashley had left. She had to, really. People in the neighbouring flats had heard them practically screaming at each other. And Charlotte was screaming threats: all rather unpleasant.'

Laura paused for a moment. 'What was I saying? Oh

yes. Amanda told the police that Charlotte didn't have any marks on her face when she saw her. Charlotte blustered a bit, said perhaps he'd come back later and done it, but by then the police were losing interest.

'Anyway, that would – and should – have been the end of the matter. But Mr Palmer wouldn't let it go. They seem to be very similar in that respect, father and daughter. He threatened to pull the funding for the Lab extension if we didn't punish Ashley in some way.'

Laura sighed. The whole incident had obviously taken its toll on her, and reliving it was doing the same thing. 'Shall we take a little break, and have some tea? I can see this is upsetting for you, Laura.'

She shook her head; her asymmetrical haircut tilted and fell back into place. 'No, I'm almost done now and it's good to get it out there, to be honest.'

'If you're sure.'

'I am. So, the university management held an emergency meeting. All very hush hush, and decided that, in the broader interests of the university, Ashley should lose his tenancy. I thought it was deeply inappropriate. They'd sacrificed him to the gods of finance, in my opinion. How he got through his finals with all that going on I really don't know.'

'The Palmers got what they wanted, in the end?'

'Well, he wasn't entirely satisfied – he obviously wanted blood – but he accepted the decision. Charlotte seemed quite triumphant about the whole thing. It's funny...' Laura looked at the photo again, wistful now. 'I think Charlotte was really in love with Ashley and I don't understand why she wanted to hurt him. I've occasionally wondered if she was trying to protect someone else, or at least if there was some other secret, she wanted to stay hidden. Oh, don't mind me: I have an overactive imagination.'

'Actually, Laura, I think you're a remarkably good witness,' Alex said. She looked at him gratefully.

'The thing is, her neighbours were adamant that she had another visitor after the screaming match with Amanda. It wasn't Ashley, he was in the common room by then, crying his eyes out – several people saw him there. Whoever it might have been the person who slapped her and left those horrible marks, I suppose we shall never know.'

'If I find out, I'll make sure to tell you. All manner of strange evidence comes out of an investigation like this.'

Laura smiled, for the first time since she had begun her story. 'I'd like that.'

**

Alex sat in the gardens of the hall of residence, collecting his thoughts and making notes. Five young people in a photograph, one of them dead. One jilted lover with a grudge. Was it enough for murder?

He discounted Tim who was obviously aloof from the whole situation, observing it with wry amusement. Ashley was too timid to kill, and Amanda had been his best friend. Charlotte? She had the motive, and someone with her money and connections could probably find the means. She had a temper, and she had made threats.

And Jeremy? He was the odd one out, the loner in the group. And he had moved away, far away, as soon as they had left university. 'I just don't know about you, Jeremy,' he mused aloud.

His thoughts turned back to the incident in the hall of residence. Whoever slapped Charlotte, hard enough to leave a livid bruise on her cheeks, was emotionally involved.

Two mysteries, where there had been only one. But in one, perhaps, lay the solution to the other. He felt as if things were, frustratingly slowly, coming together. Somewhere at the back of his mind he could feel the beginning of a resolution, an end to the puzzle. Perhaps, next time he dreamed of Amanda's accusing stare, he would have an answer for her.

He thought about Jeremy, sitting on that green bench in Paris. Something about the image of him tugged at his mind. What was it? He remembered the odd young man looking at his watch, itching to be away from his interrogator. The watch. It was on his right wrist – Jeremy was left-handed. Very interesting.

CHAPTER 19

It was early evening when Alex got back to London. He'd stayed in Bristol for a late lunch and had another look around before he got back on the motorway. He called into the office to file his notes, and to check if Jenny or Scott had left anything for him. He booted up the PC and checked his emails. There was one from Melanie, from her Met Police account: 'I've invited Steve in for a little chat tomorrow morning at eleven. I checked with Jenny and she says you're free. Just tell the desk Sergeant who you are, and she'll show you to the interview room. See you there.'

Otherwise, there was nothing to look at. He filed his notes, yawning as he did so. He realised he was hungry, but he didn't fancy going to a restaurant now. 'I'll get something from the Sainsbury local on my way home,' he told the computer, and switched it off for the night.

The puzzle of the attack on Charlotte seemed, to his tired mind, to be somehow as important as the identity of Amanda's killer. It played on his thoughts. After finishing his meal, he had a single mart whisky and ice, watched TV for a while and then went to bed.

**

'If there's nothing else for me to deal with, I'll head off to the nick.' Alex put his jacket on and headed for the door. Scott was engrossed in his PC and didn't even look up. Jenny waved goodbye and then waved him back. 'Oops, I forgot. I was doing some more background stuff on the Palmer family and I noticed – I mean it's probably just a coincidence – but her mother's maiden name is Mortimer. See you.'

**

Hammersmith police station was a flat, featureless, somehow humourless slab of brick frontage that took up most of the block. Alex walked up the entrance ramp and entered the foyer. The desk Sergeant was a business-like woman in her late forties, perfectly in keeping with the building, he thought. But she was pleasant enough and directed him through a security barrier to a long corridor humming with work traffic.

Melanie appeared from a side door and beckoned him. 'Let's just have a quick chat about how we're going to approach this,' she said, closing the door on a small, cluttered office.

'We're more or less sure the alibi doesn't check out so let's start there. If that doesn't shift him, we'll work it out as we go along.' Alex was confident Steve would crumble pretty quickly in these surroundings. He felt a bit guilty himself, as Steve hadn't done anything.

Melanie led the way down into the basement to the interview rooms. She stopped before a bank of computer screens; DI Richard Jenkins was already there, looking at Steve, sitting alone in a room decorated in a fetching shade of pale green, with lino that looked original Victorian.

'Hello, Alex, long time no see.'

The DI held out his right hand and Alex shook it.

'Richard, how are you? You're looking well.'

'Can't complain, which is a shame because I love complaining. So, do you like this fella for the murder? He looks proper shifty.'

'I'm not a hundred percent certain he has the guts for murder,' Alex replied. 'But stranger things have probably happened.'

'Well, let's go and have a chat with him. I'm thinking we'll do it mob-handed, make him think it's serious from the off.'

'Give me a second.' Alex took out a small, disposable digital camera and took a picture of Steve.

'Alex, that's not exactly kosher.' Jenkins looked more amused than annoyed.

'I know, and I'm sorry. But it's useful to have a photo of him. My associate, Scott, will be doing a bit of snooping for me, talking to Amanda's neighbours. It might be useful to show them a photo of Steve and find out if anyone saw him around her place.'

'I get that. But maybe, let me know what you're planning to do in future in the interests of good working relationship.'

A uniformed officer unlocked the door to the interview room. They entered the room in single file. Steve Mortimer looked a mess, like he hadn't slept. His eyes were bloodshot and his face was almost the same shade of green as the walls.

There were only two chairs on their side of the table. Jenkins remained standing, taking up a position by the door, and ushered Alex and Melanie to the seats. Steve looked almost relieved to see Alex.

'Mr DuPont; I wasn't expecting you to be here. Can you tell these people I haven't done anything?'

'I can do that happily, Steve, if you haven't done anything. Let's have a talk and find out first, shall we?'

Steve looked disappointed. He realised he was on his own. Melanie opened a folder and scanned it for a minute – a full minute. Even Alex began to think she was overdoing it.

'So, Steve; you told Mr DuPont that, on the day in question, you were at a football match at Tottenham Stadium. Is that correct?'

'Yes, I had a ticket. I showed him.'

Melanie smiled but it wasn't a friendly smile, more like a predator showing its teeth.

'The thing is, Steve, we've had a look at the CCTV from the ground on the day of the match, you're nowhere to be seen.'

'Well, I …' Steve stammered to a halt, had another go. 'I was probably lost in the crowd.'

There was a hearty laugh from the door. 'Lost in the crowd? It was an under-twenty friendly, out of season. You're having a laugh, son.' Jenkins was enjoying himself. 'The total attendance was,' the big DI consulted his notebook, 'two thousand, three hundred and ninety-three. Though I have a feeling they may have to revise that down to two thousand, three hundred and ninety-two.'

Steve clammed up. He folded his arms across his chest and glared first at Melanie, and then at Alex. He tried not to look at Jenkins at all.

'OK, son, I can see you're going to try and tough it out. We'll leave you to think about it for a minute while we go and have a cuppa.' Jenkins tapped on the door and the uniformed officer appeared with the keys.

'Oh, and Steve,' said Alex as they got up to go. 'You

want to think hard: giving a false alibi in a murder investigation is likely to land you in all sorts of trouble.'

Three cups of tea sat on a tray outside the interview room. Alex picked one up and sipped it. It was watery, but it was wet and somewhere above room temperature. He took his cup over to the screens. Steve looked even worse than he had when they first arrived. He was obviously terrified and could not stop himself from trembling.

'I hope he doesn't wet himself,' said Jenkins. 'Those chairs are new.'

Five minutes later they went back to the interview room. Steve started talking while they were still in the doorway, but it wasn't what they wanted to hear.

'Look, you asked me in for a chat, right? I mean, I'm free to go whenever I want, aren't I?'

Jenkins held the door open, a genial smile on his face. 'That's right, son, you're free to go whenever you want. But by the time you get one foot on the pavement outside, I'll arrest you.'

'What for?'

'Oh, I'll think of something. That suit is a disgrace for a start.' Jenkins turned deadly serious. 'Steve, you've lied about your whereabouts on the day of a murder, and you knew the victim. And you'd been pushing yourself onto her. That puts you right in the frame. Don't you think?'

Alex was impressed. Jenkins had done his homework. Steve slumped back onto the chair, defeated. Jenkins closed the door.

'OK, I wasn't being totally honest with you, Mr DuPont.'

Melanie snorted. 'That's a blatant understatement, Steve.'

'Where were you, Steve?' Alex asked gently.

'I... I was... visiting someone.'

No one spoke. Steve fidgeted in the silence. 'I mean, I was visiting a... a lady.'

'And does this... lady have a name?'

'She's... she's called Ulrika.'

Melanie suppressed a snigger behind her hand; Jenkins didn't bother suppressing his. Alex just felt sad.

'Tell us about Ulrika, Steve,' he said. He didn't feel like an interrogator now, more like a priest in a confessional.

'She's, um, a kind of specialist.'

'What kind of specialist?'

'She's a mistress of disguise. Whoever you want her to be, that's who she is.'

'And who did you want her to be?'

Steve covered his face with his hands, let them slide slowly down to his chin. 'I showed her a photo of Amanda.'

Jenkins took over. 'Steve, this is what's going to happen. You're going to give us some contact details for this lady specialist. Then I'm going to put you in a holding cell for a few hours while we check her out. If what you've told us is true, you're free to go.'

Steve nodded dumbly, numbly. He took out his phone and showed them a number. Jenkins gestured at the uniformed officer and he led Steve away.

'Well,' said Jenkins, rubbing his hands. 'I think I'll leave the lovely Ulrika to you two. I'm off to find a real cup of tea.'

**

Ulrika clearly wasn't expecting guests. Her little flat was a couple of blocks off Tottenham Court Road, looked like a tornado had recently come to read the meter. She spotted

Melanie for a copper right away. Alex, she wasn't so sure about.

'You'd better come in,' she said in a strong Birmingham accent. She swiped some underwear off the sofa and Alex sat down gingerly. Melanie remained standing.

Ulrika was attractive without quite being beautiful. Her features were bland and somehow pliable. An advantage, Alex thought, if you needed to be different people to different clients, but a little tragic if it meant the copies were always better than the original.

'We were hoping you could help us with an enquiry, Ms…?' he said.

'Protheroe, my name's Protheroe.'

'Ulrika Protheroe? That's a bit of a mouthful, isn't it?' Melanie said, trying not to smirk and failing.

'Ulrika's my working name. My regular name is Mary Protheroe. I wouldn't get many clients if I advertised under that name.'

'No, I don't expect you would.'

Alex took over. 'It's one of your clients we're interested in, Ms Protheroe.'

'I don't talk about them; confidentiality, you know.'

'Well, I hope you'll talk about this one. You are his alibi in a murder enquiry.'

'Oh.' Alex could see a struggle going on in her mind. Finally, she gave in to common sense.

'Who is this client?'

'His name is Steve Mortimer.'

'Ah, Steve. Yeah, he's been to see me a couple of times. Funny bloke. Most of my clients want me to do someone famous, you know, Britney Spears or someone like that. But he just showed me a photo.'

Alex tried to imagine her as Amanda. He couldn't see it. 'And did you "do" the woman in the photo?'

'Yes, I did. It seemed to work for Steve.'

'And did he come to see you on Sunday the fourth of June?'

'Hang on, I'll check my diary.' She took a large desk diary from under the coffee table and thumbed through it. 'Yeah, he did. He was here from three o'clock until half past four. Oh, yeah that's right; that wasn't his last visit. The last time he came to see me was a few days ago, he asked me for a little extra.'

Melanie's expression changed. 'Extra what?'

'He said he wanted me to play a joke on a mate of his. Make an anonymous phone call to him. He said, with me being such a good actress, he'd never twig.'

Now Alex chipped in. 'What kind of phone call?'

'He wrote it down for me, like a script. I was supposed to put on a mysterious voice and say, "I'm going to destroy you." Then he was going to tell his mate the next day. He gave me the name, the number and the date I had to make the call and paid for it in advance. By the way, all my clients pay in advance. Well, you never know, do you?'

'What's the name of his friend?'

'Oh.... Ashley Bradshaw.'

Mary Protheroe gave them a look that said the interview was at an end.

'Thank you for your time, Ms Protheroe. You've been very helpful, and you've got Steve out of a tight spot. I think he owes you.' Alex got up, and he and Melanie went to the door.

Melanie turned just before they left. 'A word of advice, Ms Protheroe. I'd be careful about doing little specials like that for your clients unless you know all the parties involved. You could land yourself in hot water.'

'Poor Steve,' said Alex as they tramped down three flights of stairs. 'He's got himself out of one hole only to chuck himself down another one.'

'Do you think Ashley will press charges?'

'No, not when I tell him what happened. But…' Alex stopped on the turn of the stairs, just above the entrance.

'But what?'

'I don't think we're quite finished with Steve yet. Let's get him back in the interview room and see what else he has to say.'

'Why? You don't still think he's good for murder?'

'No, probably not; but as the lovely Ulrika might say, what's in a name?'

CHAPTER 20

A couple of hours in a cell had worked a profound change in Steve. He looked haggard but resolute, as if he would do anything, now, to get himself out of the mess he was in.

Alex and Melanie had briefed Jenkins on their visit to Ulrika; now they sat in the same, pale green interview room, Jenkins again standing guard at the door. Steve really didn't look like he was about to do a runner.

Melanie took the lead. 'Well, Steve, we've got good news for you. Ulrika has confirmed your alibi, so it looks like you're in the clear, for now at least.'

Steve's look of relief was tinged with doubt. 'For now? Why? If my alibi stands, then I'm out of it, surely?'

'Until we're sure who killed Amanda, you're still a person of interest. Plus,' Melanie paused, and the brief silence filled with tension. 'Ulrika told us about a little extra game you asked her to play. A game involving an anonymous phone call to Ashley Bradshaw.'

Steve blanched. 'She had no right to tell you about that,' he said. 'That was between me and Ashley: it was meant to be a joke.'

'Ashley wasn't laughing when he told me about it,' said

Alex. 'He was terrified, and he thought he had reason to be. Can you shed any light on why that might be?'

'I might have forgotten to tell him it was a gag, now I think about it.'

'Come on, Steve. Even you aren't convinced by that explanation.' Melanie's voice was sharp.

Steve shrank into his seat. 'I can't...' he started, and then lapsed into silence.

'Let's try another tack.' Alex took the photo out. 'When I showed you this, you told me you only recognised two people in the picture. Have another look and tell me if that's still the case.'

Alex watched him closely as he looked at the photo. The way his eyes moved, Steve appeared to register more than two faces. 'No,' he said. 'Nothing's changed. I only know Ashley and Amanda.' He was looking down at the table as he replied, unable to meet Alex's eyes.

Melanie rapped the table sharply, startling Steve, and Alex too. 'You're lying. And you're a crap liar.'

'Try again, Steve,' said Alex quietly.

Steve looked at the photo again, frowning as if in concentration. 'Yeah, OK, I do know someone else here. I didn't want to say anything, because...' He shrugged. 'I don't know why.'

'Who is it, Steve?'

'Charlotte.....Charlotte Palmer. I know her, slightly.'

'How do you recognise someone slightly?' Jenkins stepped forward from his post at the door. 'Either you know her or you don't. You're wasting our time, son, and that's not clever. I'm not a patient man.'

'You're related, aren't you? Charlotte is – what – your cousin?' Alex asked.

'Second cousin. How did you know? We don't look alike.'

'Charlotte's mum's maiden name is Mortimer. It's not a big leap of logic.' Melanie fixed him with a steely glare. 'Why did you lie to us, Steve?'

'She…' He stopped and tried again. 'I didn't want to get her in trouble.'

Jenkins cut in. 'You're still lying like a cheap watch. How would it get her in trouble? We know who she is. We only had to ask the other people in the picture. You need to sort your head out, son.'

Alex changed course. 'Did Charlotte ask you to arrange the threatening phone call?'

'No, she…' Steve's lips moved but no sound came out. He looked like he was trying to chew something he couldn't swallow. 'Yes,' he said finally. 'She told… She asked me to do it. But it was a joke. She loves Ashley.'

'When Charlotte tells you to do something, so you do it.' Melanie didn't try to keep the contempt from her voice.

'It's not like that.'

'What's it like, Steve?'

'It's… complicated.' He fell silent. For the first time, he looked directly into Alex's eyes. He looked desperate: like a trapped animal begging for rescue.

Alex nodded towards the door and the three of them left the room. They huddled outside the door, ignoring the congealing cups of tea that had been left for them.

'I don't think we're going to get anything more out of him today,' said Alex. 'He's exhausted and incoherent now.'

'I don't know,' said Melanie. 'I think if we really push him, we'll get him to spill whatever it is that's behind all this.'

'I'm inclined to agree with Alex.' Jenkins looked over his shoulder, towards the interview room. 'But I think if we let him go now, he'll get in touch with Charlotte. That puts you at a disadvantage when you interview her.'

'What do you think we should do, guv?'

'I think we'll put him back in the cell until you've talked to her. Then we'll let him go. We'll make it clear we want to talk to him again, though. I want him to sweat for a while.'

'Do you think he's still in the frame for murder?' Alex didn't quite understand the DI's thinking.

'I don't think he did it. But I think he might know someone who did. Someone he knows is beginning to look good for this.'

'Charlotte's alibi is good, guv.' Melanie was puzzled too.

'It might be, but there is something iffy going on here. I can smell it. If it's not murder, it's not a million miles away.'

Melanie glanced at the station clock. 'Alex, we'd better go now; it's getting late.'

'Let's grab a sandwich on the way, I don't fancy facing Charlotte on an empty stomach.'

**

Charlotte had booked the same office for the interview. This time, though, she chose to sit behind the elaborate mahogany desk that dominated the space. 'Power move,' murmured Melanie, loud enough for Alex to hear. 'This should be fun.'

She led Alex to the leather sofa, and they made themselves comfortable, a good distance from the desk. Charlotte glowered. She hesitated for a moment, and then came over to the middle of the room, settling herself into a plush armchair. Melanie winked at Alex: one-nil.

'Why do you need to talk to me again, Alex?' Charlotte ignored Melanie.

'There are a couple of things I need to clear up, Charlotte.'

'And why do you need a police escort? Do you think I'm dangerous in some way?'

Melanie answered. 'This is a murder enquiry, Ms Palmer. I'm sure you're aware of that. It would be rather odd if the police were not involved.'

'I'm not a suspect, am I, Officer Cooper? I have an alibi, you know.'

'Detective Sergeant Cooper.' Melanie fixed her with a stare. Charlotte tried to return it, with interest. For a few moments, the two women faced each other in grim silence, then Charlotte dropped her gaze.

Melanie turned to Alex and winked again: two-nil.

'Charlotte, yesterday I went to the hall of residence in Bristol. I'd like to talk to you about that.' Alex's tone was gentle, but his expression was cold.

'Well, I don't see it has any bearing on Amanda's death, but if you wish.' Charlotte looked a bit less comfortable now.

'I think it has every bearing on Amanda's death.' Alex paused for a moment.

Charlotte wasn't the type to squirm, but it was close.

A pregnant silence followed. It was Charlotte who broke it. 'I told the police everything at the time. I don't see what else I can tell you.'

'You accused Ashley Bradshaw of assaulting you.'

'Yes, I did.'

'The police didn't seem entirely convinced by your testimony.'

Charlotte frowned. 'I was confused and upset. I was

178

injured too. They were not very sympathetic, and I don't think they handled it very well.'

Melanie broke in. 'The police didn't believe you, Ms Palmer, and they had every reason not to. Do you want to tell us what really happened?'

'It's all there in the police report. I assume you've looked at the report?'

'Yes, but we'd like to hear it from you.'

'And while you're at it,' said Alex. 'You could perhaps explain why you told me lies about both Amanda and Ashley last time we met.'

'I didn't…' Charlotte tried on outrage for size but it didn't fit. 'All right, I suppose I was a little economical with the truth. I didn't see that it was relevant, and I didn't want to open old wounds at a sensitive time.'

Alex and Melanie waited, said nothing. Eventually Charlotte twitched and began to fill the silence.

'When Ashley and I broke up, it was a bit untidy. I was very angry at him. Amanda seemed to move in on him before he'd finished saying "it's over" and I was pretty upset at that too.'

'But Ashley and Amanda were never an item, were they? They were just close friends,' said Alex.

'So they said, but I saw the way she looked at him. Ashley didn't notice. He's a bit dim that way, to be honest.'

'And Ashley didn't assault you, did he, Ms Palmer? You lied about that too.' Melanie hadn't dropped her steely glare.

'That's complicated too. He didn't actually slap me, it's true. I wasn't completely honest about that at the time. But he might as well have done. The way I see it, he did slap me; it just wasn't his hand.'

Alex and Melanie exchanged a puzzled glance. 'So,' Alex

said. 'That rather begs a question, doesn't it? Whose hand, was it?'

'I'd rather not say. I won't say, unless you arrest me and force me to, and I don't think that will work out well for you. It won't get you any closer to solving the murder, and it will bring a lot of outside pressure.'

Melanie knew what she meant. 'What you're saying, Ms Palmer, is that if we push you too hard on this, your father will get on to his golf chums.'

'Well, I wouldn't have put it like that, but more or less.'

Alex thought it was time to change the subject. 'Does the name Hugo Zelov mean anything to you?'

'I've heard the name, certainly. We have an apartment in Marseille, and I've spent a bit of time there. Zelov is some sort of criminal bigwig in the city: his name comes up a lot. We don't really move in the same circles, though.'

'So, you've never had any cause to contact him?'

'No, why should I?'

'He deals in designer drugs, amongst other things. And if the reports are to be believed, you have a taste for such things.' Melanie took a couple of police reports – one English, one French – from her bag. 'Quite a taste, by all accounts.'

'Again, you have the reports. If you want me to say more, you'll have to arrest me. And I don't think you have any grounds for doing that.' She looked serene, but the twitch at the corner of her mouth told Alex she was angry and struggling to control it.

'Tell me about Jeremy.'

She clearly wasn't expecting that. 'Oh, Jeremy,' she said. 'Why do you want to know about him? He's hardly relevant, is he?'

'We'll decide that, Ms Palmer. Answer the question, please.'

Charlotte shot Melanie a poisonous glance. 'Very well. Jeremy was part of our circle at university, but not really. I've often wondered if he's autistic: his social skills are non-existent, and he has a very odd attitude towards women.'

'Did he come on to you at university?'

She laughed at that. 'I don't think Jeremy would have the first idea how to chat a woman up. And anyway,' she smirked. 'He was soppy about Amanda. I don't think I was on his radar.' She shuddered theatrically. 'I certainly hope not.'

'Let's move on.' Melanie put the police reports away and got out her notebook. 'Your cousin, Steve Mortimer, works at Brown Legal.'

'Second cousin,' she snapped. 'Excuse me, Steve is a second cousin on my mother's side, a sort of in-law. We're not close.'

At that moment, Charlotte's phone pinged: a text coming in. She clicked the screen and put it down, frowning.

'Mr Mortimer has been helping us with our enquiries. He has said some very odd things: odd and interesting.'

Now Charlotte looked worried. Apparently, this topic wasn't covered by the umbrella of her father's influence. 'Helping you? Is he under arrest?'

'Not as such. But he is a person of interest in the enquiry.'

'You mean he's a suspect?'

Melanie didn't answer. Charlotte tried to stay silent too, but she couldn't manage it. 'Why do you want to know about Steve? What has he done? I told you, we're not close. I can't help you with this.'

'I think you can, Charlotte,' said Alex. 'After lying to us about a number of things, including telling us he didn't know you, Steve told us a very strange story, involving a specialist prostitute and a threatening phone call.'

'I don't understand.' She clearly did, though. 'Why is he threatening Ash…'

'Who said he was threatening Ashley?'

'I just… I just assumed. He works with Ashley, and he was very sweet on Amanda. It just makes sense, that's all.' Her eyes flicked to all corners of the room, looking for a way out.

Melanie pounced. 'But you told us you're not close, how do you know so much about him?'

'I said we're not close. I didn't say I know nothing about him. But if Steve's making threatening calls to Ashley, you need to talk to him, not me.'

'Ah, but there's the thing,' said Alex. 'He was reluctant to admit it, but eventually Steve said that you had told him to do it. He was very specific, you didn't ask him, you told him. Why would Steve take orders from you?'

'Steve and I have a bit of history. It's not especially pleasant, and I don't really want to go into it. But he owes me, and he resents me. What he told you is a lie. He's not much good at telling the truth – I'm sure you noticed that.'

'You're right; he lies all the time. But when he told us about you, I think he was telling truth.'

'You must decide for yourself, Alex. Steve's told you his version of the truth, and I've told you mine. Now.' She stood up and gestured to the door. 'You've taken up a good deal of my time, and I do have things to do. If there's nothing else…?'

Melanie stood up. She didn't offer her hand. 'We will

be talking to you again, Ms Palmer. Your answers have not done you any justice.'

She and Alex headed for the door. As they were about to leave, Alex turned back and asked, 'Was it Jeremy who slapped you, Charlotte?'

Charlotte stopped in her tracks. The colour drained from her face. 'I'm not going to answer that.'

This time it was Alex's turn to wink: three-nil.

**

'What made you ask that?' They were outside, walking towards the underground car park where Melanie had left her car. The city was winding down for the evening, the stream of commuters thinning to a trickle.

'Just a hunch. I have a feeling Jeremy is more deeply involved than we realise. And Charlotte is up to her neck in something, even if it's not murder.'

'Well, you were bang on the money. I'm impressed.' As they got to the entrance to the car park, Alex stopped. There was a little Italian restaurant across the road, and the smell of garlic bread and rich sauces made his mouth water.

'Let's have something to eat.'

Melanie hesitated. 'I need to make a phone call first.'

'Ah.' Alex stepped away to give her space. A few moments later she came back to join him.

'You're on. I'll deal with the fallout later.'

The restaurant was intimate and practically empty, the décor corny but cosy. They chose a corner table for privacy, but they could have sat right in the middle of the place, there was no one to overhear them.

The waiter brought garlic dough balls and olives, and they picked at them as they chose their main course. Alex looked at the wine menu. 'What do you fancy?'

'I'm driving, Alex; just water for me.'

'You're right, it's better not to have any alcoholic drinks. What do you make of Charlotte? Do you think she's good for this?'

'I don't know. She's obviously into something, and she lied through her teeth for most of the time we were there. She hated Amanda with a passion. But, much as I dislike her, I don't have her down as a murderer; conspiracy to murder, now, that would be different.'

'I agree. And that mysterious twaddle about Ashley – what was it now?' He took out his notebook and read. 'Oh, yes: "The way I see it, he did slap me: it just wasn't his hand." That came across as unhinged.'

'If we're not looking at Charlotte, at least not directly, then who is in the frame?'

'Good question. No idea.'

The main course had arrived, and Melanie paused to taste her tagliatelle. 'This is good; really good.'

They ate in congenial silence. When they finished, Melanie took up where she'd left off. 'I reckon Steve is involved somehow but I can't for the life of me see how. And if Charlotte can order him around like that, then she must be connected at the least.'

'I wonder if we're looking at two separate things here. Amanda's murder is one; but as we get closer to that we're uncovering some other strand that's linked, but perhaps not causally.'

'Sounds a bit metaphysical to me, Alex. Are you saying there's another crime here?'

'I'm not sure, I'm just speculating. At the moment, I feel as if all roads lead to Amanda, but there's some other element also. What happened in France is connected too. Then why should her murder get people in France stirred up?'

Melanie got a pen out and drew a rough diagram on a napkin: circles representing people and events, and lines connecting them. When she'd finished, she showed it to Alex.

He looked at it for a few moments and then enlightenment dawned. 'You've missed one important element out here.' He took the pen and drew a new circle and connected it to several others. Melanie leaned over to have a look.

'Jeremy! That's very interesting. When you put him into the mix, a lot of the other pieces seem to fit.'

'Yes, they do. Again, that doesn't make him the killer. But he seems to be more integral to this whole affair than the others are letting on. I'd love to know if Charlotte is still in touch with him.'

'You're good at this. I think the Met missed out when you opted for private practice. You should consider it: you'd be a fine addition to the force.'

'Funny you say that. I was thinking the same about you.'

'I'm already in the Met.'

'No, I mean the other way round. You're good at this too. I think you should consider jumping ship and joining the dark side. We've got enough work at the Agency to keep you busy.'

'Major crime is my thing. That's what gets me up in the morning. The thought I can take some criminal scumbag off the street, and bring some justice, or at least closure, to a victim's family. I don't think chasing corporate slime balls would have quite the same kick.'

'I get that but think about it. If we crack this one, the Agency's reputation will soar. Then we'll have all the major crimes you can handle. And I don't mind giving you a call to get you up in the morning.'

'Yes, well we have to crack this one first. I still feel like we're missing something here, something vital. And there's another thing.'

Alex waited.

'I don't imagine Martin would be over the moon if we were partners.'

Partners, he thought; there were two ways of understanding that word. And when he looked at Melanie, he saw she'd thought the same.

'Neither of us can sort out our existing relationships, and here we are mooning about a new one. I must be off my trolley to even think about it.' She laughed, bitterly. 'And you don't treat Claire with due care and consideration.'

'This is bit like the pot calling the kettle black. It's no different than how you treat Martin.'

'Well, do I really want that kind instability in my life?'

'It wouldn't have to be that way.'

'Maybe not; but until I see evidence to the contrary in both our personal lives, I'm best off being cynical, I reckon.'

'I think your cynicism is stopping you from living your life to the full.'

'I think my cynicism is stopping me from falling down a rabbit hole.' She seemed colder now.

Alex sighed. 'OK, have it your way. We'll fancy each other from afar and avoid all rabbit holes. It doesn't sound like much fun, though.'

Melanie chose not to respond to that. She felt she might say something and end up regretting it later.

He paid the bill and they headed back to the car park. 'Actually,' he said, 'I think I'll walk for a bit.'

Melanie shrugged and went to fetch her car. She unlocked the door and got in. Suddenly she beat the steering wheel with a fist. 'Damn you, Alex DuPont! I don't want you in my life and I can't get you out of my head.'

Alex walked down to the river and watched the sun set on the muddle of buildings, old and new, that lined the banks. 'If you could have one thing, either solve this case or be with Melanie, which one would you choose?' He asked a passing seagull that question. The gull tipped its wings from side to side and flew off. Alex laughed forlornly. 'You're right; I don't know the answer either.'

CHAPTER 21

Alex found Jenny in a state of high excitement. 'What's got you going, Jenny? You look like you've had an early birthday present.'

'We just got a call from Paris. It was that French detective, your cousin.'

'Second cousin,' Alex said, chuckling. Family relations were becoming a bit of a theme in the case.

'Whatever. He speaks beautiful English, and he has the cutest accent.'

'And did he say anything useful in his cute accent? Or are you telling me you've got a date in Paris? I should warn you he's married.'

Jenny's face fell. 'Oh, well, there goes another romantic dream. Gerard – such a lovely name – said he had some info for you about the thugs who attacked you in Paris.'

'Thanks, Jenny; I'll give him a call.' He saw the expression on her face and changed his mind. 'Tell you what, you call him and then put him through to me.'

'Alright then, I'll do that.' Jenny swiftly got back to her desk. Alex went into his office and closed the door. A minute later, Gerard was on the line.

'Hello, cousin, you have some very friendly people

working for you, very friendly indeed.' Gerard sounded perplexed.

Alex laughed. 'Sorry, Gerard; I think my personal assistant is rather taken with your sexy French accent.'

'If only it worked on French women. Never mind.'

'What have you got for me, Gerard? Did those two chumps from Marseille cough up anything useful?'

'Perhaps. They were reluctant to say anything for a while, just toughed it out while we kept asking pertinent questions. I didn't think we were getting anywhere, then Antoine started talking.'

'And what did Antoine have to say for himself?'

'I'm not sure he was saying anything for himself. He told me that an English guy had paid him and David to follow you and rough you up. He didn't say why.'

'And did this English guy have a name?'

'He did. Our Antoine is not very good with names. He has an IQ on a par with his shoe size if you ask me. He said the guy's name was Steve.'

'Steve who?' Alex was interested now.

'He struggled with the surname. It is a word of more than one syllable, so it was a chore for him.' Gerard laughed at his own joke, and Alex joined him.

'And what did he come up with?'

'He said the surname was… Multimère? Doesn't sound very English.'

'Could it be Mortimer?'

'Quite likely. That sounds like a good fit. I'll confirm it with him and text you. One other thing.'

'Go on.'

'I got the impression Antoine was reading from a script. I think someone told him to give us the name. These lowlifes don't usually want to tell the police anything, but he seemed very eager to give me the information.'

'That's interesting.' Alex's mind raced. Who was trying to frame Steve? He thought he knew the answer to that question.

'So, is there anything else I can do to help with your case? Paris is rather slow at the moment. I think all the villains are taking a holiday.'

'Actually, Gerard, there is something you could do for me. When I was in Paris, I spoke to a young Englishman called Jeremy Higgins. I'd like to ask him a few more questions, but I don't have time to go over there again, much as I'd like to. He works at a posh jeweller's shop called *Boutique Bijou.*'

'Does he now? There are rumours that *Boutique Bijou* is involved in some dodgy business with stolen gems. And the name of Hugo Zelov comes up whenever the rumour does. You want me to go and see him?'

'I was hoping you might bring him to the station.'

'Ah, you would like me to put some pressure on him.'

'Yes, something like that.'

Gerard thought about it for a few moments. 'I think that would work. I need to look into the gem business, so I can pull him in on that basis.'

'Thanks, Gerard, I owe you one.'

'No worries, cousin. I'll text you when I've set it up. Would you like to sit in?'

'How? I said I can't get to Paris.'

'I can do the whole thing on Skype. I'll let you know.'

Gerard rang off and Alex sat for a few minutes, thinking. Then he went out to the main office. 'Jenny, can you find a home phone number for Jeremy Higgins?'

'Will do,' Jenny replied.

**

Melanie sounded distant and a little morose. 'Alex, what can I do for you?'

'I just had a call from Paris. My little encounter with the Marseille criminal set was arranged and paid for by an English guy, apparently.'

'You mean there are English villains involved as well?'

'Not exactly. The person who set it up was Steve Mortimer. At least, that's what they said. Gerard thinks they were selling him a red herring.'

'Does this mean someone was setting Steve up?'

'I think so.'

'Hard to think past Charlotte for that.'

'I agree. I think we should have another chat with Steve first, and then get onto her again.'

'Ok, do you want me to pull him in?'

'I thought we might adopt a softer approach with him next time. We want him on our side for this. How about if we arrange to visit him at home?'

'I don't know if he'll be up for that. Anyway, he'll be in work, so how are we going to see him at his place?'

'I can call Walter first and get him to set the scene. It might put Steve at ease to answer our questions.'

'Alright, set it up and text me. I'll let Jenkins know.'

'There's one more thing, I'd dearly like to know how much Gerry is involved. Of course, it could be a coincidence that she was in Paris at the time I was jumped, and that she knows Hugo Zelov. But I don't like it when coincidences stack up.'

'I get that. But I don't like Gerry for this. Apart from anything else, she agreed with Walter to hire you. It seems pretty unlikely she'd have done that if she was involved, even peripherally, in Amanda's murder.'

Alex sighed. 'You're probably right. It's funny, though, how much of this mystery are linked to Paris. As far as I can tell, Amanda had no connection to Paris at all.'

'Well, let's see what happens. Anything else?' She sounded like she wanted to get rid of him. Alex could understand that.

'No. I'll text you later about the meeting.'

**

Jenny came in; now she was whistling 'Je ne Regrette Rien'. 'I've found you that number. It's not listed under Jeremy's name, it's his aunt, Katherine Manley, nee Higgins.'

'How did you find that out?'

'I've my ways, Monsieur.'

'Jenny, your French accent is terrible, even Gerard wouldn't be charmed.'

Jenny glared at him. 'Whatever.'

'Oh, that reminds me, can you set up Skype on my PC? Gerard says he can do an interview in Paris, and I can see it on Skype.'

'I'll do that for you.'

A text came in from Gerard: going to pick Jeremy up now. And Antoine confirmed it was Steve Mortimer.

Alex replied: thank you about the info on Steve Mortimer. Can you keep Jeremy in a cell for an hour before the interview?

Gerard came back: sure; why?

Alex replied: I need to make a call.

In essence, he needed to make two calls. First, he texted Melanie to let her know about the interview in Paris. She called right back and said she would be there as soon as she could.

**

When Jeremy saw the police car pulled up outside the shop, he grabbed his jacket and headed for the back door. He wasn't scared, exactly, he just knew this was about him, and this was the wrong place to be. He scurried from the back door to the rickety gate, leading to the alley that ran behind the row of shops.

As soon as he was out of the gate, he turned to his left and broke into a full sprint. It ended abruptly a few yards on, when he ran into the considerable bulk of Gerard. He wrapped his muscle-roped arms around Jeremy and pinned him to the spot. Jeremy was too dazed to struggle.

'Take it easy, Mr Higgins. There is a colleague of mine at the other end of the alley, and he is bigger than I am. It's ok, we just want to talk to you.'

'But I don't want to talk to you.'

'I'm afraid you don't have a say in the matter. If you don't come with me of your own accord, I will happily arrest you. The choice is yours. It's not much of a choice, I grant you, but at least I didn't put a bag over your head and bundle you into the back of a van. Which is what Mr Zelov's associates would do, I think.'

'Is this about…?'

'I will explain everything when we get to the station, Jeremy.'

Gerard led him off down the alley to a waiting car. Jeremy followed him, docile, wondering if the gem scam had finally broken. He wasn't bothered, he'd got what he wanted from it.

**

He thought he would give Gerard twenty minutes to

pick Jeremy up and then call his aunt.

Katherine Manley spoke elegant French with a definite Home Counties accent. After they had exchanged a few pleasantries, Alex switched to English. 'Ms Manley, you speak excellent French. Please call me Alex.'

Now her accent was all Home Counties. 'I had a French nanny, and I've lived in Paris for over ten years. I rather thought you were French. You have a Parisian accent.'

'My father is French, and I've spent a lot of time in Paris.'

'What can I do for you, Mr DuPont? I assume this is something to do with the police taking Jeremy away. Monsieur Leclerc has just informed me.'

'You seem very calm and collected in the circumstances, Ms Manley.'

'Call me Katherine. To be honest with you, Mr DuPont….Alex, yes of course, it wasn't a total surprise.'

That made Alex curious. 'How so?'

'Jeremy is my nephew, and I love him dearly. In many respects, I am his surrogate mother. But he is a rather odd young man, and that shop he works in…'

'*Boutique Bijou?*'

'Yes. That shop is also a rather peculiar place.'

'I suppose you are talking about the rumours that it is involved in some illegal activity.'

'You are very well informed, Alex. I suspect the rumours are well founded. I feel rather sorry for the manager, Monsieur Leclerc. He is a nice, pleasant and sensible man. I don't believe he's directly involved. It all seems to revolve around his goldsmith and the gem technician.'

'I'm impressed. It seems you are better informed than I. Recently, I met Monsieur Leclerc and he seemed a decent guy.'

'He is. Thierry is an old friend of the family, and he's no criminal. It's possible that he is not aware of the criminal activities taking place in his environment due to his honesty perhaps.'

Alex took a moment to collect his thoughts. Katherine waited patiently for him to speak.

'If you don't mind, I'd like to talk to you about Jeremy. If there is more to say about the shop, we'll come back to it, of course. But Jeremy is the focus of my interest.'

'Yes, I understand. Would you like the potted biography, or the full version with his medical notes?'

That startled him. 'I have some time to spare, Katherine, maybe you could tell me the full story.'

She told him about Jeremy's childhood. It sounded tragic. His father was an alcoholic, prone to violence, and his mother suffered from psychotic episodes. He was unloved, and often uncared for. While she lived in England, Katherine looked after him as best she could, while she nursed her husband, William, through the final stages of an aggressive brain cancer.

When William died, she moved to Paris, her favourite city. She persuaded Jeremy's parents to send him to a boarding school, and he would spend his school holidays in Paris with her. They readily agreed. They weren't short of money, just short of love. What little they had, each of them, they spent on themselves.

Jeremy had shown all the signs of ASD *(autistic spectrum disorder)* but his family situation meant that there was no opportunity to get him diagnosed and treated properly. He was high-functioning, and academically bright: he left Bristol with a first in Philosophy. It was only natural that he moved to Paris after graduation. By then, it was his home.

Katherine had persuaded Thierry to take him on at *Boutique Bijou*, and he had turned out to be very good at selling expensive jewellery to rich clients.

But he had soon begun to suspect that something less than legal was going on at the shop. His job meant he was responsible for stock-taking and liaising with the technicians who cut gems and repaired gold items. They had visitors who did not seem to belong to the chic world of jewellers: people who came late in the evening and left little packages, and envelopes of cash.

Jeremy didn't go to the police, and he didn't ask Thierry what was going on. He accepted the situation, and largely ignored the extra-curricular activities. Katherine suspected something traumatic had happened to him at university. Subsequently, he became even more introspective, and made no attempt to find a social life, despite offers.

'Then a few days ago he returned early from work, and I could see that he was deeply troubled. He wouldn't tell me what had happened, not really. He just told me he had seen a ghost.'

'Katherine, you said that Jeremy doesn't have much of a social life.'

'None at all, Alex.'

'So does he spend his free time at home?'

'No, not really. He goes out on his own. He says he's exploring the city, and I think he probably is. Paris is as intriguing to him as it is to me. He's often gone all day and well into the night.'

'So, if he disappeared for a day, you wouldn't think anything was amiss?'

'No. But has Jeremy done something bad? You can tell me. I've had my share of bad news and I'm rather used to it now.'

'You are a very brave woman, Katherine, extraordinarily so. What you have done for Jeremy is heroic. I can't tell you anything yet, I'm sorry, but Jeremy is a person of interest in a case I'm working on. Tell me, has Jeremy ever intimated to you that he might have fallen in love while he was at university?'

Katherine's laugh was humourless and short. 'Jeremy doesn't love people, Alex. I don't believe he's capable of it. That's the legacy of his parents. He either needs people or he wants them. Otherwise, he ignores them completely.'

'One final question - if he wanted someone, but he couldn't have them?'

'I don't know what he would be capable of in those circumstances, Alex, but I fear it might not go well for someone who spurned him.'

'Thank you, Katherine. You've been most helpful. Bye.'

**

While he riffled through his files, killing the time, the phone rang.

'Alex, I've got a Sally Prentice on the line; do you want to take it?'

'Yes, put her through.'

Sally sounded breathless: like she'd run to the phone and then kept running after she'd dialled. Her words tumbled out in a torrent. 'Alex, I'm sorry to trouble you, but I have some information that I think might be pertinent to your case.'

'Slow down, Sally. What information?'

'It's about... Steve Mortimer.'

'Go on.'

'I was out for a walk a few days ago and I saw Steve in

the Victoria Embankment garden. He was talking to a young woman. She was very smartly dressed and she had rather striking red hair.'

'Why didn't you tell me before?'

'I didn't think it was important at the time.'

Alex's ears pricked up. 'Did you hear what they were saying?'

'No, I'm afraid I was too far away to hear anything. But whatever they were talking about, it was very animated. I got the impression that Steve was quite agitated, and the young woman seemed to be angry with him.'

'Do you think you would recognise this young woman again? Say, from a photo?'

'Oh yes; I'd recognise her anywhere. That red hair, especially.'

'Well, thank you, Sally. This is valuable information. I'll send my associate, Scott, over later today with some photos. If you can pick the woman out, that would really help.'

'You can't come over in person?' Sally sounded miffed, as if Alex had snubbed her at a posh party.

'I'm sorry, Sally, but I'm rather busy right now with the case. I have to attend a police interview in Paris in about…' He looked at his watch. 'Fifteen minutes.'

'How on earth are you going to manage that?'

'Skype, apparently. Sally, thank you again for your call, and for the information. I must go now, but I'll send Scott over to see you.'

Sally mumbled something vaguely polite and ended the call.

Alex typed the new information into the file. This would make their interview with Steve more interesting.

CHAPTER 22

Alex went frantic momentarily because he was unable to deal with Skype.

Jenny rushed into Alex's office. 'What's up, are you OK?'

'Something weird is happening to the computer.' Alex was staring at the screen, spooked.

Jenny walked around the desk and giggled. 'Your Skype call is coming in. If you ever remembered to put the speakers on, you'd have heard the ringtone.'

She clicked a green button on screen and enlarged the panel that appeared. Alex saw an interview room, the view slightly tilted. Jenny nodded sagely. 'They must have linked a laptop to the surveillance camera, clever.'

Alex was surprised to see that the Parisian interview room was painted the same shade of pale green as the one at Hammersmith. 'Someone must have a monopoly franchise,' Alex said.

'Monopoly what?'

'Doesn't matter, what do I do now?'

'You switch on your speakers and mic,' Jenny said, clicking the mouse. 'And then you wait. I expect something will happen soon. Now, are you OK? Will you be able to manage on your own?'

'You might want to stay for a minute. The lovely Gerard is about to appear, I imagine.'

The lovely Gerard duly appeared via a door in the corner of the room, his face tilted up towards the camera. He moved to the table in the centre of the room. His image blurred as he walked but settled when he stopped. Alex found it disconcerting.

'Hi, Alex. And you must be Jenny. I am pleased to meet you.'

Jenny blushed and mumbled. 'Hello Gerard.'

'So, Alex, we have kept Jeremy Higgins in a holding cell for a while. We took his mugshot and his fingerprints while he was there, so he got to enjoy the full criminal experience. I think he should be nicely marinated by now.'

The Agency bell rang. 'That will be Melanie,' said Alex. 'Jenny, can you let her in?'

'Will do.' Jenny bustled out of the room, looking over her shoulder at the screen and waving demurely as she went. Gerard returned the wave and winked at Alex.

Melanie took a seat beside Alex and he introduced her. 'DS Cooper, it is a pleasure to meet you,' said Gerard.

'Likewise, Inspector Bouchard. How come you're not called DuPont? I thought you two were cousins.'

'Second cousins,' said Alex and Gerard at the same time.

'Melanie, I will conduct the interview in French. I think Jeremy would find it strange if I did otherwise.'

'That's fine, Gerard. I speak reasonably good French. I can also speak Spanish and Turkish.'

Gerard nodded his appreciation. 'I'm very impressed, Melanie. Why Turkish?'

'For the simple reason, it was sensible to do so. I discovered that Turkish was a useful language for a detective in London. I'm currently thinking about learning Russian, for the same reason.'

'In that case we are good to go. Alex, do you want to join in the interview?'

'No. Not at first, anyway.'

'Then I suggest you mute your microphone so you and Melanie can talk to each other.'

Alex threw his arms up, helpless. Melanie reached past him and muted the mic.

Gerard gave an impresario's bow. The effect was rather blunted by the pixilation. 'It's getting on, let us begin the show.'

He nodded to someone off-screen. Jeremy was led in. He wasn't cuffed, but he looked every inch the prisoner.

Gerard sat opposite him at the table and took out a digital mic, placing it on the table between them. 'So, Jeremy Higgins; you work at *Boutique Bijou*, on the Avenue des Champs-Elysees.'

'You know that, Inspector; you picked me up from there this morning.'

'Quite so, Jeremy, quite so.' Gerard's tone was genial.

'Tell me, does the name Hugo Zelov mean anything to you?'

Alex and Melanie saw the tell-tale, momentary fracture in Jeremy's features.

'No, I don't believe so.'

'I am a little surprised at your reply, Jeremy.' Gerard's tone was slightly less genial now. 'Monsieur Zelov has an unofficial connection to *Boutique Bijou*, and I think you are aware of it.'

'I am aware of some … unofficial activities at the shop, yes. I don't know if someone called Zelov is involved.'

Jeremy looked nervous, but Alex got the feeling he was protecting himself rather than Hugo Zelov.

'What kind of activities?'

'I suspect that stolen gems and jewellery are recycled through the shop. I don't think Monsieur Leclerc knows about it.'

'But you know about it, Jeremy. Why have you not come to us with your suspicions?'

Jeremy shifted in his chair. 'Some of the people who visit the technicians are clearly criminals. I think they are dangerous men. I was afraid to say anything in case they came after me.'

Gerard pressed him. 'So, you know there are criminals involved, but you don't know anything about Hugo Zelov?'

'Look.' Jeremy looked around him, as if he expected one of Zelov's thugs to appear. 'I've heard the name, and I've heard the rumours. It's quite possible this is Hugo Zelov's operation, even quite likely. I don't want to get caught up in something like that.'

'But you could have at least alerted the manager, or told him of your suspicions, eh?'

'I didn't want to get him involved. It might have put him in harm's way. I owe Monsieur Leclerc a lot. He didn't have to give me the job.' He had relaxed now, Alex noted. He probably realised this line of questioning wasn't going to get him in trouble.

'Well, there are certain advantages to you, having access to the stock cabinets and the safe, if there are illicit items lying around, no? You could help yourself to things without actually stealing from *Boutique Bijou* itself.'

Jeremy chuckled humourlessly. 'Stealing stolen gems from thieves doesn't strike me as particularly a good thing to do for one's health.'

Gerard leaned back in his chair and looked up. 'That is a very sensible approach, Jeremy. Let's move on, shall we?'

Jeremy tensed up again. He had obviously assumed the interview was about the gems, and nothing else.

'Recently you had a couple of English visitors to the shop, am I right?'

'Yes. But I don't see what that has to do with...'

Gerard interrupted him with a raised hand. 'One of the visitors was a Ms Gerry Hamilton.' It was a statement, not a question.

'Yes.'

'And this was quite a shock for you, I believe. Can you tell me why?'

Gerard was going in a direction Jeremy didn't want to follow. He swallowed hard but didn't answer immediately. 'Yes, it was. She... she reminded me of someone.'

'She reminded you of a young woman who had recently died, in suspicious circumstances, is that not so?'

'I didn't know then that her death was suspicious, but yes, you are right. Amanda was a friend and seeing her sister...' He trailed off and looked into the distance. A man remembering.

'And the shock was so great that you had to leave work for the day. Which turned out to be rather convenient, because it meant you could avoid seeing the next English visitor, Mister DuPont. Is that not also true?'

'I don't know that it was convenient, but yes, I did miss Mr DuPont's visit.'

Gerard drew himself up in his chair. 'Convenient, I say, because you were not looking forward to his visit. And, also convenient, because it presented an opportunity to a couple of thugs, hired by a certain Hugo Zelov, to apprehend Mister DuPont.'

Jeremy's face was impassive, but his fists were clenched tightly. 'I know how it looks, but I didn't set any thugs on Mr DuPont. I left him a note, arranging to meet him later that day. I wouldn't do that if I thought he was going to be attacked, would I?'

'Perhaps, Jeremy, perhaps. But there is a theme emerging here, from our conversation, actually two themes. One we might give the name Zelov, and the other the name Hamilton. Both themes appear to be intimately connected to each other and connected to you. If this situation was a wheel, you would be the hub and if it was a web, one might identify you as the spider.'

Jeremy unclenched his fists, with a visible effort. He didn't speak. His face was set tight, into an inscrutable mask.

Gerard's voice was genial again, almost gentle. 'I understand your reluctance to answer. It would be difficult to say anything without incriminating yourself.

'I see that. But think on it, Jeremy: if you say nothing, your silence is also rather incriminating, don't you think?'

Melanie exhaled sharply, almost a whistle. 'He's good, your cousin – second cousin. In fact, he hasn't accused Jeremy of having anything to do with Amanda's death, but he's led him into a tunnel of circumstances that leads that way.'

'But Jeremy is doing his best not to go down that particular path,' said Alex. 'Either he's up to his neck in this, or he's the victim of a lot of coincidences. Much as I dislike coincidences, I'm in two minds about it. He could turn out to be completely innocent. I think it's time for us to join the show.'

He started to speak, and then looked at Melanie, helpless again. 'How do I turn the bloody microphone on?'

She reached across him and clicked the mouse. As she did, her forearm brushed his. They stayed like that, arms just touching, for a moment longer than was necessary. Something crackled in the air around them. There was a look in Melanie's eyes: a look he couldn't read but desperately wanted to.

Her face was tilted up towards his and gradually, imperceptibly, he felt himself being drawn down towards her, his lips tingled with anticipation. Then, simultaneously, they remembered that they were starring on the screen of a French police laptop. Suddenly, they sat upright, like synchronised marionettes.

'Jeremy,' said Alex, the name came out as a squeak. He cleared his throat and tried again. 'Jeremy, I'd like to ask you about an incident that took place at university, involving Charlotte Palmer and Ashley Bradshaw.'

Jeremy looked around, startled: he had no idea where the voice was coming from. 'Mr DuPont, I didn't know you were here.'

'I'm not there, I'm in London.'

Jeremy looked puzzled. 'Is that allowed?'

'It's all being done in the spirit of co-operation. I hope you'll take it in the same spirit.'

'Um, yes, if it helps. What was your question?'

'There was a rather unpleasant incident in the hall of residence, during your final year. Charlotte accused Ashley Bradshaw of assaulting her. Do you remember it?'

'Yes of course. It caused quite a stir. I felt sorry for Ashley: he didn't deserve it.'

'And for Amanda?'

'Yes. For Amanda too.' A flicker of something elusive passed across his face.

'Did you believe Charlotte's account? Do you think Ashley assaulted her?'

'Not for a moment. Have you met Ashley? He's just not capable of that kind of thing.'

'I agree. So, who do you think hit her?'

'I can't say.'

'Can't, or won't?'

'Can't.'

'Jeremy, did you slap Charlotte?'

HALL OF RESIDENCE, APRIL 2005

Jeremy's eyes followed Amanda as she hurried along the corridor, her beautiful face marred by tears. His anger boiled inside him. *You're not supposed to look like that.* He didn't blame her for the imperfection, not entirely at any rate. It was Charlotte, he was sure, plotting and scheming like a spider pulling the threads of a web.

He'd worked so hard to make himself part of the group. It was purgatory trying to act as if he cared about his friends. It was struggle enough just to remember their names, or anything they said, but it was worth it. It kept him close to her. He wanted her so much. She was everything he ever wanted.

He watched until Amanda disappeared into the common room, then he turned and walked along the sun-dappled corridor towards Charlotte's flat.

PARIS, THE PRESENT

'Jeremy?'

'What? Yes, I mean, what were you saying?'

'I asked you: did you assault Charlotte?'

'Assault her? No! If she's told you that she's lying. I deny it. I absolutely deny it.'

'Then who hit her? Do you have any idea?'

HALL OF RESIDENCE, APRIL 2005

There was another knock at the door. Charlotte stomped over and opened it as if she was slamming it shut. 'Oh, it's you.'

Jeremy stood in the corridor, glowering. Instead of the slack-jawed, empty expression she pictured on the very few occasions when she actually thought about him, his face was animated, and his eyes burned with passion.

'You'd better come in. It wouldn't do for my friends to see you hanging around outside my door like the village idiot.'

He stepped in and looked around the room, as if he expected to see someone else there. Then he turned to her and, when he spoke, his voice was full of thunder. 'What have you done to Amanda?'

'I haven't done anything to her, though I was sorely tempted to. She just had a hissy fit and ran off crying, like a schoolgirl having a playground tantrum.'

'I don't believe you, Charlotte. I know you. We're more alike than you care to think. You're pushing her around like a pawn on a board for your own ends.'

'Don't you go all philosophical on me, Jeremy. You're really not up to it. And the idea that you are anything like me is, frankly, distasteful.'

Jeremy smiled and it wasn't a pleasant look. 'You're just practising a little distraction, aren't you, Charlotte, like the cheap magician that you are. You think if you insult me then I won't give you a hard time about Amanda.'

'Do stop, Jeremy, if not I'll start believing you have a

heart. If you think I've done something terrible to your precious love object, why don't you do something about it?'

'I will, just you wait. I'll…'

'No, I mean really, Jeremy. If you think I'm a terrible person, then why don't you slap me? Go on.'

He hesitated, and then he slapped her across the cheek: a gentle tap. Charlotte sneered.

'That's not a slap, you useless moron. Slap me properly.'

The impact of the blow almost lifted Charlotte off her feet. She reeled, seeing stars, leaning against her desk for support. Jeremy had gone back to that impassive robot look of his that infuriated her so much.

She gathered her senses and stood up straight again. Her voice was cold and lifeless. 'Thank you, Jeremy. You can go now.'

He turned and left. She waited a few moments, then looked in the mirror. A trio of red marks throbbed loudly on her cheek. She smiled, despite the pain. Then she stepped out into the corridor and headed for the manager's office.

PARIS, THE PRESENT

'Jeremy?' Gerard said. 'Can you answer the question? Do you know who hit Charlotte?'

Jeremy thought fast. He needed to choose his words carefully: he didn't want them coming back to haunt him. He'd tried being haunted and he didn't like it.

'I really can't say. It could have been anyone. I think you need to ask Charlotte. Perhaps, after all this time, she'll be ready to tell the truth. I'm not sure Charlotte would know the truth if it…' He looked down at his hands, relaxed now, and a grim chuckle escaped him. 'She wouldn't know the truth if it walked up and slapped her.'

CHAPTER 23

'So, are you taking me back to the cells, Inspector?' Jeremy had regained all his composure: his shoulders were square, and he was looking confident. His face was the impassive mask that Alex was beginning to get to know.

Gerard glanced over his shoulder, up at the camera. Jeremy followed his eyes. He turned back and faced the young man. 'No, Jeremy; I have nothing to charge you with, so you are free to go.'

He pointed to the door. 'The *gendarme* outside will take you to the desk. Aubert!' he called. A squat, broad man appeared. 'Aubert, take Monsieur Higgins here to the front desk and arrange for him to get his belongings back.'

'Sir.' Aubert beckoned Jeremy. 'Come with me, Monsieur Higgins, and we'll sort things out for you.'

'Oh, and Jeremy,' said Gerard. 'We will need to talk to you again. There are some issues here that we still need to resolve. I think Mister DuPont feels the same. If you feel a sudden urge to travel, I suggest you put it on hold for now.'

Jeremy nodded: understanding or acquiescence, it wasn't clear which. Then he looked up at the camera, the hint of a smile playing on his lips. 'Mr DuPont, there is one more thing you should know. Charlotte threatened to kill Amanda. I don't know if she threatened her to her face, but she certainly used those words in my hearing: "I'm going to kill her". I think that's another thing you should ask her about.'

'Why are you telling me this, Jeremy? And why now? It doesn't put you in a very good light.'

'I don't think I'm in a very good light anyway. And it's probably nothing. She was always making threatening noises. I think it made her feel better, more powerful. Make of it what you will.'

Jeremy followed Aubert out the door and disappeared from view. Gerard made a gesture to indicate he was leaving, and a few moments later reappeared on screen, this time in front of the laptop, beside a technician. 'This is Philippe; he takes care of our computer needs. He's a civilian contractor. That's why he looks like we've just dragged him in on a drug bust.'

Gerard slapped the techie on the shoulder and sat down at the laptop. 'So, that was quite a performance, eh? What do you think?'

Melanie spoke first. 'You are a master of the dark arts, Gerard. I really enjoyed watching you at work.'

Gerard gave a modest nod and shrugged. 'It's the job, Melanie, if I can't ask a few questions, I should consider being a street sweeper. It wouldn't be so bad, you know: fresh air and a steady pace of work. Either way, I would be taking trash off the street.'

Melanie grinned impishly, first at Gerard and then at Alex. 'You are quite a family.'

'Ah, you should meet Aunt Sophie. She is the queen of our little colony. Maybe, Alex will invite you over for a stay at her hotel. If not, perhaps I will have to. My wife will have kittens of course, but she loves cats.'

Melanie laughed whole-heartedly and looked over at Alex. He could see laughter lines crinkling around her eyes. She looked delicious. 'Maybe, Gerard,' she said, her eyes still on Alex. 'One day perhaps.'

Gerard clapped his hands and broke the spell. 'Now,' he announced, 'back to work. First you will help me and then I will try to help you. What do you say?'

'Right then,' said Alex. 'Let's start with our friend from Marseille. Everywhere we look, we find traces of Hugo. Apart from the murder itself, he is involved in every aspect of this case.'

'Yes,' said Melanie, frowning. 'But I'm not so sure he's worth pursuing from the angle of the murder. Also, I think there are two separate strands here, and they may not be connected at all.'

'What makes you say that?' asked Alex. He couldn't see where she was going with this.

'Hugo is obviously running an operation in Paris. Someone tipped him off that you might be nosing around his interests, and then he set his little dogs on you. But I don't think that's a clear link to Jeremy.'

'I am inclined to agree with you, Melanie,' said Gerard. 'I think perhaps Jeremy was telling the truth when he said he knew about the gem scam but didn't interfere with it. And if that's the case, why would he tip Hugo off about you, Alex? That might put him in the crosshairs. If Hugo found out he worked in *Boutique Bijou* he would think Jeremy was trying to stir the pot; or worse, trying to edge himself into Hugo's business. That way lies a corpse on a Paris street, I think.'

'So, if Jeremy didn't tip him off, we're back to Charlotte.' Alex drummed his fingers on the desk. Something didn't add up.

'Maybe, maybe not. We should not exclude Gerry Hamilton yet. If her visit to the shop was a coincidence, it was a very odd one,' said Gerard.

'On the other hand,' said Melanie, 'she was trying to get him off her company's hands. Surely, she would be only too happy if his operation was discovered?'

'I don't know. I think she would prefer if that came out after she got him off the books. Otherwise, the company would look guilty by association.'

'So, she's off the hook, then.'

'Probably. Unless she was able to time everything perfectly. Then she could drop Hugo in the soup here and rush back to London and clean the slate. But I think that would be a difficult balancing act. From what you have said, I don't see her as a high-wire artist.'

'Well then,' said Alex. 'We're back to the starting blocks. It's either Charlotte or Jeremy. And from where I'm sitting, that's the same for the murder: it's one of the two of them.'

'I think,' said Melanie, 'that the gem thing is a red herring.'

'It's possible,' Gerard agreed. 'It may just be a coincidence that Jeremy works at a shop where Hugo does some illicit business. If we take that out of the picture, what do we have?'

'We have someone using Hugo's insecurity as a cover to get rid of me.' Alex saw it clearly now. 'They could have done that without knowing for certain that *Boutique Bijou* was involved, and the same goes for Jeremy.'

'That means it wasn't Jeremy who tipped him off,' said Melanie. 'And if it wasn't Jeremy, it almost has to be Charlotte.'

'I think this makes sense. The gem thing is not linked to your case. But…' Gerard tapped his brow with his index finger. 'Jeremy's testimony is enough for us – I mean the police here in Paris – to pursue an investigation into Hugo. That will make my bosses happy. He has been a thorn in their side for a long time now.'

All three sat in silence for a few moments, gathering their thoughts. Alex stood up suddenly. 'I'm going to ask Jenny to make us some tea,' he said. He popped out of the office.

Gerard looked at Melanie solemnly. 'I think you and Alex are destined for each other, Melanie. And I think you are both fighting destiny. If you are not careful, both of you might end up regretting it one day.'

Melanie sighed heavily. 'It's not so simple, Gerard.'

'I'm sure you two will work it out.'

Alex came back in with two mugs of tea. 'Sorry, Gerard; I can't send you tea over the internet.'

'No, but my techie friend has his uses.' Gerard smiled and lifted a mug of coffee to his lips. 'Cheers.'

After a quick tea break, they got back to work. 'Let's have a think about the murder in terms of motive,' suggested Gerard. 'The means are an open question for now. I think anyone who is determined enough can get hold of poison. And as things stand, unless you can find evidence from the scene, or bust an alibi, I think everyone in the frame could be said to have the opportunity.'

'You're right, Gerard, motive is crucial here,' said Alex. 'Amanda was well-liked by almost everyone in her life, unless a lot of people are lying. And it's hard to see what anyone had to gain from her death. Therefore, we are left with looking at people who might have a personal reason to kill her.'

'And that's the difficulty,' said Melanie. 'If that's our main criterion, then Charlotte is the main suspect. But she has a good alibi. She is open about her dislike of Amanda too. She's not hiding anything in that respect.'

'On the other hand, if we include people who had a reason to hate Amanda, we ought to put Gerry back on the list. Whatever happened five years ago, when Amanda had her bout of depression, drove a wedge between them. We only have her word that they had overcome that. Amanda has no voice here.'

'And we haven't mentioned Jeremy,' said Gerard. 'That's interesting, isn't it? Do you think our conversation makes him a more or less likely suspect?'

'I like Charlotte more than him for it,' said Melanie. 'I think she has consistently lied to us and she's clearly manipulating other people around her, just look at that poor Steve. And yet…'

'And yet, there is something extremely weird about Jeremy,' added Alex. 'His alibi is tantamount to impossible to prove or disprove, and he has given us no reason to discount him.'

'But are we focussing on Jeremy merely because he is a strange – in fact deeply strange – young man?' asked Gerard. 'Weirdness isn't a crime.'

'I'm still puzzled why he told us about Charlotte threatening to kill Amanda. It seems such an obvious ploy,' said Alex.

'Perhaps he thought, in his own strange way, that he

was helping us.' Gerard scratched his head. 'To tell you the truth, a lot of what Jeremy does, puzzles me. He's not exactly going out of his way to make us think better of him. Maybe, he doesn't care what we think of him, which, I suppose, suggests he is confident in his own innocence.'

'I think there is enough there to consider him a suspect,' said Alex. 'When it comes down to it, I think it's a toss-up between him and Charlotte.'

'Yes,' said Melanie. 'Except there isn't a definitive piece of evidence linking either of them to the actual crime.'

'Maybe it's not a question of either/or,' mused Gerard. 'If I were you, I would explore the possibility of communication between them. I could more easily imagine that, than either of them is working alone.'

'It's still all about the evidence for me,' said Melanie. 'We have plenty of evidence to point at murder, but nothing to point at a murderer. That's a strange position to be in.'

'Well, let me make a suggestion.' Gerard steepled his fingers under his chin. 'I will make a request here for access to Jeremy's phone records under the pretext of an investigation into Hugo's gem operation in Paris. That's the most likely to get a result. If I find anything that relates to the murder, I can pass it on to you. Now,' he said, gathering a few sheets of paper from the desk. 'I need to be somewhere else. Otherwise, my bosses will think I have transferred to the Met.'

He disappeared off screen. Melanie closed the Skype app and they continued to mull over the case, trading suggestions and testing theories. Jenny came in to collect the tea mugs and looked at them both with a puzzled frown. It took a moment for the penny to drop.

'Ah yes,' said Melanie. 'I guess we can stop speaking French now.'

**

Melanie left a few minutes later, to update DI Jenkins on the interview with Jeremy. Alex called Ashley. He needed to tell him about the anonymous phone call, and he had a few questions that Ashley might be able to help him with.

'I don't believe it. Steve paid a prostitute to make the call. That's bizarre. Why would he do that?' Ashley sounded like he was having trouble digesting the information.

'The name of the lady concerned is Ulrika. She told us it was a joke. She said he was going to tell you afterwards.'

'But he didn't, did he?'

'No, he didn't.' Alex left that hanging. He wasn't sure yet if he wanted to tell Ashley about Charlotte's involvement.

'Well, it's a relief to know it's not a genuine threat. I haven't slept properly since it happened. I suppose I should be grateful for that. But how am I going to face him at work? For that matter, how is he going to face me?'

'I'm going to talk to Walter and suggest that Steve takes some leave. This whole affair is having a terrible effect on him. I think his confidence is shattered. It's possible…'

'What's possible, Alex?'

'I was going to say, it's possible that Steve won't be coming back to Brown Legal. I'll have to tell Walter what happened, and I don't think he'll be too impressed.'

'Well, that makes it easier for me, I suppose, but I feel sorry for Steve. I know I shouldn't, but I do.'

Alex waited a moment. 'Ashley, there are a couple of other things I wanted to ask you. First off, is it possible you mentioned my trip to Paris to Steve?'

'I may have done; I can't remember. You were a big topic of conversation at Brown Legal, you know. It was all very exciting having a private investigator on the premises.'

'Try and remember, Ashley, it's important.'

There was a strained silence for a few moments. Either Ashley was racking his brains, or he was too embarrassed to admit he'd been a tell-tale. Finally, Alex heard an out-breath, like someone had come to a big decision. 'Yes, I think I did tell him, in passing. He was asking about you a lot, pestering me really. I found it strange, as far as I knew, you were talking to him as much as to me.'

'Thank you, Ashley. I appreciate your honesty.'

'I'm sorry. I hope I didn't cause any trouble for you, did I?'

'No, not directly. I did encounter some trouble in Paris, but I don't think Steve was responsible for it. At least, I don't think so now.'

Ashley chuckled. 'Ulrika. I mean, it just sounds so wacky. Why would someone like Steve need to go to a woman like her?'

If only you knew the half of it, thought Alex. 'There's something else, Ashley; something about Amanda. Do you think she was perhaps a bit OCD.'

'Well, not so as you'd notice on casual acquaintance. But if you knew her well, like I did. Yes, she was, especially about domestic stuff.'

'Can you tell me about it?'

'I shared a flat with her for a while at Bristol. She was ferociously tidy, and she expected her flatmates to be the same. And in the kitchen? She was practically strict.' He laughed warmly, remembering.

Alex played along. 'Everything in its proper place, I guess?'

'Oh yes. The plates went in the plate cupboard, big ones at the bottom, small ones at the top. The cups went in the cup cupboard, handles pointing out, all in a line.'

'So, she wouldn't have left a wine glass in the cupboard with the mugs?'

'Ooh, not at all. That would have given her nightmares. Sorry, I'm making her sound like a lunatic, but she was a bit inflexible about that kind of thing.'

'That's very helpful, Ashley, thank you. If I think of anything else, I'll call you.'

**

Alex sat for a while, thinking. When Jenny came in with a mug of tea, she had to nudge him to get his attention. 'Hello! Earth calling Alex! Scott says his boffin friend called. Apparently, the police couldn't find a match for those prints on their system.'

'What? Oh, the prints. Oh, crap, the prints! Why didn't you tell me before?'

'Alex, what are you talking about? I've only just found out.'

'Sorry, Jenny, it's not you, it's me. There's something I forgot to ask Gerard.'

'No worries, I'll give him a call.' Jenny's eyes sparkled.

Gerard sounded like he was out on the streets of Paris somewhere. Alex could hear traffic noise in the background. 'Ah, cousin, give me a moment. I can't hear a word you're saying.' After a few moments, the traffic noise faded, and Gerard came back on. 'There, that's better, I've stepped into a café off the street. It's a little crowded, so we'd better speak English.'

'Gerard, you said you'd taken Jeremy's fingerprints.'

'Yes, we did. We haven't filed them on the system because we didn't charge him with anything. But that may happen yet, eh?'

'Do you think I could get a copy of them?'

'Hmm. That could be a problem. Since they're not on the system, they're not really ours to give away. I could send you a copy on the fly, but then you couldn't use them as evidence. Give me a couple of days, I'll see if I can untie a few of the knots in the red tape.'

Alex heard his cousin apologising in French to someone who had evidently just bumped into him. 'Huh, I think I'm a size too big for this place. Listen, let's do it this way. I'll send you a copy as soon as I can. If it turns out you need them officially as evidence, bin the copy and send me a request for the originals. What do you say?'

'That works for me, Gerard. But don't get yourself in trouble for a few daubs of ink.'

Gerard laughed, and hastily apologised again. 'I'm a big boy now, Alex; or so I've just been told in no uncertain terms. But I have to get out of this café before they call the police on me; then I will be in trouble. Speak to you soon.'

Alex decided to call it a day. He'd learned a lot, one way and another. But he had the feeling that, once he'd poured himself a large glass of red cabernet sauvignon wine and settled into his favourite armchair, it wasn't the case he would be thinking about.

CHAPTER 24

What was it about Thursdays and rain, Alex thought, adding an umbrella to his pile of work things. Late last night, as he sat and mulled over his eccentric love life, French wine in hand, rattles of thunder had disturbed his thoughts. The rain had started as he finally headed for bed: big, heavy summer raindrops falling onto the roof of his apartment, and a steady drumbeat that gradually lulled him to sleep.

He was the first to arrive at the office. A few minutes later, Jenny came in, shaking herself like a wet dog and muttering about forgetting her umbrella. Alex folded his ostentatiously and set it in the coat rack. 'Yes, well done, clever clogs, doesn't make me feel any better?'

'Never mind, Jenny, you can borrow mine when you go out later to get the sandwiches. Oh wait, here comes a man already dressed for the trip.'

Scott arrived in full wet weather gear. He was about to peel off his jacket when he noticed Alex and Jenny watching him and looking amused. 'What?'

'I wouldn't bother taking that off your gear just yet, Scott,' said Jenny. 'You're on a mission.'

'Alright, I'll do that. And Alex, after looking at the

photograph, Sally Prentice confirmed the girl she saw with Steve was Charlotte,' said Scott.

'Thank you, Scott.' Alex went back to his office to make a few calls.

**

Alex's first call was to Walter. 'I don't have much time, Alex; I have a meeting with some clients in a few minutes.'

'Then I won't keep you, Walter. I just wanted to update you on the investigation and ask you a favour.'

'Fire away.'

'I am confident we will have the case wrapped up within the next week. I mean the police and the Agency are waiting on some forensic evidence. When that arrives, we should be in a position to make an arrest. I can't say more at this point, there are some delicate evidential issues to negotiate, but I hope to have good news for you soon.'

'That's good to hear, Alex. I knew I could rely on you. I suppose you can't tell me who…'

'Sorry, Walter. Until we are in a position to charge someone, I really can't say.'

'I understand. Now, you said you needed a favour.' Walter sounded enthusiastic. Alex thought he was enjoying the idea of being part of a murder drama.

'It's about Steve Mortimer.'

'Good Lord, is Mortimer a suspect?'

'No, he isn't. But he may have inadvertently got himself involved and, to be honest with you, Walter, he has not behaved too well in the circumstances. I think it's taking a toll on him too. I was wondering if you could get someone like Sally Prentice to go and see him and tell him he looks awful and needs to take a couple of days off.'

'Does that mean, you need him out of the way for something?' Walter sounded conspiratorial now. Alex thought he'd detected a hint of Hollywood creeping into his voice. He played along.

'Let's just say it would be convenient for us if he were to be at home for the next couple of days.'

'Leave it with me, Alex, I'll arrange it before I go into the meeting. Sally will be only too glad to help.' *I bet she will*, thought Alex, grinning.

'Can you get her to call me and let me know when he's left?'

'Will do.'

Alex rang off and looked at his to do list: call Barrington arrange to meet him at Amanda's place, he wanted to ask the owner about the lovely Imelda; phone Melanie and arrange a visit to Steve; then call Claire.

**

Mr Barrington was happy to meet him later that morning but sounded distinctly nervous when Alex told him he'd like to have a chat. He didn't think the man was hiding anything significant but his reaction was puzzling. Nevermind, he thought: *let's see what the problem is when we get there.*

Melanie was chirpy, the gang shootings case was more or less sorted and she was preparing paperwork for the initial court hearing. 'What do you think Steve can tell us that he hasn't already? Or that he won't continue to lie about?'

'I'm hoping he'll be more helpful if we confront him in his den. I thought we'd arrive unannounced, catch him off guard. I'm curious about him. I don't think he's good for murder but he's still worth talking to. And we can sell it as eliminating him from our enquiries.'

'OK, you're on. Ping me when you're ready to go and I'll shove this paperwork onto someone else. I'm not keen on paperwork.' Melanie paused and the silence was palpable. 'Have you discussed anything with Claire yet?'

'Not yet.' It took a second for him to register why she was asking. 'I'll...I'll talk to her properly over the weekend. I'll let you know how it goes.'

'Alex, it's none of my business. But I would like to know what's happening.'

'That's all well and good. How about you and Martin? Have you sorted out your relationship with him yet? Remember, we both have to deal with our personal lives first before we even think of spending our time together.'

**

Alex's finger dawdled over the call button. He saw Claire in his mind's eye. Her mother was Goan, and Claire had inherited her silky, raven-black hair and golden-brown complexion. Her eyes were a dark, liquid brown, flecked with hazel. She occasionally donned a pair of round-rimmed spectacles that gave her a quirky, bookish look. Her willowy frame came from her father. She was not as tall as Alex but in heels she looked down on him.

'Alex DuPont! So, you haven't run away and joined the Foreign Legion. I haven't heard from you for a few days.' Her lilting voice was playful, but there was a less than subtle accusation in her words.

'I'm sorry, Claire, I've been horribly busy.'

'Just the occasional text, Alex, would have helped, indicating that I've at least crossed your mind.'

'You know what I'm like with phones.'

'I know what you're like.'

The silence that followed dragged on for a few seconds, and then they both spoke at once. Alex gave it a second and started again. 'I was wondering if you're free this weekend. I thought we could take a walk in St James Park and find somewhere nice for lunch.'

She sighed. 'Yes, I expect that's a good idea. What are you up to, Alex? Are you knee-deep in corporate corruption cases?'

'Actually no. I'm working on another criminal case, a murder. I'm beginning to think this is the kind of work I'm cut out for.'

'Very exciting, I'm sure.' She didn't sound excited. 'And are the police involved?'

'Of course, that's how it works.'

'Melanie Cooper, then.'

'How did you…?'

'I'm psychic. And you are so predictable. I'll see you on Saturday.'

Alex stared at the phone for a few moments after she rang off. He was fond of Claire. She was beautiful, intelligent and warm-hearted. If only… if only he truly loved her.

**

'Jenny, can you get online and find out what you can about potassium cyanide? See how easy it is to get hold of it. And have another look at Hugo Zelov and his little friends. I know they're into designer drugs and gems, but I wonder if they have more esoteric chemical interests.'

'Right, I'll get on with that.'

'Scott, you're with me. Bring the photos with you and you can have another scout round the neighbours while I talk to Barrington. Oh, and look out for our observant mate.

If he's at home, I'd like to talk to him.'

They took Scott's car, an anonymous Japanese saloon with rather too many miles on the clock. It was perfect for surveillance, though the noises it made when Scott changed gear were a tad worrying.

'Have you ever thought about getting a car that actually works properly?'

'You're the boss, Alex. If you want to buy an agency motor for me to swan around in, I'll bow to your wishes.'

They'd had this conversation before. Scott was right, they could do with a company car. Alex filed it away at the back of his mind, in the part of his brain marked 'to do, but not yet'.

As they drove along the A4, Alex's phone pinged. For a moment, he thought it might be Claire, cancelling their date, but it was from Jenny. Sally Prentice had called. Steve had been encouraged to take some leave and was on his way home.

Excellent, thought Alex. We'll give him the rest of the day to stew and swoop in on him tomorrow. He texted Melanie with the news and she agreed to be at the Agency mid-morning. There was no point in going earlier. Alex thought Steve would be drowning his sorrows tonight.

'Scott, where are we going?' Scott had turned off the main road into a narrow avenue.

'There's a little back double through here. I looked it up the other day. Gets us off the A4 and all that traffic.'

They wound through a couple of deserted streets and came to Fairfield Crescent from the other end. As they turned in, Alex saw a park, nestled between a side road and the corner shop. It was a neat place, equipped with some play equipment, recently repainted, and a few benches.

It so happened the benches were occupied by half a dozen mums and one dad. The play equipment was being colonised by a bunch of busy, chirruping toddlers. They didn't seem to mind the few raindrops still clinging to the slides. The sun was out again, and some purple-grey clouds still scudding across the sky were busy spilling micro-showers elsewhere. Alex had a fleeting thought that he ought to take a walk in that park at some point.

Mr Barrington was waiting for them at the entrance, hands clinging to each other as usual. Scott parked up right outside and took the sheaf of photos from his bag. 'Right, I'm off to get nosy with the neighbours.' He looked over at the nervous little man. 'Enjoy.'

'Mr Barrington; how are you this fine morning?' Barrington didn't share his enthusiasm for the weather, apparently.

'You said you needed to talk to me?'

'It's nothing to worry about. I just wanted to ask you about a neighbour of Amanda's. Imelda?'

'Ah, Miss Delgado. A lovely lady.' Barrington's eyes betrayed more than a hint of mousy lust. 'I mean, a lovely tenant, couldn't ask for better,' he added hastily.

'Do you happen to have some contact details for her? I assume she's at work now, and I want to ask her a couple of questions about that Sunday.' He avoided mentioning murder. Barrington had looked horribly queasy last time they had brought up the subject.

'Yes, I'm sure I have a mobile number for her, back at the office. I'll have a look when I get back and send it to you.'

'Excellent, thank you. Well, if we can just pop in for a few minutes, I'd like to have another look around.'

Barrington turned to open the front door. Just then, Scott hurried up to join them. 'Alex, I think we've got something. A lady who lives four doors away saw this lady,' he held out a photo, 'arrived here about one o'clock on the day of the murder.' Barrington cringed; Alex smirked behind his hand.

His smirk faded when Barrington spoke. 'I, um, I know that lady.'

Scott and Alex turned towards him at the same time. His hands were doing their best to disappear up his sleeves. 'Tell us more, Mr Barrington,' said Alex.

'A couple of weeks before the... before the unfortunate event, I was here doing some maintenance. Actually, it was Sunday the twenty-first of May. This lady – Charlie, I think she said – turned up and asked me some questions. She explained she was an old friend of Amanda's and wanted to give her a surprise birthday present.'

He had their attention now and that didn't seem to make him feel good. He cleared his throat noisily and went on.

'She was very charming, asked me not to let on to Amanda. And...'

'And?'

'I may have told her about the camera maintenance.' He looked, slightly aghast, at Alex and Scott, two pairs of eyes fixed on him intently. 'I mean, I told her about the camera maintenance. I think she was asking if Amanda had access to the pictures, in case she wanted to, um, sneak in. For the surprise, you know,' he finished lamely.

'And why didn't you tell us about this before now?' Alex could not keep the irritation from his voice. At the same time, he felt the first upwelling of certainty in his mind.

'I didn't think it was relevant. After all, it was a while ago, and poor Ms Hamilton won't be having a birthday party now, will she, surprise or not.'

'Mr Barrington, you have somehow contrived to be a hindrance and a great help all in one go,' said Alex. 'If we'd known this from the outset, well, never mind, we know now.'

He turned to Scott. 'I think we'd better be off.' They headed for the car, leaving Barrington, shrunken and forlorn, on the doorstep. Alex looked up as he got to the passenger door. The figure in the window was there again, and this time he did acknowledge them, with a tentative wave. Alex thought for a moment and made up his mind.

'Scott, go back to Barrington and get some sort of formal statement from him, or a recording of what he just told us. I'm going to visit our curtain twitcher.'

CHAPTER 25

Alex strode purposefully across the street. By the time he got to the gate, the front door was open. The man who filled the doorway was short but stocky; he had a full moustache, and he stood very upright. Alex had the impression of a miniaturised regimental sergeant major.

He half expected to be barked at: 'Come in 'ere, you 'horrible little man'. But the voice that greeted him was surprisingly gentle.

'Hello, I was hoping we might get a chance to talk. Won't you come in? I'm Arthur, by the way, Arthur Middleton.'

Alex stepped forward to shake hands and realised he had the photo of Charlotte in his right hand. He swapped it to his left. 'Thank you, Arthur; I was rather hoping the same thing. I'm Alex DuPont, call me Alex.' He gave Arthur his business card.

He looked at the card. 'You're a private investigator.'

Arthur ushered him into a neat sitting room adorned with framed photos: a young Arthur and his bride, a pretty, petite woman with sparkling eyes and an auburn, sixties bouffant; the same couple a few years later with a baby in her arms, a photo taken possibly some years ago, by the look of it, the woman greying now but still with that sparkle in her eyes.

'Do sit down, Alex.' Arthur stopped short and looked at the photo in Alex's hand. 'I believe I know that lady.'

Alex had been feeling impatient, as if he needed to get this interview out of the way and get back to the Agency, but now he was all ears. 'Ah, you saw her here, a couple of weeks before the murder.'

'So, it was murder, eh? I'm sorry to hear that. This place is not like it used to be, anymore. Well, I saw her on the day of the murder.'

He got excited upon hearing that news. 'The day of the murder?'

'Yes. She was here in the early afternoon, oh, about one o'clock, I think. As I recall, she was carrying something: looked like one of those bags you get from posh wine shops – actually, it was an orange carrier bag.'

'You're sure it was her?'

'Oh yes, very sure. I have a good eye for detail. She wasn't there long. I saw her come out about twenty minutes later. She looked rather angry, as I recall. And I think I can confirm it for you, if you give me a bit of time. Let's go to my little den.'

On impulse, Alex pulled out a photo of Jeremy. He showed it to Arthur, who shook his head. 'No. I haven't seen this chap before. Sorry.'

The den was kitted out as an office: there was a row of filing cabinets, and a new PC on an old but sturdy desk. Arthur touched the mouse, and the screen flickered into life. In the top right-hand corner of the screen, a panel display view of the street. Amanda's house was more or less in the centre of it.

'Please don't get the idea that I'm some sort of peeping tom, Alex. The camera is there for a good reason.' Arthur sat at the desk and brought the panel to full screen.

Alex took the only other chair in the room, a rickety folding construction, and sat beside him. 'Tell me more, Arthur.'

'Fairfield Crescent is a lovely little street: it's friendly, and leafy, an ideal place to live. That's why we chose it. But in the last few years, it's changed. We're a sort of short cut between two sections of the A4 now, and a lot of people use the short cut, particularly at rush hour. The place rather loses its charm when it's full of traffic. The trucks are the worst.'

Arthur ran his hand through his hair. 'You could say the trucks are more than a nuisance. I've been complaining to the council about them for five years now and they've never done a thing about it. Then…'

He subsided into his chair and sighed. 'Then, three years ago – three years next Wednesday, in fact – my wife, Dorothy, was crossing the street to go to the corner shop. She was hit by a truck and was killed.'

'I'm so sorry, Arthur.'

'I appreciate that.'

He smiled a thin, sad smile. 'Anyway, after I'd recovered a little – to the extent that one can recover from such a thing – I had a camera installed. The idea was both to record the volume of heavy traffic using the street, and to bear witness if anyone else were to suffer the same fate as my poor dear Dorothy.'

'You've done the right thing, Arthur. And you just might be able to provide us with some invaluable evidence. Do you keep a record of the images from the camera?'

'I do, but it will take a little time to find the relevant

material.' Arthur opened a drawer under the desk. Alex saw a large number of flash drives. 'I usually remember to label them with the date and so on, but at this time of year my mind tends to wander somewhat.'

'I understand,' said Alex. He paused and asked the inevitable question. 'How long do you think it would take to find the tape from Sunday the fourth of June? I could send someone over to help, if you like.'

'There's no need. I can sort it out in a day or two. The footage is date-stamped, as you can see.' He indicated the time and date on the screen in front of them. 'I can certainly have it for you by Monday morning, if that works for you.'

'That would be perfect, Arthur, thank you.'

'When I spotted the lady in the photo, you mentioned another date. Do you want me to check that one too?'

Alex fished for his notebook. 'That would be wonderful. It's Sunday the twenty-first of May.'

Arthur made a note on a pad in front of him on the desk. 'Right, I'll fish them both out and get back to you first thing Monday morning.'

'You can get me on the mobile number at any time,' he said. 'The office number is usually available by eight-thirty.'

Arthur gave him an amused, crooked smile. 'You were in a terrible hurry to leave when you arrived,' he said. 'You should get on, and I'll do the same.' He showed Alex to the door, and they shook hands.

'I didn't know the young woman,' Arthur said as Alex turned to go. 'But if I can help to find her killer, it will make my mind rest a little easier.' He straightened up in the doorway, the sergeant-major again. 'Good hunting, Mr DuPont.'

**

Scott made a U-turn and they headed back down Fairfield Crescent. Alex briefly considered telling him not to, but he thought Arthur would forgive them on this occasion. As they passed the park he felt the urge to go there, again, he'd get round to it.

'It looks like our Charlotte is favourite for the murder,' said Scott. Alex had filled him in on his encounter with Arthur. 'Funny, I was leaning more towards Jeremy.'

'I was too, but the evidence is stacking up the other way.' Alex took out his phone and sent Melanie a text. 'I think an arrest is in the offing.'

When they got back to the office, Jenny was waiting for them, bouncing on the balls of her feet. 'If you want to reach five foot six inches, you'll have to buy some stilettos,' said Scott.

'That's enough from you, Wallace,' she retorted. 'I've got bigger fish to fry.'

Alex grinned. 'Does that mean Scott has to make the teas?'

'In a minute. I think you both need to hear this.'

Jenny went to her desk and picked up a few sheets of printed paper, downloads, Alex saw, text with badly printed ads decorating the margins.

'I looked for stuff on potassium cyanide. It is commercially available here and there, which surprised me enormously. So, in theory, anyone could get hold of it, if they could persuade the supplier, they had a legitimate reason for it.'

'Good work, Jenny,' Alex said. 'That really moves us on.'

'Wait, that's not all. After Gerard told us about the dodgy gem technicians at *Boutique Bijou*, I thought I'd do some research on goldsmiths and gem cutters.'

She pleasingly brandished a sheet of paper in her hand. 'I think you should have a look at this.'

Alex whistled. 'So, they use potassium cyanide. And if Jeremy was nosing about in their stuff, he could have discovered it. Hmm.' He looked at Scott.

'Maybe this is still a two-horse race. OK, this is great work. I'll make the teas.'

Jenny shook her head. 'No, I'll make the tea, you've got a call to make. Katherine Manley called about half an hour ago. She sounded pretty concerned and asked if you could call her as soon as possible.'

**

Katherine Manley was more than concerned. Alex could hear a note of near panic in her voice. 'Alex, you recall what I said about Jeremy that he doesn't fall in love so much as develop a need for people?'

'Yes, I remember.'

'In the last few days, he has developed some sort of obsession for the daughter of a friend of ours, a woman I regularly play Bridge with. The girl is fairly attractive, but nothing special. But she has stunning red hair. When I asked him what was going on, that's what he said to me. He liked her because of her hair. That's when I remembered.'

She paused, waiting for Alex to respond. 'Remembered what, Katherine?'

'Some weeks ago, at the weekend – I can recall clearly it was Saturday twentieth of May – Jeremy left early. That's not unusual, but he told me he was meeting someone, and that *is* unusual.

'I rather forgot about it until a few hours later. I wanted

to get some fresh air, so I took myself off to the Jardin des Tuileries; it's a bit crowded, but the air is lovely and there is an excellent little creperie off in a corner where the tourists don't bother to go.

'Anyway, I'd been walking for an hour or so and decided to treat myself to a chocolate crepe. As I approached the creperie, I saw Jeremy, in the distance. He was having an animated conversation with a young woman.... a woman with dazzling red hair.

'I was a little worried that it was my friend's daughter. I really didn't want Jeremy to get too close to her. But when I got a little nearer, I saw it wasn't her at all. This young woman was smartly dressed, a businesswoman of sorts, I suppose.

'I kept my distance, so I couldn't hear what they were saying, but whatever it was, it had them both rather excited. Then I saw Jeremy hand her a small package. I couldn't see what it was, but it was no bigger than the size of my hand.

'The young woman kissed him. I was a little stunned by that. People don't kiss Jeremy, he's too cold for that. And I was sure they had been discussing something very important. And she didn't just peck him on the cheek, she kissed him full on the lips and lingered at it.

'From where I was standing, I got the impression that Jeremy was as stunned as I was. Then she walked away, swinging her hips like a fashion model on the catwalk. He watched her for ages, until she disappeared into the crowds.'

Alex was scribbling furiously in his notebook; it took him a moment to register that she had stopped talking. 'Katherine, this is extremely valuable information. I know it couldn't have been easy for you to tell me about this.'

He could hear her suppressing a sniffle, a prelude to tears. 'Yes, I do feel as if I'm betraying him in some way. But after what you told me, and given what I know about him, I felt I had to tell you. Is Jeremy in trouble now?'

'It's possible, Katherine, I can't pretend otherwise. But just now, it's the red-haired woman I am most interested in. If I sent you a photo, do you think you could tell me if it is the same woman that you saw in the Tuileries?'

'Yes of course.' There was a note of relief in her voice.

'Good. I'll send you the photo and stay on the line, if I can figure out how to do that.'

A moment later, he had sent the picture. Katherine gave a sharp intake of breath. 'Yes, that's her. Who is she?'

'I can't say too much, Katherine, but she is a person of interest in my investigation.'

'I can't believe that Jeremy has got himself mixed up in a murder,' she said.

'We don't know that. There may be a perfectly innocent explanation for the meeting. Maybe, they were friends, and they may just have been doing some catching up. Perhaps Jeremy simply gave her a present.'

'You don't believe that Alex, any more than I do.'

She was a perceptive woman, he had to admit. But he didn't want to dash all her hopes, not yet. 'I don't really know what to believe, Katherine. This young woman seems to have woven a very complicated web around her, and a lot of men have been caught up in it.'

'So, you think Jeremy may be a victim here?' The relief in her voice was palpable.

'It's possible, yes. At this point, anything is possible.' Alex regretted saying that immediately. He could almost hear her deflating. 'Leave it with me, Katherine, I'll let you know if anything comes of it, and soon, I promise. And Katherine….'

'Yes?' Her voice had a tremor in it now.

'Please, don't mention any of this to Jeremy. This is between us.'

'Of course. I understand.' Alex didn't think she did, not really.

CHAPTER 26

When he called Melanie, she listened for a few seconds and then interrupted him. 'I'm coming over, Alex. There's a lot to take in here, and I think we should all knock our heads together.'

An hour later, they gathered on the sofas for a case conference: Alex, Jenny, Scott and Melanie. Jenny had typed up Alex's notes and printed them and made copies for everyone. Once they were armed with tea and coffee, they set to work.

Jenny had set up a whiteboard, drawn a line down the centre of it, and written the names 'Jeremy' and 'Charlotte' on either side of it. She sat on the edge of the sofa, marker in hand. 'Right, you lot. We'll review each new item of evidence. If we think it makes Jeremy more likely for the murder, we'll put it on his side of the line and vice versa for Charlotte. If we're not unanimous, we'll take a vote.'

'Yes, ma'am,' said Alex, touching his forelock. 'I really should get a haircut.'

'Item number one,' said Jenny, studiously ignoring him. 'Ashley told Steve about Alex's trip to Paris. Steve doesn't know Jeremy, at least so far, we don't think so. Everyone happy this goes on Charlotte's tally?'

Three hands shot up in agreement. 'One-nil to Charlotte,' said Scott.

'Item two. Amanda was a bit OCD. Not sure this goes on either column.'

'Maybe; maybe not,' said Melanie. 'Think about it. They were both part of Amanda's circle of friends at university, so Charlotte must have known a fair bit about her. More than likely, she had noticed this aspect of her personality. In which case, you'd expect her to put the wine glass back in the right place.'

'On the other hand,' Scott said. 'If she wanted to frame Jeremy, she might have put it in the wrong cupboard. And if it was Jeremy, he probably just put it in a cupboard. After all, he's left-handed, so it was more natural for him to put it where we found it.'

Alex rubbed his forehead. 'Well, that's rather confusing. Are we saying it's more a vote for Charlotte?' Melanie's hand rose tentatively. 'Or for Jeremy?' Scott's hand got to about shoulder height and stayed there.

'So that's a definite maybe, unless you want the casting vote, Jenny.' She shook her head. 'OK then, we'll leave that one on the line. Next?'

'Item three: Mr Barrington's little indiscretion. He told Charlotte, in person, that the security cameras would be out of operation on the fourth of June. Seems nailed on for the Charlotte column, that one.'

'Not so fast, Jenny. I think item four may throw a little mud in that water.'

Alex looked around. 'Anyone mind if we think about these two together? Excellent. Jenny?'

'Item four: the meeting in the garden in Paris whose name I can't pronounce between Jeremy and Charlotte.'

'Tuileries.'

'Thank you; any thoughts, folks?'

'Given they met after Charlotte's tête à tête with Mr Barrington, Charlotte could have told Jeremy about it,' said Scott.

'Yes, she could. But that doesn't put him in the frame, necessarily,' argued Melanie. 'The package makes a difference, though. It makes him look like an accessory, even if he was an unwittingly one.'

'Unwittingly?' said Alex. 'I'm struggling to imagine he would just hand over a vial of cyanide, there's no innocent explanation for that. He had to know she was planning to kill someone.'

'Yes, but that kiss.' Jenny was standing in front of the whiteboard, her marker wavering between the columns. 'That sounds like she had him under her thumb, among other places.'

Scott giggled. 'Is that romantic novel speak for "by the short and curlies"?'

'You are so crude, Wallace. This place needs a refinement upgrade. If only Gerard was here.' Jenny sighed and fluttered her eyelashes theatrically.

'In all seriousness,' said Melanie. 'I think this one points firmly to collusion. Arguing about which one of them was in charge is irrelevant at this juncture.'

'I agree,' said Alex. 'It looks that way. But until we get more evidence, it's merely suggestive.'

'Item five: cyanide, and its attainment afterwards. Jeremy could have had access to it from the jewellers. He'd have had to steal it, presumably, even a couple of mobsters probably wouldn't hand over a vial of poison to any Tom, Dick or Jeremy.' Jenny looked rather pleased with herself.

'But item five muddies the waters again,' said Melanie. 'If Katherine saw him handing over a vial of cyanide to Charlotte, then access is a moot issue.'

'In fact,' said Scott. 'The more evidence we stack up, the more it looks as if they were working together. The only question in my mind is whether they were equal partners in crime, or Charlotte was manipulating Jeremy?'

Melanie nodded. 'I agree with Scott. This looks like collusion.'

'Well,' said Alex. 'Let's see if the last item gets us anywhere on that score.'

'Item six: Arthur Middleton's evidence. Some of this is still pending, but he definitely identified Charlotte and said he'd seen her at Amanda's apartment on the day of the murder. We have to wait until Monday for confirmation, but according to Alex, Arthur was very sure of what he'd seen.'

'The trouble is,' said Scott. 'The timing is off. Charlotte turns up at one o'clock with something in a posh orange carrier bag. She leaves, angry, twenty minutes later. The pathologist is fairly sure that Amanda died around four o'clock.'

'Either the pathologist got the time of death wrong, or Amanda didn't drink the poisoned wine nearly three hours after Charlotte stormed off. That doesn't work for me,' said Melanie.

'The path lab report was pretty conclusive, so let's stick with what we've got,' said Alex. 'Can we find an explanation for Amanda not drinking the wine for nearly three hours after Charlotte left?'

Jenny chimed in. 'If she was as angry as Charlotte – say if they'd had a big row – she might simply have forgotten about it. She stomped around doing angry OCD things for a period of time and then she swigged the wine.'

'Flat Prosecco, that would have made her even angrier,' said Melanie. 'I don't buy it. We're missing something here.'

Jenny wrote on the whiteboard again. 'Right then. The new evidence leans slightly more towards Charlotte than Jeremy, but it mainly suggests that they were in this together. Until we get the footage from Arthur, and the prints evidence from Gerard, we are still in the dark.'

'Not completely in the dark. We're pretty certain it was one or both of them,' said Melanie. 'If DI Jenkins was here, he'd say let's pull them both in and put lots of pressure on. One of them will crack and confess, or each of them will say something to incriminate the other one.'

'I think we should wait a few more days and we'll hopefully have all the evidence we need, between the prints and the footage,' said Alex. There were nods of agreement from everyone in the room. He clapped his hands. 'Right. Let's finish early and go for a...'

The doorbell rang. Jenny looked up at the glass panel in the door and gasped. She quickly wiped down the whiteboard.

'Jenny, what are you doing?' asked Scott.

She put her fingers to her lips, went to answer the door and let the visitor in.

Alex, Melanie and Scott turned to see, and saw a figure standing in the doorway - Charlotte Palmer. She walked into the staff common room and looked around at four pairs of eyes, glued to her. She shrugged and addressed her audience. 'I have a confession to make.'

CHAPTER 27

Four pairs of eyes widened; four pairs of eyebrows arched; four jaws did their best not to drop. Charlotte took a step back, then settled into an armchair.

'It's not what you think.'

'Then what is this confession about, Ms Palmer?' asked Melanie.

'The fact of the matter is, I've not been totally honest with you.' Charlotte glanced at Alex, and then at Jenny and Scott. 'Alex, who are these people?'

'They are my colleagues. We work as a team, Charlotte. If you have something to say, you can say it to all of us.'

She thought about that for a moment. Melanie watched a series of expressions cross Charlotte's face as she considered her situation. She was hoping to catch Alex, alone, she thought, hoping to charm him into believing her. Now she's not sure what to do.

Finally, she seemed to come to a decision. She exhaled a long breath and shrugged. 'Very well. I don't suppose it matters who is listening.'

Jenny slipped over to her desk and retrieved a notebook and pen. She sat back down and prepared to take notes. Charlotte eyed her warily and went on.

'I think I should start with Steve. You probably have the impression I have some sort of power over him, and in a way I do. But it's not as simple as that.'

She stood up. 'Sorry, sitting in that armchair makes me feel like I'm in group therapy. Where was I?'

'Steve Mortimer,' said Melanie.

'Yes, Steve. As you know, we are distant cousins, so this really shouldn't have happened really. About a year ago, we had a party celebrating our graduation and mostly members of the family attended. We all had a fantastic time. I was drunker than Steve. We had a fling. I felt disgusted and it was very embarrassing. On the other hand, Steve had become rather...... devoted.'

'So, you used Steve's devotion to manipulate him into doing stuff for you,' said Melanie, distaste was obvious on her face.

'Not at all, it wasn't like that. Not at first, at least. Steve came to me. He knew about my feelings for Ashley, and how I felt about Amanda. He said he would help me to get Ashley back. Then, he came up with a scheme: he would make friends with Ashley. They already got on well and talked about football all the time, apparently.

'He also said he could worm his way into Amanda's affections. Steve has a rather overblown idea of his effect on women, I think.'

'And you just went along with it,' Alex said, his voice dripping with incredulity.

'At first, yes. But then it seemed like he was getting somewhere. He and Ashley were best buddies, and he'd even been out on a date with Amanda. I fed him some lines to try and push Ashley and Amanda apart, you know, little hints about things they'd said about each other to him. Steve was only too keen to do things for me. Then, the whole scene changed.'

'Why?' asked Scott. 'What happened?'

'Steve came to see me. He told me he had fallen in love with Amanda. I suppose if we were talking professional football, he was asking for a transfer.'

Scott chuckled at that. Charlotte glared at him.

'From then on, Steve was working the scheme for his own ends. I don't think he got anywhere, at least not with Amanda. I may not have liked her, but I have to admit she had good taste in men.'

'You mean Ashley,' said Alex.

'Yes, I mean Ashley,' she snapped.

'So, do you think Steve had anything to do with Amanda's death?' asked Melanie.

'Steve?' Charlotte gave a curt, cursory laugh. 'God no. He's too much of a wimp for murder. If she'd been bored to death, I'd say he was a contender, but otherwise I can't see it.'

Jenny scribbled furiously, her neat shorthand hardly keeping up, she felt like she was copying a novel first-hand.

'Is that what you came to tell us, Charlotte? Only, I have a feeling there is more.' Alex did his best to sound friendly, or at least non-committal, but he didn't trust her an inch.

'I'm afraid, there's more. It's about what happened to you in Paris, Alex. I was, partly at least, responsible for that. I'm sorry.'

'Tell me about that.'

'It's a long story.'

'A story that involves Hugo Zelov,' said Melanie.

'Yes. A couple of years ago, I spent some time in Marseille, in our apartment there. It was the first time I'd been there on my own. I was excited to have the city to myself, no parents keeping an eye on me. I suppose I went a bit wild.'

'And that's where you met Hugo?'

'Not directly, and not at first. I went to a nightclub in the port area, la Joliette. The manager, André, sort of took me under his wing. He sourced some drugs for me, and we had a good time together.

'Anyway, it turned out that André was Hugo's nephew. He introduced us once. Hugo is a perfectly horrible man, but he seemed to take a shine to me. When Steve told me you were going to Paris to talk to Jeremy, I called Hugo and asked him to warn you off.

'I had no idea he was going to set some thugs on you. That was way more than I'd asked for. As I say, I'm sorry.'

She took a tissue from her bag and wiped her eyes. When she put the tissue back, it was still dry. Jenny made a note of that too.

'Why did you want to keep me away from Jeremy, Charlotte? I don't see what was in it for you.' Alex was genuinely puzzled now.

'I've always felt rather protective towards Jeremy. I've had a... soft spot for him since we met. I think he's autistic, actually. That's why he struggles socially. I was worried that if you put him under pressure, he might do something stupid.'

'You mean, like confess to killing Amanda?' Melanie asked.

Charlotte's answer took them all aback. 'Yes.' She paused for a few seconds.

'I'm not saying he killed Amanda. I have no idea who killed her. But he might have confessed to it, if he thought that's what you wanted. He is very pliable, poor thing.'

'You make him sound like a puppet, ready to use,' said Melanie. 'Perhaps you used him too, Ms Palmer.'

'It's not as simple as that. He's pliable and he's unpredictable too. He might have confessed, but he might have taken it badly, and attacked you. I think he's capable of that. In a way, getting Hugo to warn you off was a way of protecting you, Alex.'

Alex was impressed at her sheer gall. 'Let me get this straight. You called a notorious gang boss in Marseille and asked him to push me out of Paris purely for my own good?'

'In a way, but Jeremy was my main concern. He always has been.'

Scott had been quiet for a while, observing. 'When was the last time you were in Paris, Ms Palmer?'

She thought for a moment before answering. 'I suppose it must be about a year. I love Paris, but I don't often get the chance to go there.'

'That's curious. We have a reliable witness who can place you in Paris just a couple of weeks before the murder of Amanda Hamilton.'

Charlotte sat down again, heavily. She wasn't expecting that, thought Melanie.

'I… I went to see André?'

'Was that an answer or a question?' asked Scott, mildly amused.

Charlotte glared at him, silent. She could see they knew something. She tried to stall until one of them told her what it was. It didn't work. Alex and co. sat and watched her, waiting.

'Well, you obviously know already. I went to see Jeremy.' Her lips pursed into a thin line. This wasn't what she'd anticipated when she'd come here, not by a long chalk.

'Why?' Alex asked the question, but she could see it in all their faces.

'He asked me to.' Wheels went round in Charlotte's head, if someone had seen her with him… 'He said he had something for me.'

'What did he give you, Ms Palmer?' Melanie's expression had hardened, she was getting fed up with Charlotte's lies.

'There's… something you need to know first. The shop where Jeremy works, Hugo has something going on there, obviously not something legal.' She looked around at the four faces. 'Oh. You know that too.'

She was floundering now, not quite out of control, but close. 'André sent a little present for me. This is going to get Jeremy into trouble, isn't it?'

'Let us be the judges of that, Ms Palmer.'

'It was a package of drugs. Jeremy gave it to me, in the Jardin des Tuileries.'

'You're lying, Ms Palmer.'

'Prove it!' She locked eyes with Melanie, two strong women, facing off. Charlotte dropped her eyes first, and Alex broke the silence.

'On the subject of places you've been seen recently, you were at Amanda's place on the day of her death. There is camera footage to prove it.'

'That's…' She stopped herself just in time. 'Yes, I was there. I went to see if we could make up. I promised myself that, if we couldn't, I'd leave her be, her and Ashley.' Her voice caught when she said his name.

'I took a bottle of Prosecco, a rather nice and expensive one. But within five minutes we were hissing at each other like a pair of fishwives. I left in a hurry. I can't have been there more than twenty minutes. I wish I'd taken the bottle with me, such a waste.'

'Your parents told me you were with them at the time, having lunch. They lied, too.'

'They covered for me, but I went there straight from Amanda's place. Look, I didn't kill her. As far as I'm concerned, she killed herself. I've been beating myself up, thinking I might have caused her to do it. But I didn't murder her.'

She stood again, tried to regain her composure. 'I've said all I wanted to say. More than that, I've told you the truth.'

'Some of the time, perhaps. We'll be talking again, Ms Palmer, very soon.'

Melanie resisted the urge to arrest her on the spot and see what happened. She knew the evidence on its way from Paris would firm things up, one way or another. That and the footage from Arthur's camera.

Charlotte picked up her bag and went to the door. 'I think you should leave Jeremy alone. There's no telling what he might do if you push him. He's not totally in control of his own actions.' With that, she was gone.

'It's her,' said Melanie. 'I swear it's her.'

'We'll know soon enough,' said Alex. 'In the meantime, I think we need to talk to Gerard. Jenny?'

**

Gerard sat in front of Philippe's laptop. He listened as Alex recounted the new evidence they had uncovered, occasionally asking a question about some small detail. When Alex had finished, he leaned his chin on his hands and thought for a few moments.

'It seems that we have reached an impasse, my friends. You are sure in your minds that either Jeremy or Charlotte

– or both – are guilty of murder. I think you are right. All the circumstantial evidence leads to this conclusion. But until we have firm forensic evidence linking one or other of them to the actual murder scene, we cannot act.'

'That's it in a nutshell, Gerard,' said Melanie. 'However, at this point we must also assume that Jeremy and Charlotte are aware of what we know.'

'Some of what we know. I think you managed to confront Charlotte without giving everything away. That was sensible.'

'Yes, but we told her enough,' said Alex. 'Enough for her to perhaps talk to Jeremy and warn him that we are getting close.'

'Ah, yes, and this is why you are talking to me.' Gerard smiled. 'You want me to make sure that Jeremy does not fly the coop, or do something extreme, as Charlotte intimated.'

'Exactly.'

'Well, on the first count, we are already in place. Two of my guys have their eyes on him twenty-four seven. Habib and Jean-Luc are my best guys when it comes to surveillance, and I do not think he will escape their eagle eyes.' Gerard allowed himself a little chuckle.

His London audience looked on, wondering.

'Oh, don't mind me. I was just thinking that Habib and Jean-Luc are also two of the messiest individuals I know. Somewhere, in an alleyway around Jeremy's home, there is a growing pile of abandoned baguette wrappers and takeaway coffee cups. It is a little environmental tragedy, really, but I suppose it is all for a greater cause.'

'You are watching him at home and work?' asked Scott.

'He is not working,' said Gerard. 'He has taken some time off. I have a little worry about this.'

'What's the problem?' Alex didn't quite get where Gerard was going with this.

'I wonder if our Jeremy is trying to get in touch with Hugo, to warn him of our increased interest in his gem business.'

'Are you also watching *Boutique Bijou*?'

'Yes, but our resources are limited. For instance, we can watch the shop, but when the goldsmith and his friend, the gem techie leave, we don't really have enough eyes to follow them.'

'We are all in the same position,' said Melanie. 'We know what's happening, but until we can prove it, our suspects have some room to manoeuvre.'

'This is the state of play, yes. We are at the endgame, but we are not able to take out the final pawns. Checkmate is still an aspiration.'

'Gerard, have you had any luck with phone surveillance?' Jenny asked. 'It would be really useful to know if Charlotte and Jeremy are in touch.'

'Not yet. I hope we may get somewhere tomorrow. But from what you tell me, I do not think they will communicate in the next few days.'

'What makes you say that?'

'It sounds as if they are both trying to implicate each other. It's strange. It's as if each of them is guilty of murder and yet each wants to place the blame on the other. Charlotte's performance today was, I think, a limited hangout.'

Melanie, Scott and Jenny nodded sagely. Alex looked clueless. 'Is someone going to tell me what you are talking about?'

Gerard smiled. 'Cousin, you need to get out more,

especially to the movies, I think. A limited hangout is a partial confession or admission that is designed to hide the essential truth. It was invented by the CIA to cover their illegal actions in the sixties and seventies.'

Alex got it. 'Then Charlotte is not the only one. Jeremy did the same thing, didn't he?' He paused and thought. 'It is possible they were never actually working together.'

That set everyone thinking.

Alex chuckled grimly. 'So perhaps they both intended to kill Amanda, independently, and we have to work out who won the race.'

CHAPTER 28

Friday dawned, sunny but breezy. The rain had washed the heat out of the city, and now summer felt more like spring. On the previous evening, their early finish had turned into a late night at the office, accompanied by takeaway curry, beer and wine. In the morning, he went through his morning exercise routine. After that, he shaved and showered. Then, he had his usual breakfast. He dressed in a beige chino trousers, an open-necked shirt and a sports linen jacket. He wanted to keep Steve as comfortable as possible and looking informal might help.

The office was quiet when he arrived. Scott and Jenny were catching up on paperwork from their other cases. Alex couldn't think of anything they needed to do on the Hamilton case, except wait: for the results of the analysis and comparison of fingerprints, phone records for Charlotte and Jeremy, and Arthur's camera footage – a waiting game.

Melanie arrived at ten-thirty. She looked fresh as a daisy. Alex wondered how did she do it? 'Right,' he said. 'You two hold the fort, if anything comes up, text me first. I'd prefer if we weren't disturbed by a call while we talk to Steve.'

Melanie drove them to Steve's place, a Victorian

conversion in Shepherd's Bush, with a decent view of the cemetery. It took them a while to find a parking place, and they had a five-minute walk to the house. The breeze had stiffened as the morning wore on. Alex could feel it tugging at his sleeves.

'Looks a bit ominous for the weekend,' he said.

'You got plans, then?'

'I'm meeting Claire. I was hoping the weather would be good enough for a walk.'

Melanie consulted her phone. 'Sunny and breezy with the odd shower, apparently.' She waved the phone at him. 'You're allowed to do this too, you know.'

'Hmm. I suppose I'll get to like technology one day, but it hasn't happened yet. Here we are, number one eight seven.'

Melanie pressed the bell for flat B, and they waited. A few minutes passed. Alex was just going to suggest a cup of tea in a local cafe when the door creaked open. Steve looked a little the worse for wear – how Alex felt. He didn't seem especially pleased to see them.

'You'd better come in, I guess.' He led them upstairs to a small flat on the first floor. The living room was unkempt, a pizza box, which was not quite empty, lay on the table beside a few beer cans, which definitely were. 'I'd have tidied up if I knew I was getting a visit,' said Steve grumpily. Alex got the impression they had woken him up, and that he had slept in the clothes he was wearing.

He looked around the room. The furniture was mostly second-hand but decent, and the carpet was relatively new. There was a fine layer of dust on the surfaces; Steve obviously wasn't a homemaker. Alex noticed a framed photo, lying face down on an otherwise almost empty bookshelf.

'It's not mine, I rent it,' Steve said, noticing the appraisal. 'I'll think about buying somewhere when I qualify. If I qualify.' There was a hint of accusation in his voice. 'There's a good coffee shop across the road, can I get you something?'

'I'll get them,' said Melanie. She had a mental image of Steve hopping on a bus and leaving them to stew in his flat.

Alex tried to make small talk while she was away but Steve wasn't very communicative. He gave up in the end and they sat in silence until the bell rang. 'I'll get it.' Steve ambled off downstairs.

Melanie reappeared with drinks: coffee for her and Steve, tea for Alex. The hot tea perked Alex up, the coffee didn't seem to do anything for Steve's mood.

'So why are you here?' he asked angrily.

'We had a visit from Charlotte,' said Melanie. 'She told us a long story, some of which was about you. We wanted to hear your side.'

'And what did Cousin Charlotte have to say? You don't believe anything she says, do you? I don't; not anymore.'

'We're keeping an open mind. None of you have been exactly honest with us, have you?'

Steve couldn't argue with that. He slouched on an IKEA sofa, the only new piece of furniture in the room apart from the television.

'Charlotte told us that you two had a brief relationship,' said Alex.

That got a reaction. Steve spluttered into his coffee, spraying globules of froth into the air, and onto his trousers. He wiped them away carelessly. 'That's rich. What kind of relationship?' He made air quotes around the word with his free hand.

'She said you'd had a brief fling, after a drunken get-together.'

'Well, that's very romantic,' Steve sneered. 'The only word I recognise from that story is drunk.'

Alex and Melanie waited, sometimes it was best not to respond or prompt. Sure enough, Steve started talking to fill the silence.

'Charlotte told me a story too,' he said. 'Only it wasn't quite as romantic.' He put his coffee down on the table beside the abandoned pizza.

'I went to a party at her place, not long after we'd graduated. I went to Queen Mary University of London – not quite as posh as Bristol. Anyway, I had a few drinks – quite a few, as it happens – and I basically passed out. I don't remember much before I woke up in the bath with a sore head.

'By that time everyone else had gone. Charlotte came and ordered me out of the bath and sent me packing. I kind of forgot about the whole thing, but about a week later, she said we needed to talk. I went to her place again, and she accused me of raping her while we were both very drunk.'

'And did you?' asked Melanie.

'Did I what?'

'Rape her?'

Steve laughed bitterly. 'I was blotto. I couldn't have raped her if she'd come and straddled me in the bath. And anyway…' Steve's face coloured with embarrassment, maybe humiliation, thought Alex.

They waited, again, for him to continue. 'I don't mind telling you that I'm naïve in that department. I couldn't have done anything to her. She is a lying bitch and would lie to have her own way or get someone else to do things for her.'

Melanie wasn't very sympathetic. 'At the time, you had no reason to doubt her,' she said.

'Oh, I doubted her, all right. I've known Charlotte all my life and she's always been a scheming bitch. She's always tried to have things her own way. She gave me the whole works: tears, anger, threats to get the police involved and how her dad knew the senior guys at Brown Legal. I was terrified. I'd just got my trainee seat at BL, and I didn't want to lose it.'

He smiled grimly. 'Doesn't matter now, does it? I reckon they'll drop me like a hot brick. This forced leave thing was just a Dear John letter with a delay switch.'

'So, what happened then, Steve?' Alex asked.

'She explained that I was going to do a few things for her – our little arrangement, she called it. I'd met Ashley and Amanda, by this point, but I didn't know them that well. Charlotte told me to get in with them: make friends with Ashley and make eyes at Amanda.

'It wasn't difficult. Ashley and I had a shared interest in football and making eyes at Amanda was no hardship. Not that she was interested. The thing is… I knew there would be more. Charlotte wasn't ordering me to do something like that for the hell of it.'

'Did she ask you to spy on them?'

'You could say that. She wanted to hear what they said and did, that's for sure. But then she started feeding me little things she wanted me to say. She was trying to drive a wedge between them, and I was the thin end; or maybe the thick end, now I look back at it.' His laugh was humourless.

Alex stood suddenly and went to the bookshelf. He picked up the photo frame and turned it over: Amanda, smiling, on the pavement outside Brown Legal. The photo was slightly tilted in the frame, as if it had been taken out and put back in again, carelessly, or in a hurry.

'Was this the photo you showed Ulrika?'

'Yeah. I snapped it on my phone one day. I don't think she noticed.'

'Is that the only reason you went to see Ulrika?'

'Yes. A friend of mine told me about Ulrika. You know…. She could be somebody else. So, I asked her to be Amanda because I wanted to see her.

'I didn't go for the other thing. She still charged me the full fee.'

Alex put the photo back on the shelf, face up this time. 'Steve, did you tell Charlotte that I was going to Paris, as part of the investigation?'

'Probably. I told her everything I heard from Ash.'

'And did Ulrika make a call for you – for her – to warn someone about me?'

'No. What makes you ask that?'

'You've got form there, Steve,' said Melanie.

'Fair enough. But I didn't call Paris and neither did Ulrika. I mean, who would we call?'

'Hugo Zelov?'

Steve looked blank. 'Who's he?'

Alex observed him. Steve was telling the truth. He was sure of it. The man was such a bad liar he would have given it away if he knew Hugo, or even knew of him.

'Steve, what you've told us about Charlotte and the rape claim amounts to blackmail.'

'Yeah, it could be interpreted that way. But she's slippery, and her old man has his fingers in all the best pies. I'd never be able to make it stick.'

'But would you be prepared to make a formal statement,

giving your side of the story? It would be very helpful to us.'
Melanie sounded more sympathetic now. She didn't like
Steve, that was clear. But it was obvious he had been played:
for all his lies, he was the victim here.

'Yeah, why not? I don't have much to lose at this point,
do I?'

That made Alex thinks. If Jeremy really had given
Charlotte a package of cyanide, then Steve might have a lot
more to lose than he realised.

'I think you should avoid contact with Charlotte for
now, Steve,' Alex said.

'Trust me, that won't be a problem. If I never see her
again, I won't lose a minute's sleep over it.'

'I'm serious, Steve. I think it's possible that Charlotte
might try to harm you.

'She's very angry, and she knows we're on her case. She
has some reason to blame you for that.'

'You don't think she'd do anything to me, though, do
you?' Realisation dawned on his face. 'My god,' he said. 'You
think she murdered Amanda.'

'I didn't say that. Don't jump to conclusions. But if I
were you, I'd be wary of her just now.'

Melanie was less circumspect. 'What do you think,
Steve? Is she capable of murder?'

'She might be. I don't know. I think she'd be more
likely to get some poor sod to do it for her. She's officer class,
Charlotte. She wouldn't soil her boots if she could get
someone else to traipse through the mud.'

He leaned forwards, elbows on knees, thinking. 'On the
other hand, if push came to shove, I don't think she'd be
squeamish about it.'

He looked at Alex. 'Thanks for the advice, Mr DuPont.

I think I'll take it. My life may be in ruins, but it's still better than what happened to poor Amanda.'

They left him, pondering the past and the future, and walked back to the car. The breeze had calmed, and the sun was making an effort to warm the city. Shepherd's Bush high Street was alive with shoppers and traders, a hubbub of friendly noise.

'I'm tempted to lift her just to be on the safe side,' said Melanie. 'If she really is out for revenge, we can't protect Steve.'

'I don't think Steve is her top priority just now. She knows we weren't convinced by her performance yesterday. I think Charlotte is busy looking for a way out.'

'It would be ironic, wouldn't it, if she topped herself with cyanide.'

'I think some people would see it as poetic justice.'

**

Jenny looked up from her PC when he got back to the Agency. 'Your dad phoned. He'd like you to call him back. Says it's important.'

'Thanks, Jenny. I'll ring him now.' Alex didn't sound too enthusiastic.

He settled at this desk, preparing himself to make the call, when there was a tap at the door. Jenny came in with a tuna sweetcorn sandwich. 'Have your sandwich first, I expect he can wait a few minutes.'

He was grateful for the food and the pause. His dad couldn't, essentially, order him about, he was a grown-up now, and Robert understood that. But he had a way of putting pressure on him, indirectly, usually by talking about his mum. It was sneaky, but it worked.

'Hello, Dad. I hear you called. What can I do for you?'

'Ah, Alex, how are you? How is the case going?'

Alex was surprised. His dad didn't usually take much of an interest in his cases. 'We're getting there. I have a feeling it will all be settled early next week.'

'So, you have got your man, eh? Or is it your woman?' His dad sounded amused at his own joke.

'Dad, you don't usually get excited about my work here. What's up?'

'Oh yes, I bumped into an old acquaintance yesterday, at a reception for Anglo-French trade associations. Strictly speaking, it's not my business anymore, I'm retired, but I like to go along occasionally and chat to a few old friends and enemies.'

'And who was this old friend?'

'Acquaintance only, Walter Coburn, senior partner at Brown Legal, the law firm. He had a lot of good things to say about you, and about the case you are investigating. He gave me the impression you are working for him.'

'In a manner of speaking. I didn't know you knew Walter.'

'I don't know him that well, but I've seen him at a few different conferences and so on. He is a proper bigwig, I think.'

'Yes, he is.'

'He said I should be proud of you and that you've found your feet in a new world. More importantly, you've made a real success of it. I could only agree. I told him I am proud of you whatever you do.'

That was typical of him, thought Alex. When he had a criticism to make, he was blunt about it. But when he wanted to praise someone, it was indirect and vague. Still, he wasn't knocking it.

'Finally, I'm in your good books, huh? Does this mean you won't be sending Uncle Guillaume any more Arab brochures?'

'I didn't…' His dad subsided into silence. He'd been found out. 'I will tell Guillaume that I fully support you in what you are doing. I'm sure he's capable of finding his own Arab brochures.'

Immediately, he called both Jenny and Scott into his office. He was over the moon and smiling broadly. 'My parents have given me their blessings to continue with my business.'

Jenny was really pleased to hear his long overdue news. 'I'm delighted for you. Now you can relax and enjoy your life.'

Scott added. 'I fully endorse what Jenny has said. You can be more positive about your future. Wonderful news, Alex.'

CHAPTER 29

There was a fine summer mist over London on Saturday morning, but the sun had already begun to burn it away by the time Alex had completed his exercises. He then went for his five-mile run in Hyde Park and had a shower. He had time for a continental breakfast at his favourite café close by, poring over the newspapers. He didn't use his phone for newsfeeds, and he rarely went to online news sites. There was a real pleasure in the feel of a newspaper between his fingers.

After he returned, he surveyed the apartment and decided he could get away without serious domestic work. He tidied up a few loose items, emptied the bins and left it at that. He dressed in his blue chino trousers and a pale blue polo shirt and took the Tube to St James Park to meet Claire.

'Very nice to see you,' he said. He kissed her on both cheeks. 'Shall we walk a bit?'

'Yes, if you want to.' She took his arm and smiled. She had the kind of smile that made the world a warmer place. 'I've brought some food for the pelicans, if the pigeons don't get to it first.'

They wandered for a while without any clear sense of direction, talking about nothing. Claire was a chartered accountant working in the City. Although in some quarters, accountants were seen as boring people, she had a lot of interesting stories about eccentric colleagues to tell Alex which made him laugh. As it happened, he had heard these tales before. All the same, he joined in the fun.

The park was mercifully quiet for a summer weekend; the stiff breeze and falling temperatures had sent most of the tourists scurrying to the museums. Alex got the feeling they were among Londoners, reclaiming their space for a brief time. He had never been much of a tourist, so the hordes of people who invaded London at all times of the year, left him bemused.

He was enjoying himself, he realised with a little start. Then an ominous feeling began to creep up his spine. He ought to talk to her, seriously about their relationship. It was only what she deserved. He tried to put the thought away, but it kept coming back to nibble at his enjoyment, like a pigeon stealing food from a pelican.

They were at the water's edge, near the Blue Bridge. 'Come on,' said Claire. 'Let's cross the bridge and get on the right side of the pelicans.'

They stepped onto the bridge and began to cross. Up ahead, Alex saw a familiar figure. Claire tugged at his arm. 'Isn't that your policewoman friend, Melanie?'

'Yes, it is.' His heart sank.

Melanie was not alone. A few steps behind her, he could see Martin, struggling to keep up. Melanie saw him and waved. He stopped, halfway across, unsure whether to go on or wait where he was.

They met in the middle of the stretch and exchanged awkward greetings.

'What brings you to the park?' asked Claire, smiling.

'We're sort of on our way to Oxford Street,' said Melanie. 'I need to get a new suit for work, and I thought we could take the scenic route.'

Martin ambled up, blinking. He wasn't happy to see Alex. The feeling was mutual. 'Alex, were you lying in wait for us?'

Claire laughed. 'It's my fault,' she said. 'I was dragging Alex along to see the pelicans. You're not supposed to feed them, but I have some dried fish in my bag, very hush hush.'

'Shall we get a coffee?' said Melanie.

'Why not?' said Claire. 'Let's not go to the café, though. We can get takeaways and sit out somewhere. I've got goose bumps from the breeze already but I'm not ready to give in yet.'

The two women exchanged shy smiles. They all turned and walked back the way Alex and Claire had come, Melanie and Claire chatting, Alex and Martin walking along in silence.

'I'll get the drinks,' said Claire. 'Martin, why don't you come and carry some for me? I have a feeling these two may want to talk shop.' She winked at Alex and moved off, Martin reluctantly following.

Left alone, they found they had very little to say. Alex kicked at a stone by his foot, trying to think of something witty. Melanie watched him, a wry smile on her lips. 'Was I interrupting something?'

'No. We're just walking around, chatting and enjoying the surrounding.'

'Have you discussed …. with her, your situation?'

'We only arrived a few minutes ago, I haven't had the chance to say anything to her.'

He looked at the ground, at the scuff mark on his shoe,

anywhere but at Melanie. He looked away, to where Claire was leading Martin by the hand.

'I must say, she is very beautiful and has a pleasant personality.'

'I know.'

Melanie thought that was probably the reason Alex was finding it difficult to end his relationship with Claire. Also, maybe he realised that he was still in love with her. But Melanie had her own problems. How would she cope with Martin? Not easy to end her relationship with him. She felt she did not love him enough to have a lasting relationship, but she cared about him.

**

It was near four when he got back to the apartment. Claire had left him in the park, after their encounter. She told him she'd had to go home early. She'd be in touch, and her smile held a sad promise that he couldn't shake out of his mind.

He wondered if it was *a farewell smile*. He knew Claire wasn't pleased to see him spending so much of his time with such a beautiful woman like Melanie.

His phone buzzed, Gerard. 'Hello,' he said wearily.

'Ah, cousin, I have caught you at a bad time, eh?'

'Not your fault, Gerard. What's up?'

'Not good news, I'm afraid. I think Hugo and his friends are onto us. The goldsmith and his gem recycling mate didn't turn up for work this morning. I sent a couple of people round to their homes and they weren't there. Then I went to the shop and spoke to the manager. He let me take a look around in the back, and it appears that a few things have gone missing, most likely a few incriminating things.'

'That's tough luck, Gerard. I'm sorry.'

'Well, that's how things go in this job. One day you are right on track, the next day the bad guys are in the wind. But it may be good news for you.'

'What do you mean?'

'We finally got the go-ahead for a phone tap on Jeremy this morning. It came a bit too late for us, I'm afraid. Philippe looked through the call log and found that he made a call to Marseille late last night. I didn't have the manpower to watch the shop all night, and there didn't seem much point when it was closed and no one was there.'

'So, you think the gem guys came back late at night and cleaned up?'

'I'm pretty certain that's what happened. Acting on a tip-off from our friend Jeremy.'

'Alright, tell me about the good news?'

'The good news is that Jeremy is now a person of interest for us. My bosses are not pleased that this little operation sneaked out from under our noses. They want me to keep tabs on Jeremy over the weekend and pull him in on Monday.'

'That means, by the time we get the forensics and camera footage, you will have him in custody. That's convenient.'

'Yes, unless he tries to fly the coop before then. I'm going to join Habib and Jean-Luc on surveillance. It will add to the baguette heap but that can't be helped.'

'Is there anything I can do from this end?'

'I don't think so. If anything changes, I'll be in touch.' He rang off.

Alex went to the window and looked out over Hyde Park. He wondered if he should call Melanie to get someone to keep an eye on Charlotte. But Melanie had looked like she was enjoying her weekend, and he didn't want to spoil it for her.

He felt as if he had blundered with Claire, somehow.

He didn't know how, but he had the rest of the weekend to fret about it.

**

Jeremy walked around the apartment, on tenterhooks. He'd made the call, but he had no idea if Hugo had taken the advice. If he called back, grateful, he could ask him for help, if not, he was on his own. He didn't like the idea of running – he liked his life in Paris – but by now Charlotte would almost certainly have implicated him in Amanda's death, despite her saying she was on his side, he didn't trust her at all.

He felt aggrieved. He'd done what she'd asked and given her the cyanide. It was a risk, stealing poison from gangsters, and she didn't seem to appreciate that. Now she was back in London, safe, plotting.

Aunt Katherine was avoiding him. He wondered if she knew something and wasn't telling him. She had said some strange things about the red-haired girl, he hadn't realised that he'd been staring at her, but after that meeting with Charlotte in the Tuileries, it wasn't a surprise.

What was Charlotte up to? It suddenly occurred to him that she might have called Hugo too. That wasn't good news for him. There was nothing for it, he would just have to wait and see – and he really wasn't very good at that.

**

Alex hadn't slept all that well. Claire, Charlotte, Jeremy and Melanie had swirled around in his dreams, all asking awkward questions. In the morning, he checked his phone again, for the umpteenth time that weekend: nothing.

He decided to go for his five-mile run in the park. He left his phone at home unwittingly. Anyway, he thought that was not a bad thing at all: he could have a rest from checking his phone and concentrate on his run.

Still no calls, no texts. Although it was Sunday, he decided to stay in, read newspapers and watch TV. The afternoon dragged on. No contacts and no messages.

**

The call came at three o'clock. He was waiting for it, hoping for it, but it still made him jump. He took a deep breath and picked it up. 'Hello?'

The voice on the other end was guttural and gruff, the accent rough Marseille, with an undercurrent of something else, some eastern European maybe.

'I owe you my thanks. After we cleared out the shop, I sent some of my boys to keep an eye out. There are police everywhere now.'

'I'm glad it worked out.'

'So, Monsieur Higgins, you mentioned a favour. What can I do for you?'

'I need to get out of Paris for a while. Quietly. Can you help?'

'Give me some time and I'll sort something out. Be ready to go when I call.' The line went dead.

**

The phone rang – at last. Gerard again. 'Something is happening; Jeremy received a call from Hugo. I've sent for a little backup in case it gets lively.'

'I wish there was something I could do.'

'Actually, there is. If we bring him in, we ought to have someone from London here when we question him, from the police, I mean. Can you call Melanie and get her to arrange it?'

'It probably won't be until the first thing on Monday morning, Gerard. I don't think the Met works that fast.'

'Well, see what you can do. I must go now; we're trying to keep a low profile.'

Alex called Melanie and updated her.

**

The phone rang again, same gruff voice, same rough accent. 'At midnight, a black Mercedes saloon will pull up at the end of the street. The driver will get out and light a cigarette. You will walk up to him and say the word "Joliette". Once he's sure it's you, you are away.'

'It's a bit cloak and dagger, isn't it?'

'What, you would prefer if we turned up with balloons and party hats?'

'No, of course not. Sorry.'

'Midnight. Be there.'

**

Alex woke up with a start. He looked at the clock: nearly midnight. His dream had been a moving tableau of faces. Amanda: first, the smiling, beautiful young woman from the photo Steve had surreptitiously taken, and then used as a fetish, then the awful rictus of her last moments.

Claire: the knowing wink as she took Martin off to get drinks, a sad smile that he couldn't recall seeing in real life.

Melanie: her face tilted up towards his, their lips almost brushing, her scornful expression in the park.

He checked his phone again: no calls, no texts. He lay back down again, and was soon fast asleep.

**

At the same time in Paris, Gerard swung into action. 'Ah,

Jeremy, the urge to travel was too strong to resist, eh?'

He knew that voice: Bouchard. The inspector stepped out from a shadowy recess beside the entrance, placed a sizeable hand on his shoulder.

'And where were you planning to go, Jeremy? I hear Marseille is nice at this time of year; quiet and safe.' He slipped the rucksack from Jeremy's grasp, put it over his own shoulder.

Jeremy said nothing. He considered breaking free, making a run for it. But two burly figures appeared under the streetlight in front of the block, as if from nowhere.

'In fact, there is nowhere to go, Jeremy. Nowhere else to go, at least. I think you know what I mean. Jean-Luc, Habib; take our guest to the car.' He smiled, a feline smile. 'Take a few hours rest, Jeremy, and then we will talk. I think we have a lot to talk about, eh?'

At the end of the street, a figure in a dark hoodie threw away his cigarette, got into a black Mercedes saloon and drove away.

CHAPTER 30

Alex hadn't realised he'd been sleeping until the phone woke him up. Light filtered into the bedroom from the edges of the curtains, strong sunlight. He sat bolt upright, grabbed the phone, looked at the clock: seven-thirty.

'The DI's cleared me to go to Paris. I should be there around noon.' Melanie sounded fresh and eager. 'I'm looking forward to meeting Gerard in person, less so to meeting Jeremy, but let's see how that goes.'

'OK. I need to wait for the call from Arthur on the footage. What else do we need to do?'

'Well, Richard and I were planning on pulling Charlotte in this morning. Now he thinks we should wait for a while, see what we get from the prints and the camera. In the meantime, we've put her under surveillance, in case she does a runner – or "flies the coop" as Gerard would say.'

'Good. I'm glad surveillance has been organised for Charlotte. I think you two are going to get on like a house on fire. I'll keep you posted on the footage, I expect Richard will do the same with the prints. And if Philippe comes up with anything useful from Jeremy's phone, he'll let us both know.' Alex could feel the blood rushing through his veins, this was it, the final sprint.

'It all comes down to the forensics. If it puts Jeremy in the frame, I'll arrest him in Paris. If it's Charlotte, Richard will arrest her. It looks like we've got a result either way. You've done it again, Alex, if you hadn't stepped in, we'd still be none the wiser.'

Alex felt the glow of pride, but he suppressed it, for now. 'Let's see what happens through the day. Anyway, I've some excellent news to share with you: my parents have given me their full support to carry on with my new career.'

'That's marvellous news, Alex. I'm very pleased for you.'

'Thanks. I hope you have a successful outcome in Paris.'

Melanie rang off and Alex jumped out of bed and did the usual things in the morning. He dressed up in his blue striped suit, blue shirt and fuchsia tie and headed for the Agency. There was a lot to do, even if it still felt like most of it was waiting.

**

Gerard finally gave up after two hours. Jeremy had said nothing, not a word. The young Englishman had sat, serene and utterly silent, through a barrage of questions. Gerard had begun to worry if he had become catatonic. It was time for a break, they both needed it, Gerard maybe more than Jeremy. He went out and bought a coffee from a kiosk outside. If he drank any more of the awful stuff that came out of the machine in the station he would explode.

Paris was shimmering in the dry heat. Across the street, the little park in front of the church was an arid vista, grass gone brown in the sun and flowers hanging on by a dry thread. There was a taste of dust in the air. He stifled a yawn, and went back inside. 'I think Jeremy slept better than I did,' he muttered as he passed the desk. The desk sergeant looked at him, with puzzlement on her face.

'Ah, I was speaking English, right?' he said, in English. 'Oh, never mind.'

The interview rooms were located in an above-ground basement at the rear of the station. Gerard looked through the observation panel. Sunlight filtered into the room from the small windows set high in the room's walls, one beam bathed Jeremy in its golden glow, giving him an unexpected halo.

'Well, Saint Jeremy,' said Gerard, looking at the figure bathed in gold, still as a statue. 'It seems the gods are on your side, for now. Let's see if the glow of sanctity fades as the evidence mounts.'

Gerard put his takeaway coffee cup on the table. Jeremy's eyes flicked towards it, just for a second, and his tongue traced a thirsty line along his upper lip, then his face settled, and his gaze returned to the surface of the table in front of him.

'I can get you a coffee, if you like. It won't take a moment.' Again, a momentary flicker of… something.

'I get that, you don't want to say anything yet. I get that you are silent; but you don't have to suffer in silence, as the English say.'

'Black, one sugar.' Jeremy's eyes met Gerard's, briefly, when he spoke.

Gerard looked up at the observation camera and gave a brief nod. 'It won't be a moment,' he said, resting his elbows on the table, his chin on his clasped hands, the ghost of a smile on his face. 'So, we have established that you have not been struck dumb since we last spoke. That's good. That's progress.'

Again, Jeremy's eyes momentarily met his. Gerard

thought he'd caught a flicker of a smile. He let the moment last.

Aubert bustled in with the coffee. He placed the cup on the table, exactly halfway between the two men, as if he wasn't sure who to give it to.

'It's for Monsieur Higgins, Aubert. Don't be shy, man.' Aubert slid the coffee towards Jeremy, looked at his boss, one eyebrow arched. Then he turned and left the room. Jeremy removed the lid off the cup and took a sip. 'Mm. Good.'

'Perhaps you are ready to talk now?'

'About coffee, yes. About anything else, no.'

**

Jenny was looking into Eurostar and tried to establish how easy it was to travel unnoticed. There were passenger lists of a sort, if you knew the right database to sneak into: Jenny did. But she had no luck on the days she was interested in.

'There are a couple of obvious loopholes in the system,' she explained. 'The database captures people who pay with credit or debit card. But if you pay by cash, you're invisible.'

'Not to the security cameras,' said Scott.

'No, but I can't hack into those. We'll have to leave that to the police.' She mused for a moment, the end of a biro tapping on her lower lip. 'There's another way to stay off the radar.'

'Go on,' said Alex.

'Get someone else to pay for your ticket.' She beamed, like she'd just got the last clue in a crossword puzzle. 'If you think about it, that probably covers both Jeremy and Charlotte.'

'Despite your smile, we're still none the wiser.'

'We know what we don't know, which means we know

what to look for. I'll call one of Melanie's tame plods and get them on the camera thing.'

Alex paced around the main office. He needed something to do, something that wasn't waiting. Scott was relaxing on the sofa. After all his years on surveillance duty, first as a police detective and now as a private one, he was used to waiting and took it all in his stride. Alex wished he had the same patience and composure.

Then the office phone rang. He hurried towards it, but Jenny got there first. 'Mayfair Investigative Agency; how can I help?'

She listened for a moment and held out the phone. 'It's for you, Arthur.'

**

Gerard sat, sharing the silence with Jeremy. The young man had talked about his favourite coffee kiosk, a few blocks from the shop. Then he'd clammed up again.

A uniformed *gendarme* came in. She leaned over his chair and whispered in his ear. 'Ah, excellent.' He stood up and stretched. 'I really must get some sleep soon. A friend has arrived, Jeremy. Excuse me for a few minutes.'

He got to the station entrance just as a squad car pulled up. Melanie Cooper got out of the passenger side. She stood for a moment and adjusted to the shockwave of heat. Gerard hurried over to greet her. 'Melanie, it's good to meet you in person. I trust your journey was pleasant.'

'It was fine, Gerard. Aubert here,' she flicked her thumb over her shoulder at the waiting squad car, 'has been practising his English on me. I think he was a bit disappointed when I changed to French.'

They walked into the station entrance, and the blessing of air-conditioning.

'Wonderful,' she said. 'Tell me about Jeremy. Has he said anything interesting yet?'

'He has recommended a coffee kiosk in Paris: good information, but not quite what we need. Now you are here, we can change the subject. I think he was a bit bored of me talking about Hugo all the time. Would you like some coffee before we start? I'm afraid it's not from Jeremy's favourite place.'

'No, I'm good. Eurostar is basically a mobile snack wagon.'

He led her down to the interview rooms. They paused at the observation panel and Melanie looked at her target, mentally preparing herself. 'Right, well, there's no point in leaving him there thinking up plots on how to lie to us. Let's get to it.'

**

'I've found the two files in question, Alex.' Arthur sounded quietly excited.

'Thank you, Arthur; hopefully this is the last piece of the puzzle. Can you email them to us?'

'Afraid not, old chap. The files are huge, and my email doesn't allow it. Can you pop over?'

Alex was momentarily deflated. He thought about asking Jenny to do something clever. Then he remembered the park and changed his mind. 'Yes, I can do that, Arthur. I'll see you in about an hour.'

He rang off and clapped his hands. 'Scott, we're on. Let's get to Fairfield Crescent and see what the cyber gods have got for us.'

**

Jeremy looked disinterested when Melanie walked into the

room with Gerard. That changed when she spoke in English.

'Jeremy, you remember me, I take it. I have some questions for you regarding the death of Amanda Hamilton. Let's get started, shall we?'

He seemed almost relieved. 'I'm glad you're here. I was expecting Mr DuPont, though.'

'He's rather busy in London. And this is police business now, Jeremy. We are talking about a murder, after all.'

'Yes, I suppose we are. Well, first things first, Ms Cooper. I have something to tell Mr DuPont, if you'd be kind enough to pass it on to him.'

'Let's hear what you have to say, Jeremy. I'll decide if we need to pass it on to Mr DuPont.'

'Ah, a power play. You should have brought in a higher chair, Ms Cooper.'

Melanie didn't answer. She took off her jacket and sat beside Gerard, took out a notepad and pencil, and set them on the table.

Jeremy watched with amused detachment.

The silence went on for several minutes. Finally, Jeremy broke it. 'I think Mr DuPont will want to hear this. He seemed very… concerned.'

'I'm listening, Jeremy.'

He hesitated, as if he's changed his mind. 'I would rather tell him in person, if that's all right.'

'That's not possible, Jeremy. Alex – Mr DuPont – is very busy today. And you don't have much time.'

'I don't understand. It seems to me that I have all the time in the world.'

'There was another camera across the road. Mr DuPont will have the footage today.'

'Ah.' Jeremy appeared deflated a little. He didn't look

unhappy; more like an adventure had come to an end, and he was giving himself permission to rest.

'Then I suppose you will have to do. You need to tell him that I said… That I said this: She told me to do it.'

Just for a moment, the room became a vacuum, as if all the air had been sucked out of it by Jeremy's words. Melanie and Gerard were taken off guard; they sat and stared at him. They were hoping for more, but Jeremy seemed satisfied with his testimony.

'Who told you?'

'Charlotte; Charlotte Palmer. She told me to do it.'

Finally, Gerard spoke. 'She told you to do what, Jeremy?'

Jeremy smiled. 'To slap her, of course.'

Melanie was about to speak and stopped abruptly. She was confused. Then she remembered Alex's question to Jeremy: *Did you slap Charlotte?*

'Yes. Twice, in fact. I didn't slap her hard enough the first time. Then I did. She said thank you. Charlotte is a very weird person.'

His smile was blissful now; his sun-halo had moved on, but he still seemed to shine with an inner light. Melanie looked at Gerard, and her eyes flicked towards the door.

'I need to talk to Inspector Bouchard. We'll be right back.'

CHAPTER 31

'Stick to the main road, Scott,' said Alex.

'Why? We'll save five minutes and about twenty percent of our lung capacity if we go the back double.'

'For Arthur's sake.' Scott looked confused, but he did as Alex asked.

Arthur was waiting for them at the door. 'Come in, gentlemen. I've got everything ready.'

He led them straight to the den. The camera panel was already on full screen. Alex could see the date stamp: Sunday the twenty-first of May. He smiled inwardly, though he felt impatient; Arthur was saving the best bits for later.

'I've already run through this a couple of times. I've paused it just before the part you need to see.'

He clicked the play button and the footage began to roll. Barrington appeared, with a dustpan and brush in his hands. He stopped and looked up as a woman walked up the driveway. Charlotte.

They talked for several minutes. Charlotte was playful, flirtatious. Barrington was too embarrassed to enjoy it properly, but he was doing his best. Finally, she took her leave. She walked back down the driveway and turned to wave; then she moved away to the edge of the frame, her hips swinging seductively.

Barrington was rooted to the spot for a second. Alex wondered if Arthur had hit the pause button by mistake. Eventually, he stirred, shaking his head, and went back towards the corner of the house. The contents of his dustpan spilled onto a flower bed and they watched as he stooped to recover them, every so often looking up and into the distance.

'I've written down the time she arrives and leaves. Your people can go straight to it.'

'Thank you, Arthur. So…'

'I know, Alex, the main event. Here,' He took out the first flash drive and inserted a second; this time the date stamp showed Sunday the fourth of June. 'There are two different things to look at here. I've rolled it on to about one o'clock so you can see the first part. Then I'm afraid we'll have to bugger around a bit – excuse my French – until we get to the other part.'

He clicked play and Charlotte appeared again carrying a posh orange carrier bag; no Barrington this time. She walked up to the door, rang the bell and waited. The image of the door shifted. 'Automatic lock release,' said Scott. Charlotte stepped through the door and disappeared.

'Then we'll fast forward until… Ah, there she is.' Arthur was enjoying himself.

Charlotte came out of the front door and slammed it behind her. Alex could almost hear the sound. She stormed off down the driveway, looked as if she was mumbling to herself and gesticulating in the air without looking back. She did not have the orange carrier bag with her. She was out of shot in a few seconds.

'Now,' said Arthur. 'I know you're interested in visitors later in the afternoon. I checked quickly through the footage yesterday evening. There's a bit of coming and going; it starts about two-thirty. I'll fast forward in between the shots that might interest you.'

Alex was impressed at how adept Arthur was with the PC. 'I should come here and take lessons, Arthur,' he said. 'My colleagues think I'm still stuck in the nineteenth century.'

'To tell you the truth, Alex, I don't like computers much. But if I have to use a tool, I like to think I can use it properly. Right, here we are.'

The time stamp read two-thirty. The door opened and a glamourous woman stepped out. She had extravagant curls of dark hair and a curvaceous figure.

'That must be Imelda,' said Scott. 'I can see why Ashley got a bit tongue-tied.'

Arthur hit fast forward. Most of the time, the screen registered a view of the house, its outlines blurring slightly as if it was moving quickly too. Occasionally a figure passed, at impossible speed, like a surreal marionette with soft edges and jerky limbs.

As the time stamp rolled towards three o'clock, a figure popped onto the left-hand edge of the screen. 'Ah, I think this is it,' said Arthur, and slowed it down. The figure walked towards the house and then walked past it.

'Damn, I thought that was... Ah, here it is.'

Another figure came on from stage left. A man, walking without hurry. He had a small, blue rucksack slung over his left shoulder. Scott and Alex leaned towards the screen, trying to catch a glimpse of his face. No luck: he kept his head down and turned towards the house.

He walked up the driveway, came to the door and rang the bell. Then he leaned down to the bell panel, and there was a brief conversation. The door opened and he stepped in.

Arthur hit fast forward again. Plenty of people passed the house but no one went up the driveway. 'No Imelda,' said Scott. 'Pity.'

Arthur and Alex looked at him, grinning. Scott explained, 'No, I mean, pity she didn't come back when he was there. She might have heard something.'

'Jenny will have a field day with this, Scott. You'll be making tea until Christmas.'

Arthur coughed politely and they turned back to the screen. A figure emerged from the house at impossible speed. 'Sorry,' said Arthur. 'I'll rewind it a bit.'

The house seemed to judder to a halt. The door opened, and a figure emerged at real-world speed. Alex recognised him immediately. 'Bingo!'

They continued to watch. The man had his blue rucksack and was carrying an orange carrier bag.

'He wasn't carrying the orange carrier bag when he went in,' said Scott.

The man crossed the street, towards Arthur's house. He didn't look at the camera; he didn't have to. They could see his face now. He turned right and headed out of view.

'I bet I know where he's heading,' said Alex. 'Scott, take these flash drives and get them to Hammersmith nick, quick as you can. Copy the date and time stamps,' he pointed to Arthur's notepad. 'And get their techies to send the relevant frames to Gerard and Melanie. I'll text them to let them know the stuff is coming.'

'How will you get back?' asked Scott.

'Oh, I'll get a cab; it won't take long.' He turned to Arthur. 'Arthur Middleton, you are a star. I imagine there will be a Crime Stoppers reward for this. But for now, I think we should reward ourselves with a little walk in the park, don't you?'

**

Scott drove straight into the staff car park at Hammersmith and jumped out. He would deal with the complaints later. He hurried up the stairs into reception. A burly man was waiting for him. 'Hello, Scott. Come on. I'll show you where our techies live.'

They hustled through a couple of security barriers. Jenkins was following him. The tech hub was a sea of PCs, and there were laptops perched on desks everywhere. Jenkins shouted at no one in particular. 'Right, who's got two minutes to wrap up a murder case?'

A couple of hands went up. Jenkins headed for the nearest one. 'Surinder, I've got some footage here, and I need you to isolate the best bits and send them to our colleagues in Paris, marked for the attention of Inspector Bouchard and DS Cooper.'

Scott handed Surinder the flash drives and his notes on the date and time stamps. The skinny young man in a scruffy Oasis T-shirt slammed them both into a couple of ports and opened two screens. In what felt like seconds, he'd sent the two files off. 'Anything else, guv?' he asked in a broad Scouse accent.

'No, you can go back to playing Tetris. We're off to forensics.'

He rushed out of the room and Scott hurried to catch up with him. 'So, they've got somewhere with the prints?'

'Oh yes. They've got a fairly conclusive match. I can feel an arrest is coming on.' Scott grinned and followed him up the stairs.

**

Alex and Arthur walked down Fairfield Crescent towards the

park. Arthur stopped in his tracks. 'Alex, I don't know how I feel about accepting a reward for this. I'm not really doing it for the money.'

'I know, Arthur, but think of it this way. You could do something good with the money. Maybe, donate it to the park so they can buy some new play equipment for the little ones or you might consider getting a memorial bench in there, for Dorothy.'

Arthur's eyes filmed over with tears. He smiled then and began walking again. 'The bench is a rather nice idea, Alex. I might just do that.'

The park was quiet. Two toddlers clambered around a small climbing frame, watched by their doting mums. Alex and Arthur walked around the perimeter, eyes peeled. Arthur spoke first. 'There. Behind that rhododendron.'

Alex looked where he was pointing. A thick, elderly rhododendron sat surrounded by the remains of its flowers, a carpet of purple petals. Behind its gnarled trunk, he could see the edge of an orange carrier bag.

He snapped on a pair of latex gloves. Arthur smiled. 'Were you a boy scout, Alex?'

'Dib dib dib, Arthur. And no, I wasn't.' He stepped gingerly onto the flowerbed and knelt in front of the old shrub. With a little effort, he teased the carrier bag out from its hiding place.

'Let's see what we've got, then.'

He stepped back onto the grass and opened the bag. Inside he saw a wine bottle – Prosecco – and a mobile phone, the sim card taken out and snapped in half. 'Well, well. I think this about wraps thing up. Arthur, let's get back to your place. I need to call a cab.' Alex thought: *for some time, he had been drawn to the park, probably because, the evidence was hidden behind the rhododendron bush all the time, waiting for his attention.*

**

Melanie was alone in the interview room with Jeremy. Aubert had called Gerard away for something. Jeremy seemed at ease. He was talking now, freely, but it didn't all make sense.

'I think poor aunt Katherine believes she betrayed me. She was so worried about that girl down the street; the one with the red hair. I don't know what got into her. I wasn't obsessed, I was just confused. After that kiss, I didn't quite know what was going on. But I'm over it now. That happens, doesn't it, Ms Cooper? A stray kiss can lead a person down all sorts of blind alleys.'

Melanie's heart skipped a beat. The button he had inadvertently pressed had released a flock of butterflies. She fished around for a suitable reply.

'Charlotte again?'

'Always Charlotte,' he smiled. 'The funny thing is she's not important; not as important as she thinks. I've gone my own way despite her; apart from the slap, of course. Mr DuPont will understand. He *is* important, isn't he, Ms Cooper?'

'Yes, he is.'

She was saved from falling any further down that rabbit hole when Gerard reappeared, a laptop in his grasp. He set it on the table, turned to one side so they could all see the screen. 'I've just received an email from our colleagues in London,' he said. 'A little gift from Alex.'

He clicked an icon on screen and a video panel came on. The front of Amanda's house, on a summer afternoon.

'As we said, there was another camera.'

The three of them watched in silence as the footage played through. At the end, Jeremy sighed; it sounded like relief to Melanie.

'What was in the carrier bag, Jeremy?' As she asked, her phone pinged. She read the text and answered the question for him. 'A wine bottle – Prosecco, and a very expensive one – and the remains of a mobile phone; Amanda's phone. The sim card has been snapped, but our tech people reckon they can retrieve everything from it.'

Gerard folded the laptop. 'Jeremy, we're going to give you a few minutes to think. I'll get someone to bring you another coffee.'

They had hardly left the room when Melanie's phone pinged again. 'They've matched the prints on the glass to the ones you took from him,' she said. 'I'd say we're home and dry, Gerard.'

'I think so, Melanie. Come. Let's get some fresh air before we go back and clear up the final details. I think we deserve it.'

The angle of the afternoon sun cast shadows all the way across the street; it wasn't cool, but it was cooler. Melanie took a series of deep breaths; the air in the interview room had become stultifying, and Jeremy's remarks had got to her. When she felt calmer, she said, 'So what happens now, Gerard? Do you think he's ready to give it all up?'

'Oh yes. I think he will tell us everything. He looked very tranquil when we left. I think it's all over for him now. That's to say, I think it's all history for him; it's gone, and he can tell us the story without pain or guilt. The murderer? That was another person in another place. He wants to be rid of him now.'

'So, we'll take a statement and have done with it?'

'I think we should make – you should make – the formal arrest when we go back. Then we'll let him talk for a while. I think he'll be ready to make a full statement after that.'

Back in the interview room, Gerard sat at the table; Melanie remained standing. Jeremy looked almost noble; he held himself with a kind of pride that she should have found repulsive, but actually it was poignant and impressive.

'Jeremy, there are some formalities we need to get out of the way,' said Gerard. 'Detective Sergeant?'

'Jeremy Higgins, you are under arrest for the murder of Amanda Hamilton, on Sunday the fourth of June, two thousand and six.' She read him his rights, and he sat calmly through the recital.

'Are you ready to tell us what happened?' asked Gerard.

'Yes of course.' He seemed impatient to get on with it. 'You didn't need the fingerprints and the bottle, you know. Once I realised you had the footage, I was ready.'

He flexed his fingers, as if he was about to play a difficult piece on the piano.

'I got the cyanide from the shop storeroom, as you've probably worked out. It's used for cleaning gold, among other things; seemed appropriate.

'I told Amanda I'd be there in the early evening. I arrived early to take her by surprise; and because I thought the camera maintenance people would be finished and the cameras would be back on. I'm not sure how long it took her to die; I stayed until I was sure and then let myself out.'

'Why did you kill her?' asked Melanie.

'Ah, yes. There's the crux of the matter. I wanted her; I'd wanted her from the moment I saw her. When I realised it wasn't going to happen, I decided if I couldn't have her, then no one else could.'

'Did you know that Charlotte had been there?'

'Yes. She went there to deliver the wine. I don't usually drink, so I wouldn't know anything about a decent bottle of wine like Prosecco. I didn't explicitly tell her what it was for but I think she knew. She sent me a lot of texts, you know; I imagine your technical people are looking at them now. They will have fun with that. She wanted me to do it, I know she did. But I didn't do it because she wanted me to.'

'I don't understand,' said Melanie. 'Are you telling us that Charlotte was involved or not?'

He smiled at that, impishly. 'I think you'll have to work that out for yourselves or ask Charlotte. I'm sure she believes she made me do it. But I can't speak for her; I have my own story to tell.'

'Jeremy, I think we should let you do just that,' said Gerard. 'I will send in some officers to take a formal statement from you. Are you ready?'

'Of course. Tell them to bring coffee; this may take a while.'

Melanie and Gerard got up to go. 'Ms Cooper,' he said. She turned back.

'Don't forget to tell Mr DuPont what I told you. I'm not sure it will be part of my statement, but he will want to know.'

**

'He's making a full statement now,' said Melanie. 'Then Gerard is lending me a couple of his people as an escort, and I'll take him back to London.' Alex's phone was on speaker, and they crowded around it. Jenny was trying to take notes but she gave up pretty quickly; it was too exciting to miss.

'So, all that evidence left him no choice,' said Scott. 'He was bang to rights.'

'Hmm. It was funny how that panned out. Gerard brought in the laptop with the video footage; and your text about the bottle arrived as we watched it. Then Jenkins pinged me with the forensics about two seconds later. Turned out we didn't need the half of it; once he'd seen the video, he was ready to confess.'

'He was just waiting for a sign,' said Alex. 'He needed permission from something or someone to tell the story.'

'Yes, it felt that way. Now he's keeping two people busy telling that story.'

'And what about Charlotte?' asked Jenny. 'Is her limited hangout going to blow up in her face?'

'I really don't know.' Melanie's uncertainty was clear in her voice. 'Some of things Jeremy said seem to incriminate her; others sound like he's absolving her. I think we'll have to wait for the full statement, and even then, we'll need evidence to prosecute her.'

'I spoke to DI Jenkins an hour ago,' said Alex. 'I'm meeting him tomorrow morning, and we're going to see her. Whether Jenkins is going to arrest her or not depends on Jeremy's statement and maybe the evidence from his phone.'

'Yes, the phone may help. I've only heard snippets from the tech people here in Paris but it sounds like there's some pretty weird stuff on there. Philippe hinted there was some rather explicit material; I don't quite know what to make of that. He also said that the traffic was very one-sided.'

'Perhaps Jeremy was keeping quiet for his own protection,' said Scott. 'Then if things fell apart – like they have done – he might have been able to make out he was the innocent party.'

'When you say explicit,' said Jenny. 'Do you mean she came right out with it and asked him to kill Amanda?'

'No. I don't think Charlotte is stupid enough to do that, though I could be wrong. I mean some of the texts – they included photos, apparently – were sexually explicit.'

That brought a collective intake of breath. It was a few seconds before anyone spoke.

'So, she was offering herself as an alternative to Amanda, or a prize if he killed her,' said Alex. 'That would explain the strange story that his aunt told me about their meeting in the Jardin des Tuileries.'

'Yes, I think it was something like that. The thing is...' Melanie paused, thinking. 'I don't know if I'm seeing things that aren't there, but I suspect something weird was going on. I think maybe Charlotte was trying to provoke him into doing something terrible to Amanda, but Jeremy acted independently. I wonder if he had been planning to kill the poor girl for a long time, perhaps since university.'

'I believe both Charlotte and Jeremy wanted to see Amanda dead. And I agree Jeremy acted independently. He had a fixation on her. From the very beginning, he realised that Amanda was not interested in him at all. He felt rejected. That meant he would not be able to have her. He decided then that nobody else would have her. Hence, he developed the malicious intent to kill her. Yes, he had been planning to kill Amanda since his university days. He was just biding his time to achieve his goal. On Sunday the fourth of June, he had the opportunity to carry out his deadly plan. According to his aunt Katherine, he had a sad and troubled childhood, deprived of parental love. She said, as a result, he still cannot cope with rejection and reacts badly. In this instance, he ended up killing Amanda.'

'Very interesting indeed. It explains his motive to kill her,' said Melanie.

'Charlotte may have landed herself into trouble for nothing,' said Scott. 'That's kind of ironic.'

'Still richly deserved,' said Alex. 'If it was a kind of karmic accident, it couldn't have happened to a nicer person.'

'Right,' said Melanie. 'I need to go; we're getting ready to ship Jeremy back to London and I need to sort things out with Jean-Luc and Aubert, my escorts. There's one more thing, though. Alex?'

'Yes.'

'Jeremy wanted to tell you something. At first, he said he would only tell you, but in the end he told me so I could tell you. It's about Bristol.'

'Go on.'

'He said to tell you that Charlotte told him to slap her. He said he did so, and she said it wasn't hard enough. Then, he really clattered her; and she thanked him for it. Weird, huh?'

Melanie rang off. Scott, Jenny and Alex looked at each other. 'What's that?' said Scott. 'But I get the feeling we've solved a crime, and it's solved itself, all at the same time.'

'That's mystical garbage, Wallace,' said Jenny. 'If Alex hadn't stepped in, the crime would have gone unsolved.'

'I think I know what Scott means, though,' said Alex. 'I wonder if, in time, Jeremy would have felt the need to confess. I think the person we've arrested, and the one who might have got away with it, is Charlotte.' He got up and headed for his office. 'I think we can knock off for the day,' he said. 'We've still got plenty to do tomorrow. In the meantime, I need to make a call.'

**

Melanie looked up; she had almost finished reading the statement for the second time. The train had emerged from the Eurotunnel and, through the windows, she could see the lights of the coastal terminal.

'Home or not, Jeremy, you'd better get used to it. You're going to be here for a long time.'

His eyes met hers for a brief moment, and then he turned back to gaze out the window. 'I never liked the place; no good memories here. And what have I come back to?'

'Justice, Jeremy. Justice.'

His laugh was short and derisory. 'That's very British of you, Detective Sergeant.'

Jean-Luc woke up from his nap and nudged Aubert. 'Look, we're in England. We should have time for a wander around London before we go back. Maybe, get some fish and chips, eh?'

'English food isn't fit for dogs,' grumbled Aubert. 'I've brought a packed lunch.'

CHAPTER 32

Alex had finished reading Jeremy's statement. He looked over at Jenkins; he'd finished reading the report on the text messages between Charlotte and Jeremy and was drinking tea from an enormous mug. 'Swap you?'

'Go on then. I hope you're not of a nervous disposition, Alex. There's some strong stuff in here.'

'Can't be any worse than Jeremy's blow by blow account of poisoning Amanda; and then watching her die. He has a grisly eye for anatomical detail.'

'Yeah, you could say that of Charlotte too.' Jenkins laughed. 'And while you could accuse her of all sorts – and we will in a bit – being shy is definitely not one of them.'

Melanie came into the DI's office, fresh as a spring breeze. 'Morning, guv, Alex.'

'I don't know how you do it, Melanie. You don't look like you've just crawled out of a long tunnel under the sea.'

'I managed to get a few hours' kip, guv. Plus getting Mr Higgins safely banged up in an English nick took a weight off my mind.'

'And where are your *gendarme* mates?'

'Probably out sightseeing. They've got a few hours

before they go back and they signed off everything they needed to last night.'

'And what about you?'

'I need to do a few things this morning. It wasn't strictly speaking an extradition, but there's a bit of EU paperwork to get through. Plus, I need to talk to Inspector Bouchard and see how he's getting on.'

Alex had just read a particularly fruity text. He whistled through his teeth. 'I don't know about conspiracy to murder, but that…' he pointed to the report, 'doesn't sound legal to me.'

Richard and Melanie laughed. 'You've obviously led a sheltered life,' said Richard.

'Maybe, I should give Ulrika a call and get some tuition.' He turned to Melanie. 'So, what's Gerard up to?'

'Is he a mate of yours?' asked Richard.

'Cousin,' said Melanie.

'Second cousin,' said Alex. Now it was their turn to laugh.

'He's back at *Boutique Bijou*, checking if Hugo's little friends left any evidence behind. He's not optimistic; still, he knows a place where they sell good coffee.'

She blanked Richard's bemused look and sat in a spare chair. 'Now you've had a look at the paperwork, what's the score with Charlotte?'

'I think there's more than enough for conspiracy. With Mr Mortimer's statement, there might be enough for blackmail too. I'll get over to Angleton Insurance in a bit and pull her in. Do you want to come along, Alex?'

'I'd like that, Richard, thank you. I want to see the look on her face when it all catches up with her.'

'Yeah, she thinks she's Teflon, doesn't she?' said

Melanie. 'Daddy's money and friends won't help her this time, though.'

**

Nicki popped her head round the office door. 'That's all booked for you, Ms Palmer. You can pick the ticket up from St Pancras; I've texted you the booking reference number. I've booked it on my personal debit card, as you asked.'

'I'm just transferring the money to your account now, Nicki.' Charlotte's fingers flew over the keyboard. She wasn't transferring money; she was sending another email to André. Cheating her PA out of the money for the fare made her feel good; she'd never liked the uppity little bitch.

'I still think you should get a flight from City Airport. It's direct and much quicker. I can't see the advantage of taking the train.'

Anonymity, thought Charlotte; that was the advantage. Travelling incognito and on someone else's money was next to impossible by air. And she'd be off the radar for a few hours.

'Will there be anything else?'

'No, Nicki, that's everything.' Charlotte gave her a big, false smile and thought good riddance.

Alone in her office, she checked that she had everything she needed: passport, travel bag and a good book for the long train journey, a couldn't-put-it-down thriller. She'd be exhausted by the time she got to Marseille, but hopefully André would have a nice little pick-me-up waiting for her.

She glanced at the clock on the PC; she had more than an hour to spare, but she felt too agitated and impatient to stay in the office; she needed to be moving. She rang a cab and headed for the exit, ignoring Nicki as she passed her desk. She'd have coffee at the station and keep a lookout for anyone following her. She had a momentary vision of Jeremy, lurking in the shadows on the station platform, and shuddered.

**

'Nice place they've got here,' said Jenkins as they crossed the foyer of Angleton Insurance. 'The statues are a bit over the top, though.'

Alex had to agree; where Brown Legal was all elegance and greenery, Angleton Insurance was all money and bad taste.

Jenkins stopped briefly at the reception desk. 'Charlotte Palmer?' he asked, waving his warrant card.

'Fifth floor. But…'

'But nothing, love; we're the police.'

He commandeered a lift and they whizzed upwards. Jenkins looked pained. 'Why do posh lifts always generate such high G-forces?'

Nicki looked up from her PC when they got to the fifth floor reception. 'Can I help you gentlemen? Oh, it's you, Mr DuPont. May I ask who…?'

'DI Jenkins, love, and I'm in a hurry. Is that Charlotte Palmer's office?'

'Yes, but…'

'Does everyone here have a speech impediment?' Jenkins hustled past Nicki's desk and Alex followed him, gesturing an apology to the PA.

The room was empty. 'Looks like she's only just left,' said Alex. 'This coffee is still warm.'

Nicki's head appeared around the door, pert and annoyed. 'That's what I was trying to tell you. Ms Palmer left about fifteen minutes ago.'

Alex and Richard followed her out. 'And where has Ms Palmer gone?' asked the big DI.

'I'm not sure I am obliged to…'

Jenkins leaned over her desk and gave her 'The Look'.

'Eurostar,' she said meekly.

He dropped a business card on Nicki's desk. 'If she happens to come back, give me a call, pronto. And Nicki…'

'Yes, DI Jenkins?'

'You never even offered us a cuppa; what kind of reception is that?'

When Alex DuPont and the rude policeman had left, Nicki logged on to her bank account. No transfer from Charlotte; typical of her to cheat on something so trivial. Nicki reached into a drawer and took out the Post-it with Charlotte's bank card details and made the transfer. She didn't care if it was technically stealing; it looked as if her ex-boss was in enough trouble to keep her occupied for a while. And anyway, she'd never liked the pompous cow.

**

'And then he produced a rabbit out of my secretary's handbag.' Charlotte laughed politely and finished her coffee. She stood up and left the forecourt, offering a brief, finger-wagging wave to the businessman she'd been flirting with.

He looked disappointed. But then, he looked fat and middle-aged too. She had already picked up the ticket, so she headed straight for the platform to board the train. The doors to the first-class carriage hissed open and she stepped in. The carriage was practically empty; perfect. She took a window seat with a table and got the book out of her bag.

**

Jenkins put the blues and twos on as soon as he'd made the call. 'I've told the transport police to hold the train. But we might as well get a shift on. Don't want to keep our Charlotte waiting.'

They weaved in and out of the city traffic, Jenkins giving a one-fingered salute to the few drivers with the temerity to complain. Alex looked a little pale, and Jenkins laughed good-naturedly. 'You'll be all right, Alex. Driving badly at high speed is one of the perks of the job.'

The weather had warmed up again, and the streets were full of tourists. One or two of them snapped the police car as it passed. 'Yeah, I've never really thought of myself as a London landmark before,' said Jenkins. 'Look out, you idiot! Cycle couriers ought to carry road-kill points on their hats.'

They screamed to a halt on the service ramp at St Pancras. Jenkins collared the first person he saw in uniform. 'Which platform for the Eurostar to Marseille?'

'Platform seven,' she said, pointing. 'A few yards past the food court.'

Alex surged ahead; Jenkins was sweating in his suit and wheezing. 'I really ought to do some exercise,' he panted. 'My missus will kill me if I have a heart attack.'

Alex got to the platform and scanned the carriages. 'There,' he said, 'in first class.'

'Only the best for the upper criminal classes,' said Jenkins. 'Give me a minute to get my breath back or I'll fall over when I'm reading her rights.'

**

The train should have left ten minutes ago. Charlotte closed the book and tapped her fingers on the cover, irritated. Why did nothing ever work properly in this country? A few more business travellers had taken their seats in the carriage, taking out laptops and Blackberries and getting straight to work.

Charlotte sighed and went back to her book. A few murderous pages in and she'd relaxed. Every so often she thought of André, his darkly good looks and his romantic attitude towards her.

A shadow passed over the pages. Alex DuPont sat down in the seat opposite. 'I don't think André will have much time for you today, Charlotte. He'll be too busy answering awkward questions from the French police. And anyway, I think you've got some unfinished business in London.'

A couple of the other passengers looked over at them. She ignored them and scanned the carriage for a way out. She probably couldn't get past DuPont. She looked behind her, to the other end of the carriage; a large man in an ill-fitting suit filled the doorway. He looked like he'd been running.

She turned to Alex, fuming. 'What are you doing here, Mr DuPont? I'm not the person you should be looking for. It's Jeremy…'

'Jeremy is in safe hands, Charlotte. He won't be going anywhere for a long while; nowhere nice at least.'

'And what are you going to do, Mr DuPont? It's not as if you can arrest me, is it?'

'No, but I can.' The man in the ill-fitting suit loomed over her, flashing a warrant card. She read it, a mixture of venom and panic in her eyes.

'My father…'

'Your father won't be able to golf you out of this one, Ms Palmer. I expect he might be a bit shy with the Christmas money this year, too.' Jenkins grinned.

'So shall we get on with it?' said Alex. 'I imagine the

other passengers would like to be off.'

'You, on the other hand, are just getting off,' said Jenkins. 'With us.' He drew himself up and looked a long way down at her. 'Charlotte Palmer, you are under arrest for conspiracy to murder Amanda Hamilton.'

'Conspiracy?' she sneered. 'You'll never make it stick.'

'Maybe not, but I shall have a lot of fun trying. And I might just add blackmail into the mix.'

'Steve, you treacherous little bastard,' she said.

Alex stood up. 'Shall we, Charlotte? I think your time's up.'

**

'You'll be assigned a duty solicitor, Jeremy,' said Melanie. 'If you're not satisfied with them, you're free to find someone else, but you'll have to pay for that out of your own funds.'

She had finished all the paperwork an hour earlier. Since then, she'd taken Jeremy to be photographed, and have his fingerprints taken again for the record, and logged his confession statement.

Now they were walking along the corridor leading to the holding cells. Jeremy wasn't handcuffed, but they were accompanied by a solid-looking uniformed officer. In any case, she thought, Jeremy didn't look like he had any plans to try and escape.

'I don't think that's an issue,' he said. 'It's not as if I have any sort of defence. I'd like to call Aunt Katherine, though, if I may. I want to reassure her that none of this is her fault. She's really the only person who's ever cared for me.'

'I'm sure we can arrange that. I'll just pop you back in the holding cell and go and sort it out. Ah.' Melanie came to a halt and looked along the corridor.

Alex emerged from the stairwell, followed by DI Jenkins. He was holding Charlotte Palmer by the upper arm. She looked dishevelled and very angry.

'Well, that's rather awkward,' said Jeremy, sounding amused. 'I hope you didn't arrange this among yourselves; Charlotte will be very upset with you.'

Charlotte had been murmuring something baleful to Jenkins. Now she looked up and caught sight of Jeremy. Her eyes narrowed. 'You,' she hissed.

The two trios, prisoners and their captors, came to a halt a few feet apart. Alex smiled at Melanie, and Jenkins winked. 'Well, fancy meeting you here.'

They stood in silence for a few moments. Jenkins tightened his grip on Charlotte's arm. She was coiled like a spring, ready to launch herself at Jeremy. Alex stepped between them and turned sideways so he could see them both at the same time. 'This is an unfortunate coincidence,' he said. 'But it's not the worst thing that could have happened. Whether or not you two worked together, you've ended up in the same situation. It may not be any comfort to Amanda, but justice has been done. The two people who wanted her dead are where they belong.'

Suddenly, Charlotte tore herself free from Jenkins' grasp, a howling, spitting ball of murderous energy. Jeremy took a step back, and raised his arms to ward her off, but Alex got there first. He enveloped her in his arms and pushed her back, surprisingly gently, towards the big DI.

'I'm afraid you've run out of space and time for revenge, Charlotte. I don't suppose you two will see each other again.'

'I'll think of something,' she muttered.

Melanie tugged Jeremy's sleeve, and they stepped

carefully around Charlotte; he couldn't resist a sardonic smile, but he said nothing. Jenkins relaxed his bear hug and Charlotte shrugged, haughtily. 'Well, let's get this over with,' she said. 'And then I can get talking to a very expensive lawyer.'

She walked down the corridor, head held high, ignoring everyone around her. Alex and DI Jenkins followed like lowly retainers, but the smirk on Jenkins' face was anything but respectful. Charlotte didn't seem to care; she was already scheming.

CHAPTER 33

Alex watched on the observation screen as Charlotte was led into the interview room. She looked as if a few days in the cells had not done her any favours; her complexion had paled a couple of shades and her hair was a mess. The sweatshirt and joggers she had been given to wear hung off her spare frame like laundry in a breeze.

Her lawyer, on the other hand, positively glowed. Her ebony skin bore the traces of minimally applied makeup; her hair was cut close to her scalp and oiled. Her dark grey trouser suit, worn over a plain white shirt, was elegantly tailored for her tall figure.

She stood as Charlotte was brought in. Alex saw cold indignation in her eyes. Her voice, clipped and commanding, came through the speakers. 'My client looks dreadful; what on earth have you done with her?'

Melanie bristled at the implication. 'Your client has been given every opportunity to look after herself; up to this point, she has refused. Ms Ndombele, if you have a genuine request to make for Ms Palmer's welfare, I am ready to listen to it. Otherwise, I think we should stick to the matter at hand.'

DI Jenkins had spruced himself up for the interview

too, Alex noticed. His suit was freshly pressed and his tie was straight for a change. Once Charlotte was seated, and Ms Ndombele reluctantly sat back down beside her, he gave the time and date, and the names of those present.

He took a photo from the folder on the table in front of him and showed it to Charlotte. 'Do you recognise this, Ms Palmer?'

Charlotte glanced sideways at her lawyer and returned her truculent stare to Jenkins. 'No.'

'For the record, the image labelled Exhibit A is a small package containing a vial. The contents of the vial are thirty milligrams of potassium cyanide.'

Melanie tapped the photo with impatient, imperious fingers. 'This vial was found at your flat, Ms Palmer. For the record, the prisoner's address is apartment number eighteen, Kensington Towers, Westbourne Park Road.'

She tapped the photo again. 'As I said, Charlotte, this was found at your flat. It matches the description given to us by a witness of a package handed to you by Jeremy Higgins in the Jardin des Tuileries, in Paris, on Saturday the twentieth of May, two thousand and six. Did you somehow forget about it in between him handing it to you and us finding it in your flat?'

Charlotte said nothing. The lawyer's nostrils flared. 'You're just badgering my client, Detective Sergeant; if this… item is to be presented as evidence in any future court hearing, you don't need Ms Palmer's approval.'

'Ms Ndombele, this vial contains enough potassium cyanide to kill approximately twenty people. It was found in Ms Palmer's flat and it bears her fingerprints. Given this is a murder investigation, and the victim died of cyanide poisoning, I think this is a legitimate, not to say pertinent, line of questioning.'

She turned back to Charlotte. 'Tell us about the cyanide, Charlotte. What were you planning to do with it?'

Charlotte shrugged. 'I was planning to kill myself.'

'What, twenty times over?' Jenkins sounded incredulous. 'Come on, Ms Palmer. You can do a lot better than that.'

'My client has answered your question. It's up to you whether you believe her or not. Can we move on?'

Jenkins acknowledged the lawyer's comment with a wave of his hand. 'OK, let's do that, shall we? Let's move on to a series of text messages you sent to Jeremy Higgins.' He slid a couple of printed pages out of the folder; even via the camera, Alex could see they included images as well as text. He saw Ms Ndombele's eyes widened too.

'Over the course of four weeks up to the date of Amanda Hamilton's death, one hundred and sixty messages passed between you and Jeremy. Only four of them were from Jeremy to you; the rest went the other way. You were busy, Charlotte; busy and… well, let's say creative.'

Charlotte leaned towards her lawyer and whispered something in her ear. Ms Ndombele addressed the two police officers as if she had just scraped them off the sole of her shoe. 'My client and I need a few moments alone.'

'Interview terminated at eleven forty-one; to be continued.' When Jenkins had completed the formalities, he and Melanie left the room. They joined Alex a few moments later. 'I have a horrible feeling that she's going to skate,' said Jenkins. 'That brief of hers is so far up my nose my brain tickles.'

'And she's just the first in a long line of lawyers, each one more expensive than the last, all of them itching to get a slice of the Palmer's pie.'

'What are you saying, Alex? Do you think we're on a loser here?' asked Melanie.

'I'm beginning to think so. The circumstantial evidence is really good, and the texts are at the very least suggestive. It's illegal to possess potassium cyanide without an EPP licence, so we could convict her on that. But that's two years maximum. And the blackmail charge will fall down in court. It's only Steve's word against hers, and if a half decent barrister gets him in the witness box they'll make mincemeat of him.'

'Well, we've got until five o'clock this afternoon to either remand her or let her go. What do you think we should do?'

Alex mused, stroking his chin with thumb and forefinger. 'I think we should talk to Jeremy again; see if we can persuade him to say something more definite. I'll go and see him, if you like; it will only take me a few minutes and then I'll let you know if he's changed his mind.'

'Yeah, I think that's our only play if we want to get her on the conspiracy thing,' said Jenkins. 'I think we should push the possession charge to keep her inside in any case. We can't let her get away scot free.'

'So, we do her for possession, she gets two years max, gets out in about twelve months and otherwise she walks.' Melanie wasn't happy, but she couldn't see another way out.

'She'll get bail for the possession charge too,' said Jenkins. 'It's a regulatory infringement; she only has to claim she didn't know what was in the vial and she's off.'

'But she specifically asks Jeremy for cyanide in the texts,' said Melanie.

'A good barrister will ditch that on a technicality,' said Alex. 'They'll argue she asked, but didn't know he delivered. So, shall I go and see Jeremy or not?'

Melanie exhaled, long and hard, defeated. 'There's no point, Alex. He's said all he's going to say. He's not going to change his story just to help us out. I think he's quietly proud of himself, like he did the right thing and he's happy to carry the can for it.'

'Well, that's that, then.' Jenkins pushed a weary hand through his hair. 'Let's charge her with possession, drop the rest, and let Ms Ndombele walk her out of here on bail. Then we can all go home and weep into our favourite tipple.'

**

Alex was in the station reception hall, waiting for Melanie, when Charlotte Palmer came out from the cells, accompanied by a triumphant lawyer. Ms Ndombele was taller than he'd imagined from seeing her in the interview room; he had to look up to meet her eyes – not that she returned his gaze.

Charlotte was only too keen to lock eyes with him. She stalked over and confronted him. 'You've ruined my life, Alex DuPont, and I won't forget that. I'm going to prison, I know that. But it won't be for long. And I know people, Alex, serious people; you know that.'

She stepped away from him, smiled. 'So you should keep an eye over your shoulder, Mr DuPont. You never know what might creep up behind you. Don't forget me; I won't forget you.'

She walked back to join her lawyer; together they left the station and got into a sleek black car with a uniformed chauffeur at the wheel. Alex watched them go, and had an ominous feeling in the pit of his stomach.

'What's up, Alex? You look like you've seen a ghost.'

'It's nothing, Melanie. Don't mind me, I'm fine – just fine.' As they left the station, he wondered if the ghost he had seen was his own.

CHAPTER 34

Alex watched in horror as half of the text he had just typed disappeared. 'Jenny!' he shouted. 'This bloody machine has eaten half of my report. What do I do now?'

Jenny came into his office, giggling behind her hand. 'Control Z, Alex.'

'What?'

'Press Control Z.'

He did so, and the text reappeared. 'What just happened?' he asked, confused and relieved.

'When you press Control Z it undoes your mistake,' Jenny explained. 'It's there because most people don't have a clue what they're doing on a computer.'

'I say, I don't suppose you know a Control Z for my life, do you?'

'Sorry, but my life programming skills are pretty basic. Like you on a computer. When are you presenting the report?'

'Tomorrow at two o'clock. There's lots of stuff I can't tell them, of course. It's still *sub judice*.'

'Is that posh speak for off the record?'

'No. Just the opposite. *Sub judice* means it's subject to

the legal process and can't be revealed.'

Jenny filed that one away for later perusal. 'So, what are you able to tell them?'

'Well, I can tell them the steps we took, how we worked with the police and where we got in terms of arrests and charges. I'm sure it's all fine. Walter knows he got his money's worth, even if I still don't really know why he spent the money in the first place.'

'Gerry Hamilton will be satisfied at least. She knows who killed her sister, she knows he's going to prison for a very long time and her family's got some closure. I'd say that's a result.'

'I suppose so, Jenny. Though I don't know how meaningful closure is when something so awful happens to a family.'

He went back to typing the report. He felt as if half of his mind was elsewhere; had Charlotte's threat been serious, he wondered, or was it just her anger bubbling to the surface? Alex had an uncomfortable feeling that he hadn't heard the last of Charlotte Palmer.

**

'I think you should come to the meeting, Melanie. Walter will expect someone from the Met to be there, and you were the SIO on the case.'

'Yeah, I can do that. Things are pretty quiet here. Who else will be there?'

'I've invited Walter, Sally Prentice, Ashley, Steve… and Timothy Williams. I know he wasn't involved in any way but I felt it would be good to have all of the gang along, if only for old time's sake.'

'All except Charlotte. And Amanda.'

'Yes; men only as far as the Famous Five go. I'd like you to have a quick look over the report, and make sure I haven't included anything I'm not allowed to say. And, to make sure I haven't made any criticisms of the police that might impact on you. I'll email it to you.'

'OK, thanks, I'll have a look. Richard and I have had a chat about the court stuff. We think it would be a good idea if you were part of our team. It's only a formality in Jeremy's case, obviously.'

'And in Charlotte's case?'

'I'm not sure we'll need you for that one. Like Richard said, it's basically a regulatory infringement.'

Alex was relieved to hear that. He didn't fancy facing Charlotte again, not yet.

**

Alex said good night to Scott and Jenny and walked back to his apartment, picking up some groceries on the way. The evening sun was warm and mild, lending an amber glow to the buildings around him. He decided he'd go for a decent run before he had his dinner, to build up an appetite and to push all the unpleasantness out of his system.

After running five miles at a good pace, he felt ready for food and rest. He sprinted to the gate of the park, and then walked the rest of the way. His mind was clearer now, and the exertion had done him good; he realised he'd missed out on a lot of quality exercises while he'd been pursuing the case.

He'd realised something else, too. This was the kind of work he really wanted to do; this was the kind of work he was good at. Corporate crime was lucrative and it built his reputation; but crime, particularly murder, had an edge to it that he couldn't find elsewhere. It was a thrilling experience. He thought Melanie was right about getting bad guys off the street, bringing justice to victims, was satisfying in a completely different way. He thought it was the right time for the Agency to implement a new strategy. Maybe, he'd need to concentrate mostly on corporate issues and major crimes in future.

He also thought if by any chance he saw Amanda in his dream again, he would tell her that *her killer had been caught and justice was achieved.*

Alex slipped his key into the lock and stepped inside his apartment. He had other thing to think about, especially, his relationship with Claire.

Down at the end of the street, a man in a dark hoodie watched him until he was safely indoors; then he got in an anonymous car and drove away.

CHAPTER 35

J ean greeted him like an old friend. 'Well done, dragon
boy; I hear you got your man, then. Should I be asking
for your autograph?'

'I'm disappointed, Jean. I thought you'd be asking for
my phone number.'

Jean tapped the side of her nose conspiratorially. 'I have
access to all the firm's secrets, Alex. If I need to find you, I
can just look you up. Anyway, shouldn't you be asking for
mine? It's only polite.'

Melanie came over; she had been sitting on one of the
many luxurious sofas scattered around the atrium, enjoying
the performance. 'Dragon boy, eh? Am I missing something?'

Jean blushed. 'Oops; you're not Mrs Alex, are you?'

'Melanie is a detective sergeant; she actually arrested the
murderer. She's here to make sure I don't do anything
illegal.' He winked at Jean and turned to Melanie. 'I'll
explain the dragon thing later, after you've met Sally
Prentice.'

'Well, I hope you can keep him in order, Sergeant; I
think he could be a bit of a handful. Look, there's Ms
Hamilton.'

Just for a second, Alex caught his breath; beside him, he

heard Melanie do the same. She looked so like Amanda. Gerry came over and shook Alex's hand, then she gave him an awkward hug. 'I'm glad I caught you before the meeting, Alex. I wanted to say thank you, on behalf of all the family.'

Alex nodded in acknowledgement. 'How are your parents, Gerry?'

'Better, I suppose. I don't think they'll ever get over it but knowing that Amanda's killer is behind bars has brought them some kind of relief. Closure, they call it; isn't that right?'

'Yes, that's right. A rather impersonal term for something so emotionally connected; like the end of a book.' Alex heard a polite cough from Jean, behind them. 'Is it time for the meeting, then? We'll go up now. Where is it? In the interview room?'

'Ooh, no. Mr Coburn is holding it in his office. I think he wants to be part of the show.'

'Thanks, Jean. I'll see you later.'

'You never know, mate. I'm free the odd evening.'

Melanie smirked all the way to the eighth floor.

**

'And Jeremy Higgins was arrested for murder – by Detective Sergeant Cooper here – on Monday. He has made a full confession, so the court proceedings should be a formality.'

There had been a hushed, breathless silence as Alex read his report. Now, the people gathered in a ring of comfortable seats, arranged in the centre of the huge space that Walter called an office, exhaled all at once.

'Thank you, Alex. I believe you have set all our minds at rest. And thank you too, for your discretion; yours too, Detective Sergeant. Brown Legal's reputation could so easily have been tarnished by this tawdry affair.' Walter's eyes strayed for a second towards Gerry; an unreadable expression flicked across his face and was gone.

'We owe you a debt of thanks, too, Walter,' said Alex. 'First, for funding the investigation and making it possible. But also, for using your influence at crucial times to – ah – ease the process.'

Walter smiled paternally. 'Not at all, dear boy. There is little point having influence if one does not get to use it occasionally; I'm only too glad I could help.'

'I'd like to think the HR department helped too, in our own small way.' Sally Prentice had puffed herself up for the occasion; but there was a hint of pleading in her voice.

'Your help was invaluable, Ms Prentice.'

'Sally.' She blushed meaningfully.

'Sally. In fact, everyone here helped us, in one way or another. That's why I wanted you all to be here when I delivered my report.'

Steve had made himself very small during the meeting, as if he thought Walter wouldn't be able to see him. But now he rose a little in his seat and pointed to the elephant in the room. 'And what about Charlotte?'

Ashley and Tim nodded. Alex hadn't left her out of the report completely, but he had played down her role in the affair. It didn't impinge on Jeremy's guilt, after all, not in legal terms. But Steve was right; he owed the survivors of the Famous Five that much at least.

'I can't say too much, because a certain amount of information is still *sub judice,* as you'll all appreciate. But there was insufficient evidence to prosecute Charlotte for conspiracy to murder, so we must presume her innocence, as the law demands.

'Now, I've taken up enough of your time. I think we should all move on with our lives. Having said that,' he paused and looked at Gerry. 'I do hope that Amanda will live on in all our memories. That's the least she deserves.'

**

They formed a loose group in the atrium: Alex and Melanie; Ashley and Tim; Gerry and Steve. Walter had said his farewells in the office, and Alex had managed to shoo Sally away before they got to the lifts, which brought a mock-theatrical whisper of 'dragon boy' from Melanie.

Gerry didn't stay long; there were clearly too many bad memories here. She said her goodbyes and fled. Tim didn't stay long either. 'I enjoyed the show, Alex,' he said. 'And I'm glad to know what happened. But it all belongs to a past I'm already beginning to forget. If you ever need any financial advice, though, you know where to find me.'

Steve shook hands with both Melanie and Alex. 'I didn't think so last week, but you have done me a favour. I realise this isn't my life, and I think I've got a lot to learn before I find out what it is. And anyway, Uncle Walter made it clear I don't have a future at Brown Legal. He laced it with a few 'dear boy' noises, but I could see the sneer.'

'Take care, Steve,' said Alex. 'And remember what I said. Keep away from Charlotte; it will be better for you.' Steve nodded and took a last look around the grand atrium, shrugged his shoulders and left. He looked over his shoulder at Ashley and gave a conciliatory wave; then he was gone.

That left Ashley: he was fidgeting with a pen, trying to look casual, but Alex could see he had something to say. 'What is it, Ashley?'

'I would like to express my sincere thanks to you for

finding Amanda's killer, solving the allegation against me and clearing my name,' Ashley said.

'You're very welcome, Ashley.'

'Also, I was thinking about that text from Amanda. She wanted to ask me about Jeremy, didn't she? If I thought she could trust him. If I'd twigged, I might have been able…'

'Don't go there, Ashley,' said Alex. 'Jeremy was determined to kill Amanda. He had it all planned and you couldn't have stopped him. Don't blame yourself for not being psychic.'

'I guess you're right.'

'Go and enjoy Hong Kong,' said Alex. 'You've been through a lot, and you deserve it. I'm still attached to the legal grapevine, even if it's more as a weed than a fruit; I expect I'll hear about you in the future, doing good things at Brown Legal.'

'Thank you, Alex. I should go back up. I'm supposed to be working and the old man doesn't care for slackers.' He turned and headed for the lifts.

'So, there you go; end of the story, eh?' Jean sauntered over. 'What now, then? Do you just ride off into the sunset, looking for more dragons?'

'Something like that, Jean. If you see any, give me a shout.'

'I will, dragon boy. Oh, and look after that nice police lady. I think she might be sweet on you.' She winked solemnly, and turned back to her desk.

Melanie chuckled. 'You should hire her, Alex. I think she'd be good for you. Anyway, I should get back and see if any crime's broken out while I've been hobnobbing.'

'OK.'

'Before I go, let me say, I got a call from Gerard. The

shop was clean as a whistle. He says they're closing down the investigation for now. His bosses think it's not a fruitful line of enquiry anymore.'

'He'll find something else to get his teeth into soon enough. Paris can be quite a lively place; I can attest to that.'

Melanie laughed at that, and then her expression turned pensive. 'You don't think Charlotte is a serious threat, do you? She does seem to have a well-developed sense of revenge.'

'I'm sure she'll find better things to do with her life. Once she's served her time. If she serves any time. And anyway, if I think I'm in danger, I can always call the police, can't I?'

'I've enjoyed working with you, Alex. You're very good at this.'

'So are you, Melanie. I loved working with you too. I think we make an effective team. Twice we've worked together and twice we've produced excellent results.'

'To be fair, on both occasions, you've been superb and most of the credits must go to you.'

'It's nice of you to say that, but you, Richard and your colleagues have made a significant contribution as well.'

'Well whatever….., I ought to go now,' Melanie said. 'I hope we don't have to wait for another year before we see each other again.'

'I hope not. I'll ring you in a few days, I promise,' Alex said. They looked at each other with warm eyes. Words were not exchanged. Then, Melanie left to get back to the Department.

Alex turned round and had a good look at the atrium, waved goodbye to Jean and then walked out of the Brown Legal building with a tremendous sense of satisfaction.

Whilst travelling back to his apartment, he had the time to reflect on recent events. He felt a lot had taken place both professionally and personally. Now, he'd be able to spend some time to try and resolve the sensitive issues in his personal life.

Printed in Great Britain
by Amazon